Between the Walls

www.tinyghostpress.com

ISBN:
E-book 978-1-915585-29-5
Paperback 978-1-915585-30-1
Hardback 978-1-915585-31-8

Cover Art by: Fiona O'Shea

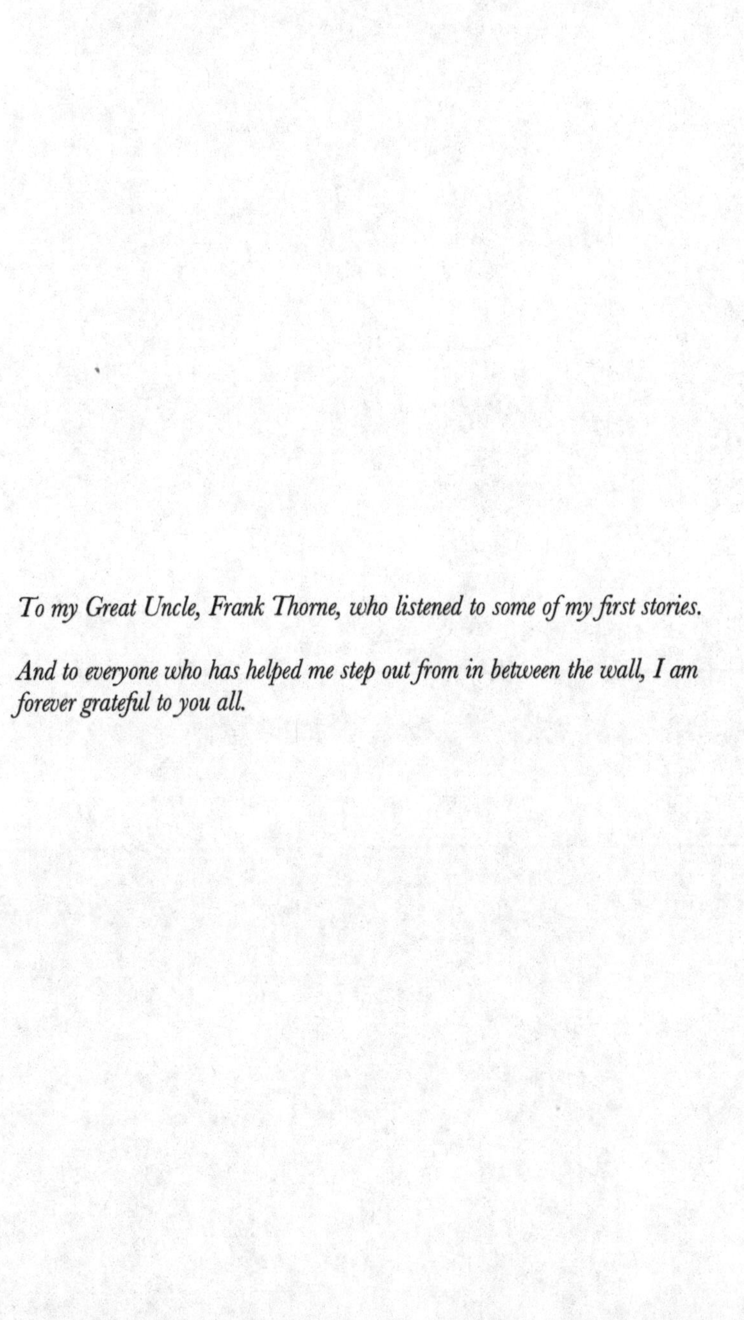

To my Great Uncle, Frank Thorne, who listened to some of my first stories.

And to everyone who has helped me step out from in between the wall, I am forever grateful to you all.

Between the Walls

Caspian Faye

Tiny Ghost Press

James

James flopped down onto the mattress behind him, regretting it immediately as the cloud of dust from the plastic covering erupted around his face. He coughed and sat up, staring around the room – *his* room now, though it didn't feel like it yet. He looked at the cardboard boxes piled in the corner. Maybe it would seem more like home once he'd unpacked. Maybe doing the unpacking would help him to miss his old house – his old life – a bit less.

He stared blankly at the large sash window for a moment, the dust motes dancing in the last rays of sunlight. He needed to summon the energy to get started or he was going to have an uncomfortable night. He sighed. His dad was far too busy with his own tasks to help out; this had to be a solo effort.

He stood up, pulling the bunch of keys from his jeans pocket, and opened out the pen knife, cutting through the plastic sheeting on the mattress. He would focus on the essentials: sort the bed out, find some sheets and leave the actual unpacking for the next few days. He had more than a week before his classes started, enough time to settle in.

If he even wanted to settle in. None of this was his choice; the thought returned with accompanying anger and frustration. He was in an impossible situation. He tore the plastic off and tossed it onto the floor; the clean-up could wait. Next, he started opening the boxes labelled *Bedroom – James* in his mum's perfect handwriting. He paused a moment, tracing the letters she'd formed with the black permanent marker.

He wanted to go home. This sprawling old house in the middle of nowhere was not home, no matter how cheerful his dad pretended to be and how many times he heard optimistic proclamations of DIY plans.

His phone buzzing was a welcome relief from the sense of melancholy that threatened to settle in. It was his boyfriend, Will. *Made it yet? X*

Caspian Faye

Yeah baby, it's as crap here as I thought it would be. Just unpacking. Miss u so much. X

There weren't that many queer kids at his old college, but once he met Will, he hadn't cared about that. Will was the only one he had eyes for, and after a whole year as a couple, he was sure they were endgame material. He couldn't imagine his life without him, his quirky, whip-smart joker with a softer side that only he was lucky enough to know.

I know, long distance is hard. But really looking forward to seeing U some weekend soon, it'll be intense…X

James stared at the message. Some vague, unspecified weekend felt like a lifetime away, especially when he was used to seeing Will almost every day. There would be no more grabbing coffees before school, or cosy lunchtimes by the football pitch, or takeaways at the weekend. Or film nights. Or—

'JAMES!' His dad's bellow reverberated around the unfurnished house.

James shoved his phone in his pocket and went out onto the gloomy landing. His dad was standing at the bottom of the stairs, leaning on the banister.

'What's up?'

'Have you given any thought to what you want for dinner?'

James considered a moment. A knot had settled in his stomach as the car pulled out of the old driveway and was still there; his appetite was non-existent. 'Nope, not really.'

'Want to go out for something?'

'Yeah, maybe.'

'I mean, if we stay in, I think we've got…plain rice with marmalade?'

'In which case I definitely want to go out. I'll just grab my jacket.'

James ran back to his room, humouring his dad with the performance of enthusiasm. He swung around the heavy oak door to grab his jacket off the hook he'd hung it on, but it wasn't there. He stopped, confused. He had definitely put it there when he'd arrived, slightly sweaty from hauling and stacking boxes in here, and he knew he hadn't touched it since. It wasn't on the floor, though, so it hadn't fallen. He checked on the bed, under the bed and the sparse furniture that was in the room – the bedside table and his desk – but there was no sign of it. Giving up, he tore into a nearby box and grabbed an extra jumper instead.

Nathaniel

Nathaniel was awake again, his consciousness sparking and returning in little fragments. He clung to them, same as before, and bit by bit, he was back.

He blinked his eyes open, yawned and looked around, orienting himself through the blur of recently recovered awareness.

He was still in his house, as always. He drifted from the wall and looked around his room. It looked the same as last time and yet not quite the same. It was dustier than he remembered; boxes were stacked in the corners. He knew what that meant: new people had arrived.

He wondered what year it was now, how long he had slept for. The last time he'd been awake, it had been… He paused, calling to mind the calendar that had hung on the wall opposite, drifting over to where the old nail still remained in the cracked plaster, slightly bent. He stared at the familiar metal, and it came back to him – 1997! He pictured the pages of the calendar as if it still hung there now. It had been brightly coloured, a group of captivating women in eye-catching clothing – The Spice Girls, that was it. He remembered now.

He vaguely recalled the people who had lived here then. They had stayed far too long; their loud voices and powerful emotions had made him want to hide away forever – but their energy had disturbed him regardless of how far into the wall he retreated. Eventually, they had left, and he had been able to go back to sleep. It was so much less lonely when he was asleep.

He hoped these new people would be quiet and tolerable, or else leave him in peace and not force him to expend any effort to drive them away.

He was drifting already, pulled further into the room by the lingering life force already there. A jacket was hanging on the back of the door; it was unlike anything he would have been permitted to wear. Not that he had ever really been permitted to wear what he wanted, except in private, of course. In the darkness, in the shadows – that was when he had tasted his own existence, his true self.

He looked down with fondness. The familiar olive-green frock coat he had sewn by hand, the brown waistcoat, the breeches that clung to his lean legs, the soft shirt against the skin of his chest – all of it was so right. All of it was exactly fitting for a young man of 1712.

Nathaniel turned around to scan the room, shaking his head and feeling his hair settle itself in the ribbon he had tied it with. He knew he looked every bit the way he was always supposed to, only no-one could see him now. He sighed, running his hand down the side of the strange jacket hanging on the old coat hook. The residual energy of its owner crackled back into his palm, giving him a little taste of life. It was a dangerously pleasant sensation, and he didn't mean to, but he lifted the jacket, carrying it with him as he ventured over to the boxes, peering inside them. He was reaching out his other hand to explore the items inside and gain clues about their owner – and perhaps how best to drive them away if it came to it – when he heard footsteps. Someone was running back towards this room. He could feel their energy; it was so close, so startlingly vibrant.

He knew he likely couldn't be seen but realised too late that the jacket dangling from his hand could be. A split second before the door opened, he stepped back into the wall, taking it with him.

The dark, cold space enveloped him, safe and familiar. He waited, listening intently. When the human left, he would have time to put the jacket back where he had found it.

There were noises coming from the room and, unable to resist his curiosity, he peered through the wall. There was a boy about his own age, with a friendly face and warm eyes that made Nathaniel like him immediately despite himself. He wanted to step nearer, to properly read the boy's energy and make a conclusive judgement. He could do it so easily: step out of the wall and walk to him. He inched forward impulsively and then hesitated. It was a bad idea and he knew it. He couldn't allow himself to fall into this trap again; taking a liking to someone would only lead to guilt and misery. This boy would leave in the end, terrified like the others. Getting close was always a terrible idea. If the boy sensed him somehow, he would undoubtedly be frightened, but perhaps it was better that he be frightened now and leave immediately. What was the point in drawing it out? Then again, if the boy left, whoever came after was an unknown quantity – not to mention they were unlikely to possess such enthralling energy.

Indecision kept him frozen as the boy continued his erratic movement around the room, returning to stare at the back of the door in confusion. Then Nathaniel realised why with a little spark of panic: the boy was searching for the jacket that was still clutched in his hand. He stared at it; he had made a mistake already. He waited a few moments more, and the boy abandoned his hunt for his jacket and left, the bedroom door shutting behind him.

Nathaniel shook himself, stepping out of the wall now that the coast was clear and placing the jacket carefully back on the hook where it belonged. This one little indiscretion he would likely get away with; he just had to make sure he didn't slip up again, he mustn't create a pattern for the boy to notice. He needed to be sensible, see if these humans were tolerable enough and if they were, leave them well alone.

As the sound of the humans leaving echoed around the house, Nathaniel relaxed and took stock of his old home. He drifted to the window and stared wistfully at the overgrown garden, wishing he could see it restored to its former glory, even just for a moment. His favourite tree was still there, the trunk broader and the canopy of leaves wider every time he awoke. When he gazed at it, he could still feel the rough bark against his palms, could still recall the footholds and handholds that had defined his childhood sanctuary.

The last rays of sunlight were casting shadows on the grass, just as they had on the day Theodore had made that carving, in the last year of Nathaniel's mortal life. He wondered if it was still visible, tucked away behind the branch he used to climb up to, or if centuries of weather had worn it away.

Nathaniel stared at the leaves dancing in the breeze, and for a moment, it was as if he could see the two of them again, sat with their backs to the tree trunk, fingers intertwined.

Theodore producing his little whittling knife, his dark eyes shining, 'I'm going to make our mark for eternity!' *Our* mark.

Nathaniel sighed, tearing his gaze and the direction of his thoughts away from that moment, looking around the rest of the garden instead. The benches that had bordered the lawn were long gone, but his mother's rose bushes lingered, less orderly now, yet somehow more captivating in their wildness. The other plants that had grown in amongst them, sending them creeping and clambering around the trellises, lent them a more authentic beauty than before. He watched a bumblebee hover over a nearby bush before settling and contemplated how wonderful it could all look once again with a bit of work. He considered the changes he would make if he were able. It had looked its best during the days when the Victorian twins, Agatha and Arthur, had lived here, adding character to the space with their artistic choices. He smiled sadly to think of them again; the memories of the twins always returned quickly and with the most clarity every time he awoke. They were the strongest fragments, and with a little concentration, he could pull the threads all together and revisit the golden months when he had been the happiest in his afterlife. His chest began to ache, the familiar pain rising out of the haze and wrapping itself around his heart, everything beginning to devolve into a painful, confused blur. He opened his eyes with a snap. It was too much, too soon. He couldn't bear it; he must force himself to focus on the present. There would be time enough to remember.

'Maybe this boy will have green fingers,' he pondered out loud, his voice echoing around the room. 'Perhaps I could hint to him somehow, leave a little sign or—'

He stopped. 'No, *no*, I mustn't; what is wrong with me? I cannot think like this again. He'll only be petrified like the others. You know this, you utter fool.'

He stared miserably at the floorboards for a moment, struck once more by the hopelessness of his predicament. He had spoken to no-one but himself now for over a hundred years. At first, he hadn't fully grasped his situation, expecting more humans like the twins to move in someday, open to conversation and able to see him, but they never did. For a long time, he had held out hope that maybe the next guests would be different, so he had made blunder after blunder, terrifying and confusing every human who entered his house – and himself sometimes into the bargain.

Over the long centuries, he had finally come to understand enough to have some idea of what the rules were, what he could and could not do. He could not let them know he was here; he must not meddle with their things nor try to communicate. He must sustain himself only with his memories, return to those days with the twins, the days before everything went wrong.

The time before *it* had arrived and spoilt everything.

Nathaniel shivered; he didn't want to think about that. The details were murky and confusing, but the fear was crystal clear. He was safe now, though, wasn't he? It was gone.

He sighed. On the one hand, he always found himself frustrated when he awoke to find his memories had grown so hazy whilst he slept. It made him yearn for clarity, for the puzzle pieces to fit into place and form a complete picture again. He would clutch at them impulsively, trying to come home to a full idea of himself, somehow wanting to stay awake and retain it all despite his other yearning, the yearning that had grown more powerful over the decades: the conflicting desire for an escape to an uninterrupted sleep in the wall, an end to the relentless disappointment, the painless peace of nothingness and the silence of the void.

James

'I just want to say, for what it's worth, I'm sorry about all this,' James's dad said, gesturing vaguely with a piece of naan bread.

'It's not…I don't blame you,' James told him. 'I mean, I'm obviously not super happy about it – I really miss Will and my friends and my old life already; it's a lot of change. But it's not your fault.'

'That's very mature,' his dad responded, his eyes narrowed. 'You're not…blaming your mum instead, are you?'

James looked away. 'Not entirely, but if she hadn't cheated…well, then you wouldn't have moved out and changed jobs, and then this relocation thing wouldn't have happened either.'

His dad shook his head. 'It's really not that simple. I don't mean to patronize you by saying this, but at your age, things seem a lot more straightforward. When you get to my stage in life, you just…there's more nuance to it all.'

'But actions have consequences, and Mum made certain choices, and now here we are.'

His dad nodded. 'Those are valid points, yes, but ultimately…your mum's affair wasn't the catalytic event you might see it as. Things between us hadn't been right for a while, and some of that is on me – I was tired of my old job, and that was an entirely separate issue. It was just time for change, for both of us. And sadly, it has also affected you greatly.'

'OK.' James nodded. 'So, you were going to end up here anyway?'

His dad sipped his drink and considered. 'Very likely. I suppose if your mum and I hadn't had problems, then maybe we would both be here, or perhaps elsewhere – there's no way to tell, really.'

'So, either way, I'd have had to move and be apart from Will? That was unavoidable?'

'I would say so. Does that bring you some kind of peace around the divorce?'

James shrugged. 'I suppose, in a way.'

'So, will you please message your mum back then? She's been on at me about it.'

James pulled his phone out and looked at the last few messages she'd sent, inquiring after his wellbeing with increasing urgency. He typed, *All good here thanks Mum, just been really busy with everything. Talk soon. XXX*

His dad grinned. 'Thank you; I appreciate that.'

For a moment, James saw through his grin to the cracks underneath, the pain he was trying to hide.

'Everything okay with your meals?' The server appeared at the side of the table; a customer-service smile plastered on her face.

James's dad returned the smile. 'Absolutely perfect, thank you. Really great to have found such a nice spot to eat on our first night in the area.'

'Oh, are you on holiday here?' she asked, her tone becoming more conversational and genuine.

'No, we just moved! Myself and my son here.'

The server smiled at James. She was about his age, and he wondered if they'd be going to college together. 'Welcome to the area! Are you living in the town?'

James shook his head. 'No, we're up near the woods. A bit of a—'

'Needs work!' his dad interjected, before he could finish his sentence. 'A fixer-upper, as they say, but a great price. "The Coach House" on Old Horse Lane, do you know it?'

The server swallowed, her features becoming slightly rigid. 'Oh…yes, I do. I do know it, but not well. Anyway, I'll stop bothering you and let you enjoy the rest of your meal. Let me know if you need anything!'

She turned and left before either of them could respond. James found himself staring after her, wanting to know why she'd shut down so abruptly at the mention of their new address. He glanced at his dad and saw the same thought was clearly on his mind.

'That was odd. I hope there's nothing wrong with the house,' he mused. 'The surveyor said it was sound, but maybe there's something the locals know that they didn't pick up on.'

'Maybe something awful happened there,' James said, voicing the direction of his own thoughts. 'I mean, that was a classic horror movie *you've just moved into a murder house* style reaction.'

His dad laughed, but it sounded hollow.

James looked around the cosy restaurant, with its comfortable booths and warm lighting, and realised he didn't want to go back to the house. He pushed the last bit of rice around his plate with his fork while his dad gave the dessert menu a cursory look.

'Do you want anything?'

James shook his head. He wished he had the appetite to force something sweet down and delay their return, but the thought of attempting it made him feel slightly ill.

'Right, I'll sort out the bill then.'

While his dad was at the counter, James pulled his phone out again and messaged Will a photo of his dinner. *Went for dinner in a cute restaurant, will bring you when you visit. X*

***

As the car pulled up to the house, James looked up at the darkened windows and neglected exterior; the house appeared even more unwelcoming at night. A shiver ran down his spine. It was far too easy to imagine someone – or something – waiting inside for the new occupants to arrive. He wondered if his dad felt it as he switched off the ignition and paused a moment.

'Will you be alright here tomorrow while I go into the office?'

'Dad, I'm eighteen now. I'm legally an adult.'

'I know, I know, I just don't want you to feel abandoned.'

'No need to worry; I've got all that fun unpacking to do. And I might go for a run, set up my weights bench – I'll be too busy to feel anything, least of all abandoned.'

His dad nodded and got out of the car, looking unconvinced. 'Well, you won't forget to eat lunch, will you? There are some sandwich bits in the fridge that I brought with us and—'

'I'll be fine! You just focus on your first day at your new job, okay?'

As they stepped up onto the porch, James noticed the crumbling white paint took on a slight luminescence in the moonlight. 'I guess this is kind of beautiful, in a weird way. Nova is going to love it here!'

His dad fumbled with the key and opened the front door. 'I agree! You can really feel the history here; it's remarkable.'

He flicked the dim hall light on, taking a deep breath as the shadows receded. James bent down and picked up the letters on the mat, flicking through them. Their first bit of post, all of them bearing his dad's name, *Frank Thorne*. He straightened up, staring at it and wondering if his Mum had started the process of changing her name yet.

'So, when is Nova coming to visit?'

James passed him the letters with a shrug as he led the way into the kitchen. 'Not sure yet, but hopefully soon, if that's OK?'

'Of course; your friends are always welcome. Just give me a few days' notice if you can.'

James grinned at him as he filled the kettle. His parents had always assumed Nova was his girlfriend or was going to end up his girlfriend – until he'd brought Will home. If he were straight, they probably would have been right.

He dug around in a nearby box for teabags and laid them out on the counter. 'What do you want, Dad?'

'Decaf green for me. I need an early night after today.'

James poured the tea, his mind back on what he'd left behind. He fished his phone out and saw a reply from Will. *Looks amaze, can't wait. X*

He replied, *Free for a video call in a bit? X*

Frank leant against the cracked counter and blew on his tea. 'Don't stay up too late, will you?'

James shook his head. 'Not planning on it. I'll have a quick chat with Will and then probably head to bed.'

12

Frank smiled. 'Ah, young love! Say hello for me.'

James nodded. 'I will. Sleep well!'

His dad left, the creaking of the staircase audible in the kitchen as he made his way upstairs. James sipped his tea, looking at his reflection in the window opposite. He looked tired; his brown hair was on the shaggy side of tidy, and his jaw was a little tense. He hadn't realised how clenched it was and took a deep belly breath like his football coach back home had taught him.

His phone buzzed again. Will had replied, *Sorry babe, not tonight. Out for Stevie's birthday, remember? Wish you were here.* X

James's stomach dropped at the reminder of what he was missing out on, and he sent a message to Nova instead. *Would love to have a quick chat if you're free now?* X

He was fairly sure she would be. She wasn't likely to be at Stevie's birthday; he was a football teammate, and while Nova had often come to his games to be a good friend, it wasn't really her scene.

He was staring at his phone, waiting for her reply, when he heard a noise. It sounded as though it had come from just outside the window.

'Probably an animal,' he said out loud to reassure himself, but he was suddenly very aware of how visible he was from a fair distance around with no blinds on the windows and the light on. Not to mention with the reflection on the glass and the darkness outside, he couldn't see a thing out there.

His skin began to crawl with the uncomfortable sensation of being watched and the urge to get out of the kitchen as quickly as possible. He turned and switched the light off, the darkness momentarily feeling safer, shielding him from prying eyes, but then the uncomfortable feeling he was no longer alone in the kitchen hit him.

Grabbing his tea and snatching his phone up, he left the room at a swift pace, feeling foolish as he went up the stairs, but he couldn't deny the sense of relief when he reached his room and closed the door behind him.

He flicked the light on, and his breath caught. His missing jacket was back on the hook. For a moment, his heart raced, but then he made sense of it. His dad must have put it there; no doubt he'd dropped it somewhere around the house and his dad had brought it back up on his way to bed. He must have been wrong about leaving it hung up on the door earlier. Calming himself down and dismissing the jacket situation, he settled down at his desk and switched on his laptop.

Five minutes later, Nova's face was beaming back at him from the screen, her dark hair swinging in its loose ponytail as she waved.

'Hey, you! I miss you so much already!'

He grinned back. 'Same. So good to see your face.'

'So, tell me everything! How's it been?'

He laughed. 'Not much to tell you. The drive was long and dull, got here, pretty much dodged unpacking, moped a bit. Went for dinner with Dad; he's gone to bed now.'

Nova nodded, her eyes taking on a searching look. 'Right, but I mean…how are you doing, really?'

James sighed. 'Honestly, at the moment, I just feel a bit…lost. Like I've been dropped into another reality that doesn't make sense and I'm just waiting to wake up with my arms around Will, back home.'

'I get that. It doesn't feel real to me either. I keep thinking I'm going to just, like, hang out with you tomorrow.'

James shrugged. 'As we said before, it is what it is, right?'

'Right, got to make the best of it. And remember, when I read my tarot the other night, I—' She stopped, staring intently into the camera, a sudden frown on her face. 'Wait, what was that?'

James turned, following her eyeline to the wall and the door behind him. 'What was what?'

Nova leant forward slightly, still staring.

'What was *what*, Nova? Stop it, you're freaking me out!'

'Is Posey there?'

James shook his head. 'No, the pet transport people are dropping her off in a few days, when we're more settled in. Why? Did you see something that looked like a cat?'

She turned her gaze back to him. 'No, not exactly. Sorry dude, I just…it was probably just a trick of the light. Did a car drive past just then?'

'No, my room overlooks the garden and the woods; there's no light out there. What the hell did you see?'

Nova looked away. 'Probably nothing, honestly. Eyes playing tricks, I bet. You know me, too witchy for my own good sometimes, spooking us out, sorry! Not what you need first night in your new house. Do you want to hear the gossip I heard today from Amanda? She said—'

'No! Come on, Nova, don't do this to me! Tell me what you saw.'

She sighed. 'Okay, fine, but don't blame me if it stops you sleeping. It just looked for a moment like a shadow on the wall behind you, a figure. It was only there for a second or two, and then it just sort of…flitted away.'

'Oh, fantastic! On top of everything else, this dump that I now live in is haunted?'

Nova bit her lip. 'I mean, maybe. It is very old!'

James sipped his tea and watched various competing emotions cross her face. He sighed. 'It's alright, Nova, you can let it out.'

Her eyes lit up. 'Thank you! I mean, obviously, this is shit for you, but I'm so excited! When I come to visit, maybe we can do a séance or a Ouija board, find out if there really is anything there?'

James nodded along. 'Alright, you can go full *Scooby-Doo* or whatever when you come up here. But seriously, what can I do in the meantime? I'd really like to just…get on with things, focus on getting onto the football team here and making a good start on my coursework. I don't want to be bothered by any restless weirdness right now.'

'Of course, you've got enough on your plate! Okay, well, I don't suppose you have any sage or Paulo Santo wood on you, but I bet you've got salt.'

'No, funnily enough I don't. But yeah, got salt – it's in the kitchen.'

'Get it and create a circle around your bed for tonight. I'll cast a little protection spell for you, and just keep imagining yourself inside a protective bubble of white or golden light that nothing that wishes you harm can penetrate.'

'Okay, thanks. So, what's new with you?'

Caspian Faye

Nova launched into the day's news about their friends in detail, and James relaxed, drinking his tea and immersing himself in his old world. By the time she'd finished, he felt like himself again. When her mum started shouting to turn her laptop off and go to bed, he wanted to beg her to stay on; he wasn't ready to go back to the silence and strangeness of his new environment.

She waved goodnight. 'Look, we can chat as much as you want, Jamesy; just message me whenever if you're having a hard time. I'm always here for you, you know that.'

'Thank you, and likewise. Sleep well! Sweet dreams, night!'

A click and she was gone, his room suddenly feeling very large and empty again. He shut his laptop, got up, and giving up on the idea of making the bed properly, he went rifling through the boxes until he found his sleeping bag and a pillow, throwing them onto the mattress. A few minutes more digging and he found the framed photo of him and Will taken not long after they'd started dating. They were smiling together on the edge of the football field. He grinned, remembering how he had noticed Will in a school play and started deliberately lingering behind after football practice just so they'd run into each other when Will came out of drama club rehearsals. And how Will had later admitted that he'd also started tracking the football practice schedule and coming to watch games whenever he could. They were clearly meant to be.

James put it on the bedside table, running a finger gently along the top to remove any dust.

He turned his phone torch on, ran down to the kitchen, grabbed the salt out of the sparse cupboard without lingering and made his way back up to follow Nova's advice. Once that was done, he felt a little bit better about what she'd seen. He knew it would play on his mind for a while, even though he was almost certain it was some kind of camera glitch or trick of the light. But it didn't hurt to be careful, and if there was anything that made him feel a bit better while he was settling in, he'd take it.

The upstairs bathroom was chilly, with harsh white lighting, groaning pipes and uneven tiles that were cold on his bare feet, so he got ready for bed as quickly as possible, returning to his room and settling into his sleeping bag with his phone. He checked Will's social media, but nothing had been posted since earlier, so he sent him a quick, *Good night, love you. X* before settling down to sleep.

Nathaniel

He shouldn't have done it, he knew that, but the voice he'd overheard was so musical, so enticing, he'd only wanted to see who it belonged to. The boy was back in his room and talking with someone, so Nathaniel had stepped out for a moment to watch, and it had been fine at first. He'd learnt the boy's name: James. A lovely name that suited him. It had been so nice to see him smile like that, his face lighting up when he saw his friend on the modern device. His energy had lifted a little; the sadness was still there, but now Nathaniel could feel joy and love emanating from him too. He had been really enjoying the reflected warmth; it had been so pleasant to bask in that, to linger on the edge of such a strong human connection – and then the girl had seen him!

He'd moved away as quickly as he could, but they were still talking about him. They were saying that awful word: *haunted.* Hearing it spoken out loud sent an instant jolt of fear through him. Suddenly, he was right back there, surrounded by the garish furnishings that had dominated the room in that time – the orange lights, the scattered art supplies and the leather diary on the desk with *1976* in gold lettering. He heard her voice again – much too loud – the woman in his room, screaming. 'It's haunted! *Haunted!* We have to leave!' Her coiffed hair bouncing as she grabbed at her daughter in a frenzy, pulling her away. The recollections were so startling, emerging from the haze of vagueness as violent technicolour visions, all triggered by the utterance of one word.

Pulled back into those days, he felt the regret as a downward drag on his heart. He had really liked Emily, the girl who had lived in his room, with her paint-stained jumpsuits and easel. It had been so soothing to watch her paint, an activity he couldn't stop himself joining in with once he realised he could. Although she had never been able to hear or see him, her gleeful reactions to him lifting the brush, dipping it in the paint and depicting scenes from his life and memories had always warmed his heart. Many times, he painted the twins for her, always under a shining sun, sometimes in the garden. Occasionally, he allowed himself to imagine moments that had never happened: him outside and alive in the sun with them. Emily didn't really know him off the canvas, but they had still been friends. Or so he'd thought. Until she told her mother about him, showed her his muddled artist's impression of the night he died. Instantly, Nathaniel went from her 'invisible friend' to an apparent threat; then the screaming started, and the house filled with fear.

He thought he saw regret in the backwards glance Emily gave the room as she was pulled away, but he'd never know for sure. The front door had slammed so violently it reverberated around the house, then silence fell until the noisy men with boxes came to collect everything, invading his space, sunlight searing his eyes as they tore down the curtains. When they'd finally gone and the dust had settled, Nathaniel found all that was left of his friend was a single paint-encrusted brush and a broken pencil, lying where they'd fallen over the ridge in the old floorboard.

In that moment, he'd made a decision: he would never try to connect directly with a human again. Then he had sunk back into sleep once more.

He drifted his hand through a cobweb idly as he considered his predicament. No, it didn't matter that James made him curious in a way he hadn't felt in decades; ultimately, he was still a human, and connecting with humans was a doomed venture. He sighed. In many ways, that moment in the autumn of 1976 felt like yesterday and yet like an age ago, a story from someone else's life.

In the last few decades, something had shifted. The reality that this was it now, this was *forever*, had truly sunk in. The two occasions he had been woken in the time since felt so different to before – an annoyance, not an adventure.

He felt so tired and yet somehow restless…frustrated and many other things he couldn't even name, all at once. The sleep lately had felt different too, not so deep and not satisfying. He stared blankly into the darkness within the wall, wishing he could somehow fathom a way to make his interminable existence tolerable.

There was the euphoria he felt occasionally glimpsing his reflection in mirrors and windowpanes and seeing himself, at least. That sometimes helped to stave off the loneliness a little – and perhaps if he was smarter this time and remained strong with James, he could make it work. He must not risk a similar outcome; James seemed nice, so if Nathaniel's first impression was correct, he could keep his distance and they would co-exist peacefully. He would remain unnoticed, knowing he had the option of diversion, entertainment, a life to watch and a way to feel invested in the passage of time once more – but he would refrain from doing anything obvious. He would be cautious.

He heard the conversation draw to a close, so he drifted back out again. The girl with the rare ability to see him was no longer present. It had taken him a while to understand how modern devices worked, and they changed so much between sleeps, but the delicious power he could draw from them remained the same.

He drifted to the one on the desk where the girl's face had been and brushed it lightly with a hand, drawing out what remained in the battery. It was so thin and much smaller than anything he'd seen last time, the screen so much clearer and louder. He paused for a moment, pondering how shocked he would have been to imagine such a thing when he was alive. The accusations of witchcraft that would have been spat at someone who even suggested such a powerful thing could exist. He shuddered, pushing the thought away.

James was rummaging in his boxes, so Nathaniel watched him, eager for the distraction from his swirling thoughts. He was intrigued to see what items would be unwrapped and what they would tell him about his new guest. First, it was bedclothes that were tossed casually aside, but then James found something that clearly meant a lot to him – he took it out with reverence and handled it carefully.

Whatever it was, it made him smile again, his eyes lighting up. Nathaniel smiled too, reflexively, enjoying the sensation and becoming curious to see the object in James's hand. As soon as James left the room, Nathaniel went to the bedside table to look.

A small picture frame with one of those exceptional modern images in it. He stared, captured by the two joyful faces looking back at him: James and another boy. They looked so happy together, as if they fit. They were both so beautiful. Nathaniel wondered what it would feel like to be one of them – so alive, so present and so loved.

A sudden noise out on the landing startled him from his musing. His first impulse was to flee back to the safety of his wall, but he fought it. He needed to know if it had happened again; he needed to know if *it* was back. Many years had passed since it had last roamed the house, but Nathaniel's fear had never lessened in intensity.

He made his way carefully to the doorway. So long as he stayed in his room, he was safe. It wouldn't come in here, wouldn't hunt Nathaniel, so long as he stayed out of the way. Nathaniel looked out into the hallway; it looked clear. Relief flooded through him when James came out of the bathroom – he had probably shut a cupboard door too hard or something. He certainly didn't sense any malevolent energy in his immediate vicinity. No, he was definitely being paranoid. He had ventured downstairs earlier, and he would have felt any disturbances or lingering evil had the entity escaped.

He wracked his fragmented memory. The people who had been here before Emily and her parents arrived, some time ago, they had done it, the binding. The people who had arrived in a group with their bright-coloured clothing and loud music. He had liked them; they had radiated freedom and joy. That was…the 1960s. He was sure of it.

They had brought such energy for him to bask in. Dancing and singing, they were too focused on each other to ever notice Nathaniel, but they had noticed *it*. The entity had grown strong and started disturbing the peace, feeding on their growing fear. Then came knowledgeable people from outside, and with their smoke, candles and chanting, they bound the entity that scared them so much. Peace, after years of terror and hiding. Nathaniel wasn't sure where or how they had bound it, but they had. He hadn't ventured from his room very much after their ritual—but he had felt better knowing that in theory, he *could*.

The energy in the house had felt lighter, the people even happier. Nathaniel vaguely remembered considering some of them almost-friends. They didn't know him, but he was sure they felt him as a part of the house, the collective energy – and it was almost enough. But they had left in the end anyway. The memories were still hazy when he tugged at the threads of them, but he knew the longer he was awake, the more they would become clear. He had to be patient.

He calmed himself with the assertion that the entity was bound. It was still gone; the house was safe.

Despite having soothed his fear, he was still relieved to see James was spreading salt around his bed. If James was careful and knowledgeable about such things, then Nathaniel wouldn't have to worry so much about *it* returning and preying on him.

As James got into bed and started to settle down, Nathaniel drifted back into the wall; he knew humans liked to sleep in peace.

James

James woke with a start, his alarm amplified by the acoustics of the high ceilings in his new room combined with the lack of furniture. The cold winter sun was streaming into the room, highlighting all the boxes that needed unpacking. He groaned and wriggled out of his sleeping bag, grabbing his phone to silence the alarm. Automatically, he checked for messages. There was a picture from Nova of her dog Zed with a new toy, some college registration stuff in his email and some heart emojis from his mum – but nothing from Will yet. He took a deep breath and shook it off. He couldn't become clingy or this long-distance thing wouldn't work. Will had been out last night; he was probably sleeping off a hangover, knowing him. It wasn't personal, and they both needed to make allowances for each other's separate lives now within their relationship – or at least, that's what the advice videos he'd watched online had said. Searching 'how to make long distance relationships work' had brought up a lot of information, some of it conflicting, but most people seemed to be in agreement on the trust and compromise part being crucial.

He pulled on his joggers and went downstairs to make some porridge, which he ate perched on one of his dad's favourite bar stools by the window. His mum had hated them and called them 'tacky', but his dad thought the cracked upholstery gave them a vintage US diner aesthetic. James was indifferent, but they were a handy height for his long legs.

The garden really was a wilderness, but in quite an interesting way. He watched a variety of birds hopping around on the frosty grass and hoped his dad wouldn't tidy it up too much.

When he'd finished eating, he made coffee and took it back up to his room, determined to make a start on setting up.

He passed the first few hours unpacking and sorting things into piles, then dragged his chest of drawers out from underneath the boxes he'd cleared and chose an alcove for it. Once most of his clothes were put away, the room looked a lot better, and he went downstairs to set up his workout area. His dad had promised him the garage, as the driveway was big enough for the car and the road isolated enough that it would be perfectly safe there. He knew it was an offer made out of guilt, but he wasn't going to argue.

He dragged all of the bits he needed into the garage and started reassembling everything. Once the bench was set up and he'd brought all of his weights, his mat, and his foam roller down, it was starting to look pretty good. The garage was a fairly new extension to the main house, with a concrete floor and exterior bricks that didn't quite match the aged ones the house was made of. The plaster on the walls looked quite fresh, and there were a few cobwebs and a bit of dust, but it only took him a few minutes to make it look fairly clean. He decided he'd get a mini fridge to keep his pre- and post-workout snacks in and started to look for a plug socket. There were a few shelves in the corner that he guessed the last occupants had used for tools, so he went over to have a look there.

As he approached, he spotted a dark patch between two of the shelves. It looked like mould but was oddly rectangular. He ran a finger along it; it was cold but didn't feel damp. He noted it as something to flag up to his dad later.

Underneath the shelving unit was the power source he was looking for, and he put aside concerns about damp and went back to his kit, determined to squeeze in a workout before lunch. It was the best way he had to make himself feel more in control of his life and a great distraction from the feelings of loss that kept coming up every time he thought of his old home.

***

As James knocked back his protein shake, he checked his phone and saw Will had finally sent a message: *Party was CHAOS baby! Missed you, love you. X*

James grinned at the screen and replied, *How are u feeling today? Chat later? X*

There is not enough coffee in this world…that's how I'm feeling! Worth it though. I would love to, but have so much to get done…tomorrow night maybe? X

OK, you're on! Good luck with all the stuff to do. X

James stared out at the grey day, put aside his disappointment with Will's busy schedule and pondered whether or not to go for a short run. After a moment's deliberation, he decided he would – he could use the fresh air and couldn't afford to slack on his cardio if he wanted to make the football team. He wasn't looking forward to having to prove himself all over again, and it had been weighing on his mind that maybe the team here wouldn't be as welcoming to a gay guy as his last team had been. If that was the case, he might have a battle ahead – both socially and physically. He might have to win them over by being such an indispensable asset that any bigots among them put their views aside for the good of the team.

In general, he wondered what this area was going to be like; it was so much more rural than he was used to.

He dumped his empty protein shaker in the sink along with his plate from lunch and opened the back door. A gust of wind blew rain into his face as he stepped out, and he zipped his hoodie right up, stuck his earphones in and set off.

Nathaniel

Nathaniel drifted from the wall while the outside world was still in darkness and waited patiently to watch the sun rise from the large bedroom window. It was something he had always done in his physical form, a ritual that had brought immense comfort in the hardest of times, and he liked to revisit it.

The slowly spreading light began to illuminate his favourite tree as he heard James's dad get up and move around the house, the front door closing behind him when he left for work. He looked back at James's face, still sleeping peacefully as the first rays of the morning fell on his features. The sudden sound that woke him was harsh and unpleasant; Nathaniel hated it so much he considered whether he should drain the power out of the horrible portable phone device to prevent it making such a jarring noise. He remembered the phones from last time being far less strident in their sounds, and never in the bedroom.

James got up and thankfully made the noise stop, pausing at the phone for a moment in just a T-shirt and boxer shorts. Nathaniel was acquainted with these styles of garments, but somehow, the way James wore them made them look so much more appealing than he had ever seen before. Nathaniel gazed at him a moment. The T-shirt lightly grazed the muscles in his chest, the sleeves settled on the curve of his biceps, and the muscles in his legs on display were a sight to behold. Nathaniel suddenly remembered an old sensation: that of blushing, the heat, the energy, and for a split second he almost felt…alive again.

Then James moved, putting his phone down and walking from the room, shattering the moment. Nathaniel stared after him, realizing he was drifting towards the door as if pulled by some magnetic force. He stopped with effort and shook himself. After setting his intent to keep his distance, here he was risking detection by staring inappropriately like a damn fool. It mustn't happen again. He knew lingering gazes could sometimes be felt by sensitive individuals and make them uncomfortable. He must exercise restraint and remember to avert his eyes like a gentleman.

When James returned to the room a while later and began to move his belongings around, Nathaniel retreated to the windowsill and settled. There was nothing wrong with staying there, out of the way where he wouldn't be walked through and keeping an eye on his new guest. The fact that James was moving heavy boxes and furniture, sweating a little and still wearing that tight T-shirt, was just a harmless little treat. When he left and went back downstairs, Nathaniel turned back to the garden, pushing aside his disappointment. The view of the garden helped to ground him and remind him of his place. It wasn't such a bad thing to look occasionally and admire, but no good lay in developing delusions or fixations on what he could never have. He had learnt that lesson already and learnt it well. Attachment and misplaced hope were dangerous beasts, and with all the time he'd had to reflect on it, there was no excuse to entertain such weaknesses again.

But there was no harm in dreaming of how things had once been, of the dreams for a happy future that he'd enjoyed before he knew better. He could gaze out into the outside world all he wanted, remember the simple sensation of the breeze on his skin and the warm touch of another human. The summers when he'd spent time with his siblings, the laughter and the games. He wished he'd not taken it for granted at the time, assuming it would always be like that. Swimming in the river for hours, happily lying on the bank afterwards and drying off in the sun, with his feet lightly coated in mud. Days that stretched on, making summer seem endless. It was the most himself he had been in life, existing without much thought past the present moment, skimming stones, stealing apples and wearing his older brother's clothes.

He smiled as he recalled taunting his newly appointed governess alongside his brother and sister as she scolded them from the riverbank, her protestations about the sour apples spoiling their supper and the messy state they were in. Looking back, he had a little more sympathy for her constant futile struggle to control any of them.

He remembered how much his face ached with laughter on the afternoon that she slipped in the mud and fell in, having to drag herself from the water in her heavy skirts, incandescent with rage and striding away dripping wet to try and recover her dignity.

He allowed himself to indulge in one of his favourite fantasies, the one where his body had not betrayed him with unwanted changes, one where he had grown tall and strong like his brother. Being able to cast off his shirt and swim in breeches alongside him, even as he grew into adulthood. Being free, being just like he was.

In this other reality, he could imagine everything had gone differently. His brother had never been sent off to boarding school, and Nathaniel hadn't had to watch the carriage leave, taking his best friend away.

He imagined if James had been his friend back then, how he would have loved to see him laugh too and watch him swim, the ripples in the water those muscles would make. The way his wet torso would glisten in the sunlight.

He played out this new version, being outside on the riverbank like before, but with the addition of James, the shiny new focus in this happy daydream. He closed his eyes and saw it in his mind's eye: James looking at him the way he looked at the boy in the picture on his bedside table. A big smile, light in his eyes, and then as they grew closer, his hand reaching out. Nathaniel focused and could almost feel it: James's hand taking his, the warmth and solidity of it, his imagination transporting him from his current reality and into a better one.

A noise downstairs shook him out of his fantasy. He opened his eyes and tuned in to the energy of the house. It hadn't shifted; it was fine. He knew it was fine, but the fear of *it*, of the dreadful entity coming back, still rose so immediately at every unexpected sound, even after all this time. It was probably for the best that his reverie was interrupted, however – he needed to be more careful with the direction of his fantasies. He took a pause and refocused on the present. He would have to get used to sudden noises again; humans tended to make them a lot.

Likely the noise he'd heard was just James sorting out his new home, settling in. Nathaniel noticed a feeling of contentment at this notion and realised he was decided on matters: he really wanted James to make changes, to feel at home here. To not leave. The realisation came with added resolve to not mess things up this time – to not overstep, to not be too much, to never risk driving James away.

He could feel James's energy from here; he was somewhere on the left side of the ground floor, but Nathaniel could connect with him, pick him out of the general atmosphere of the house. His energy shone out of the mundane hum, more distinct than anything Nathaniel had felt before.

A door banged, and Nathaniel both saw and felt James leave the house, a little wrench somewhere in his chest as the sensation of lightness and connection withdrew, the source of it jogging away into the grey day.

James

A prickling sensation across his back made James pause and look back, his eyes drawn to his bedroom window. It was inexplicable, but he felt like he was being watched again. It wasn't unpleasant, just a sense of observation and the instinctive urge to find the source of the feeling. He knew there was no-one in the house, so he looked around once more, wondering if his dad was back early or a neighbour had come calling.

He couldn't see anyone, but then visibility wasn't great in this weather, so he was likely missing something. No doubt they'd leave a message. He pulled his hood tighter around his face, turned his running playlist up and jogged on.

Halfway through his run, his phone rang, interrupting the music. He stopped to decline the call, expecting it to be spam – but it was Will.

'Hey, baby, how are you?' Will sounded enthusiastically buoyant.

'Hey!' James answered, caught off guard by the call and trying to recover his breath. 'Just in the middle of a run, great to hear your voice, though. I miss you!'

'I miss you too. So much.'

James slowed to a walk, stepping around a puddle and into some mulch. He swore as the slimy substance coated his shoes.

'Sorry, wrecking my trainers out here in the middle of nowhere! I also really miss my usual running routes.'

'I bet! But still, my guy keeping himself in peak condition. I approve.'

'It's not *just* for you, y'know.' James laughed.

'Well, I like to think it is.' Will paused. 'So, the thing is, I'm not free to video chat this week, sorry.'

'Oh, that's…it's okay. I get it – you're busy,' James replied, fighting to keep the dismay out of his voice.

'But I was thinking…instead, when can I come and visit?'

'When are you free?'

'I thought if I get ahead on my coursework and get Taz to take notes for me on Friday and Monday, maybe I could come for a long weekend?'

'Of course, when are you thinking?'

'This weekend?'

James felt the massive grin break out on his face. 'Are you serious?'

'Of course I am! Does that work for you?'

'Yes, please!' James answered without thinking about it. Will was his priority; he'd figure out how to arrange anything else that came up around seeing him. He sat down on a log while they worked out how Will would get to the nearest station and then finished his run with renewed energy despite the breeze repeatedly blowing icy gusts of drizzle into his face.

When he got back, he took a hot shower and made a start on unpacking some kitchen utensils, not quite sure how the day had gone so fast.

His dad arrived back from work not long after sunset bearing pasta, and they ate dinner on the stools around the breakfast bar while they gave each other a brief rundown of their days. He was predictably happy enough with the news of James's first visitor and confirmed he'd be back from work in time to pick Will up from the station on the Friday.

James pushed a forkful of penne around his plate and mopped up some more of the arrabiatta sauce. 'Oh, yeah, Dad, also, I spotted some damp in the garage earlier when I was setting up my workout stuff.'

'Damp? Since when are you a property expert?'

James laughed. 'Whatever. It's a nasty mouldy-looking stain on the wall – might not be damp, but it's very cold, and it looks slimy.'

Frank made a face. 'Thanks for letting me know. I'll have a look at it in a bit. Doesn't sound like something we want to leave unaddressed.' He pushed his plate to one side. 'Oh, also, your mum called earlier. the pet carrier folks will be dropping Posey off tomorrow. Apparently, we'll get a more precise timeslot in the morning, but are you okay to wait in for her?'

'Of course, Dad!' James felt his mood lift instantly; having his cat around the house would definitely help to make it feel more like home.

***

'Hmm…it does feel a bit cold.' Frank ran his hand over the wall. 'Not wet, exactly, but the coldness definitely isn't a good sign.'

He ran his hands over the brickwork. 'It's an outside wall, so I'll have to have a look on the other side and see if I can spot anything. Weird positioning, though. If it was a pipe or something, it'd be more linear.'

He reached into his toolbox and pulled out a flathead screwdriver, tapping along the wall gently with the handle. When he reached the dark patch of plaster, the sound changed.

'That's odd.' He tapped again, a bit harder.

'Different resonance, definitely.' James leant in and took the screwdriver. 'What happens if you…'

He flipped it and poked the wall hard. The plaster cracked and shattered, releasing a cold breath of air into the room.

'Oh, well bloody done, Mr Muscles…' Frank trailed off at the sight of a small cavity underneath the plaster. They both stared at it for a moment, and then James reached in and picked away the remaining edges, the darkened plaster coming away easily.

'May as well carry on; it's going to need fixing up now anyway,' his dad said with a little sigh.

'Is there something in there?' James asked, peering into the small space. It was about the size of three bricks – not a large cavity, but it did look deliberately hollowed out. He pulled out his phone and switched on the torch, illuminating the space. Inside was a small box. He drew it out and placed it on the floor.

'An imaginative child's game, I reckon,' Frank said.

The box was styled in the manner of an old treasure chest. He reached down and snapped the small metal padlock off with a flick of the screwdriver, and James opened it.

The lid was slightly damp with condensation, and the interior of the box was no more pleasant. It was stained on the inside with something dark and sticky, and some old dried-up vegetation sat on top of the mess. A small, charred piece of paper was rolled up with it.

Frank unrolled it and peered at it. 'We've got an unintelligible scrawl; that's utterly useless.'

James poked at the dried-up plant and felt something hard underneath, he lifted it out: a very old-looking pocket watch. 'This doesn't look like a child's game.'

He held it up, and his dad frowned. 'Maybe they stole it from a grandparent or something.' Frank straightened up. 'Well, mystery solved. Whatever that rotting crap is has obviously leaked out into the plaster. I'll have to patch it up at the weekend. Whoever's kid pulled this one owes me a drink!'

James looked down at the watch, the metal heavy in his hands.

Frank stifled a yawn. 'Right, well, fun little diversion though this was, I'm going to get on with unpacking the living room. We need somewhere cosy to unwind pronto, especially now that you've got a guest booked in, eh?'

James lingered for a moment, turning the watch over, the chain sliding between his fingers. He fiddled with it, and the catch popped open with an odd puff of air. The glass over the watch face was cracked, and the hands looked rusted in place. On the inside of the case was an engraving. he rubbed at it with a finger until he could make it out: *A.G.*

Nathaniel

Upstairs, Nathaniel started awake to a wave of terror, knowing with awful certainty: *it was back.*

James

'I'm making tea; do you want one?' James stuck his head around the living room door, grinning at his dad fussing with the exact positioning of a clock on the mantelpiece.

'I'm alright for now, thanks,' Frank replied. 'I'll probably head up to bed soonish.'

'Ah, ok. Sleep well. Do you have—'

A sudden bang from outside the room drove the rest of the thought out of James's mind. 'What the hell was that?'

His dad joined him at the door, his posture cautious as he made his way out into the hall and back towards the kitchen. James followed him, his heart rate increasing. Together they checked the kitchen thoroughly, but there was no sign of anything amiss.

'It sounded like it came from out here…' Frank trailed off, his gaze landing on the corridor leading through to the garage.

James led the way, flicking the light back on. Everything looked as they had left it, except for the dumbbell that was now in the middle of the floor, on top of the crushed remains of the little treasure box.

'I didn't – that was stacked away under my weights bench!' James blurted out.

'I know,' Frank cut him off, his face a little pale. He looked back and forth between the bench and where the weight sat now amongst splinters of wood. 'It must have been a freak gust of wind, maybe – caused an extreme draft or something. Don't worry about it; I'll sort it out.'

James stared after him as he went to the corridor to fetch the dustpan and brush. It was bewildering to see him try and rationalise such an odd occurrence with such an unlikely explanation. He picked the weight up and put it back where it belonged as Frank began sweeping up the mess.

'Dad, are you sure there's no one else here?'

'Of course. There's nowhere for them to hide, for a start, and they would have had to pass us to get out of here.' He gestured at the way they'd come in and then towards the garage door, which was coated in cobwebs and a layer of rust; it clearly hadn't been opened in a long time.

James felt a shiver pass down his spine at the realisation that something very unnatural had taken place in this room just minutes ago – not that it was a much better proposition to believe there was another human hiding somewhere in their new house.

'A draft, then,' he said out loud, humouring his dad. James had his doubts that Frank believed his own theory, but it was much more comforting to agree than to discuss the alternative. For a moment, he was tempted to tell him what Nova had seen the other night, but he dismissed the idea. His dad had enough on his plate without adding to it, and he would probably call it fanciful nonsense anyway.

Nathaniel

Nathaniel had been fighting waves of panic ever since he sensed it: the return of the dark heaviness that had hung over the house for so long. When the bang sounded from below, accompanied by a burst of aggressive energy, he shrank further into himself, cringing within the wall.

Now that *it* was back, so distinct and intense, Nathaniel wondered how he had ever mistaken slight energetic shifts for *this*. It was worse than he remembered. He kept reminding himself that he was safe so long as he didn't leave his room – but there was James to think of now. James and his wonderful energy that felt like sunshine; Nathaniel couldn't bear the thought of some terrible thing befalling him. Already, he could feel James's light obscured by the growing darkness downstairs, his energetic signature more distant.

He willed him to come upstairs, to the safety of this room, to the one place Nathaniel knew he was protected. Finally, after what seemed like forever, he did, his steady footsteps on the stairs, a steaming cup of tea in one hand and his phone in the other.

Nathaniel slipped from the wall and watched him, his rich brown eyes flicking from side to side as he read something on the phone screen, a slight frown on his face. His expression reminded Nathaniel of Theodore in that moment, of how he would frown over his notebooks and poetry. It was one of the first things Nathaniel had found so endearing about him: the complete absorption in his scribblings.

He had loved to watch Theodore writing his spells and constructing his plans, the special moments when he would look up from whatever he was working on. His automatic smile when he met Nathaniel's gaze, his inky fingers reaching out and twirling strands of his hair, making him feel like he was the only person in the world who mattered to him. The only distraction worth taking time away from his occult studies.

Caspian Faye

The days they had spent together, lying in the shade, both absorbed in their own writing, comfortable in the glow of each other's company. The happiness Nathaniel had derived from all the wonderful adventures Theodore planned, their exciting imagined future together. The loss of that future had hurt almost as much as the loss of his past when the dark edges came creeping into his memories, the sourness of betrayal curdling those happy times, spoiling them too. He shook it off, wishing he had more control over the memories that came back to him. Dwelling on Theodore after all these years was pointless and painful, and yet he could never seem to stop himself. So many things reminded him of Theodore. He supposed, despite the pain, there was some strange pleasure in the recollections too. Perhaps the illusion of past love was better than no love at all.

Nathaniel pushed the memories away and focused instead on what was right before him now, moving towards James slowly, carefully, coming to a stop close enough to read James's energy but not so close that he would accidentally make contact with him. Nathaniel had learnt a long time ago that people didn't like that – they would move, complain of coldness, seem revolted in some way.

James was concerned about something, that much was clear. As he watched, James pulled something from his pocket and tossed it onto his desk. Nathaniel stared; it was *the* pocket watch. Seeing it again after all these years was a shock, especially in its current state. It was profoundly wrong to see it filthy and uncared for when it used to be prized, always gleaming, catching the light against Arthur's dark waistcoats. Arthur flashed into his mind's eye, always impeccably dressed in perfectly tailored suits. Nathaniel often used to covet them, wishing he had someone to make him custom clothing. Wishing he could wear a range of things in the afterlife for a bit of variety. He drifted over and examined the watch, the initials still clear. He lightly tapped it with a finger. A sticky energetic residue came away with his touch, enough for him to know the object had been tainted by the awful presence trapped within, and a trace signature of the magic from the visitors who'd trapped it inside, but otherwise empty now that the entity roamed the house once more.

He withdrew his hand and turned, only to find James staring right at him. His focus seemed slightly off, but it felt very much as though he could somehow sense he was there.

'Hello?' Nathaniel said immediately, but he wasn't sure why he did it. James was not a Victorian occultist; he was unlikely to hear a word, and even if he did, that outcome was even worse.

James's eyes narrowed, almost as though he was trying to hear. He looked curious, not scared. Nathaniel felt a sudden kindling of hope despite himself.

'James?' Nathaniel tried again, willing him to somehow hear him now. Perhaps it was worth the risk. A little test – if James recoiled, then Nathaniel could go back into hiding, knowing not to try making further contact.

James cocked his head, his eyes still on the space where Nathaniel stood. He was frowning now, but he still didn't seem uncomfortable or frightened. He wasn't reacting like the children in the 1940s who arrived covered in city grime and complained to the owner of the house of 'sharp whispers' that hurt their ears, or the man who came after them who would jump and scratch at his skin every time Nathaniel uttered a sound.

He knew attempting this contact was a reckless loss of control and went against all his resolutions, but he reached out and drained the power from James's phone anyway. Channelling what he had drawn from it, he summoned the courage to speak again, 'Hello?'

James startled a little this time, his eyes widening as he looked around the room.

'Hello?'

'Yes! I'm here!' Nathaniel answered, unable to believe his luck. James had heard him, for the first time in over a hundred years, not a tap, a bang or a whisper – his real, actual voice. Most importantly of all; James wasn't screaming; he wasn't running; he was still here.

James was breathing heavily, looking all around him as if hoping to spot Nathaniel, but he knew he didn't have enough energy to fully show himself.

'Did you…are you what moved my weight earlier and smashed that box?'

'No!' Nathaniel answered, but he could feel his ability to use his voice already fading.

James looked around expectantly then sighed. 'Didn't like that question, then?' He waited another moment, then shook his head. 'I'm actually going mad, properly mad.'

Nathaniel wanted to reassure him that he wasn't, but he couldn't do it without using power from the lights, and he knew from experience that humans particularly hated lights flickering. They'd hated it even more on the rare occasions he'd overdone it and exploded a bulb or two. Not wanting to send James running from the room when everything was seeming so promising, he held himself back despite desperately hungering for more contact.

James looked down at his phone and sighed again, going to the wall to plug it in. Nathaniel watched him switch it back on and send messages but forced himself to move away. It would be very ungentlemanly of him to read private correspondence, and he prided himself on having never lost his manners.

Besides, nothing good had ever come of reading another's letters. He had done it once, in life – reading his mother's account of his apparent insanity to his aunt when she'd left it open on her bureau – and he had never regretted an imprudence more. Despite the years of sleep, some moments never faded from his mind, and some words could never be unread.

He moved to the window, staring out into the darkness at the trees rustling in the wind, trying to calm himself. The exhilaration of having communicated with James, however briefly, was surging through him. It was triggering impulses he hadn't had in a long time. He looked at the mirror leaning against the wall in the corner of the room and contemplated it. Throwing caution to the wind, he moved, drawing on the power from the phone now connected to the wall. Then he waited, focusing on his intention in front of the mirror; he saw himself appearing more solidly again. Not the wispy, faded, transparent reflection, but one that almost looked human, to him, at least.

It would likely only last minutes, but the rush was as good as the very first time. Even better, perhaps – extinguishing candles and gas lamps had all been very well, but the power on offer had become better every time he awoke, and the potential of new ways to absorb it was something he was still exploring.

He never got tired of it: looking at his reflection and seeing his truest self. He felt a smile spread across his face as he stared at the young man looking back at him. His grey eyes might be a little sad-looking, but they were clear and strong. His face had lost the softness it had once had, the shadows along his jaw and chin lending him the masculinity he had always hungered for. His flat chest, the lack of anything that didn't belong. And even better, the shape of muscle underneath his tailored clothing, the fullness and hardness of his body. The sense that he was becoming complete, not lacking anything.

James's gasp jolted him from the study of his reflection and back into the present. He turned and found him staring not through or past him, but right *at him*. Nathaniel gazed into those searching eyes and knew they were firmly fixed on him, taking in his appearance. James had dropped his phone on the bed, his mouth remaining partly open; he was frozen.

Nathaniel moved towards him and smiled as he did so. He hoped he looked friendly and that James's stare wasn't that of terror or revulsion. It would be particularly devastating to be perceived as a frightening, freakish apparition; he wanted James to know he meant well.

He stopped an arm's length from James, not wanting to intrude on his personal space but desperately wishing he could get closer. They stared at one another, eyes locked, as Nathaniel noted the encouraging sign that he had not backed away. He couldn't help but wish James would make a move towards him, though, step into the space between them and make it clear he wasn't afraid.

Caspian Faye

The moment stretched on, then a bang from downstairs shattered it. James sucked in a deep breath, grabbed his phone and sprang from the bed, running from the room. Nathaniel made a move to follow him, opening his mouth to call out – but his energy was fading fast, and he couldn't make a sound.

James

'NOVA, oh my God, Nova!' James panted into the phone as he fled out the back door into the garden.

'Jamesy? Are you ok? Sweetie, what's wrong?'

'I…I saw…I heard…I—'

'James, deep breath, okay? I want you to take three deep breaths with me and then tell me, from the beginning, what happened. I've got you; let's do it together, alright. I'm here. One…two…three…four, and out for six, one…two…three…four…five…six.'

James followed her voice, focused on his chest expanding and taking in the cool night air, and slowly, he began to feel better.

'Right, so what's going on? Take your time.'

James sat down on the back doorstep and huddled into his hoodie, hoping his limited phone battery would hold out.

'Okay, so, I just saw something – a ghost! – in my room.'

'What? Oh my Goddess, okay, go on!'

'That's not all – so much weird stuff has happened. First, there was this feeling I was getting of being watched, then I found a strange stain on the garage wall which turned out to be a small cavity with a box in it, and a pocket watch. Then something smashed it with my dumbbell when me and my dad were nowhere near it – the box, not the watch. Also, I heard something earlier; I'm sure I did! Faint and almost in my head, but now I'm pretty sure it wasn't my imagination because I just looked up from checking my emails to see this guy looking into my mirror! And he looked so real!'

'Wow! Yeah, that's a lot. It sounds like a very active site!'

'It's not a *site*; it's my home now. I have to live here, Nova! I have to sleep in that room! And he saw me. It wasn't like this unaware-replay type thing; he saw me and moved closer and looked back at me.'

'Oh, wow! Whoops, yeah, sorry, it's just, I can't lie, this is so fascinating! Okay, the ghost you saw, details?'

'About my age but definitely from another time, I'm guessing 1600s or 1700s, maybe? Highwayman aesthetic, y'know? Long sandy hair in a little ponytail, maybe five foot six-ish, athletic—'

Nova laughed. 'I didn't mean, like, dating app details, I meant—did he seem threatening or aggressive? Did you feel any malicious intent?'

'I was too busy being shocked by a ghost appearing right in front of me to conduct a vibe check.' James paused and recalled the moment. 'But…he didn't seem aggressive. More, I don't know, a bit confused, perhaps? Almost as if he didn't expect me to see him.'

'Hmm, that makes sense.'

'It does?'

'Look, James, while most if not all people – in my opinion, anyway – have the potential ability to see past the veil or communicate with entities no longer in the physical form if they're open to it and cultivate it, most people don't. They're closed off, and they don't want to open up.'

'I haven't opened up or cultivated anything!' James objected. 'I don't want this. I've got enough to be dealing with, especially right now.'

'I know, but here's the thing – I think you're naturally psychic whether you like it or not. I'm not at all surprised by this, taking your astrological chart into account and your intuitive leanings.'

James picked at the flaking wood on the side of the step. 'Well, what can I do about it? Apart from the stuff you already told me about.'

'You've got, like, three options here: either you protect yourself, close off as best you can and get on with things, or you start looking into having your house cleansed, or…you investigate further.'

James considered for a moment, remembering the ghost's eyes on his, recalling the loneliness he thought he sensed in that moment.

'I don't think I want to do the first one; it feels too much like denial. The second one seems…hostile and cruel. The third one is scary but seems the most right, though I hate to say it.'

'There are different ways to get rid of spirits – you can banish them, but you don't have to. So, space cleansing is not hostile necessarily; it can just be releasing the spirit to move on.'

'But I feel like I want that to be his choice. He was here first, after all.'

'Option three, then?'

James felt a little rush of fear and excitement mingled together. 'Yeah, option three.'

Nova appeared to be trying to keep the enthusiasm out of her voice but didn't succeed. 'Right, I'm going to come and visit as soon as I can. In the meantime, I'll send you a protective spell bottle to wear and some resources to work with, and I'll start doing some research, but don't forget to do all the things I already told you to stay safe, especially until we know what we're dealing with.'

James exhaled, feeling much better now that they had a plan. 'OK, let me know as soon as you figure out when you can visit—oh, Will is coming this weekend, though.'

Nova laughed. 'Oh, brilliant. I hope the ghost shows up, I can only imagine his reaction.'

'I'd rather not, thanks!' James replied. 'That's a drama I could do without.'

He heard his low battery alert go off. 'My phone is going to die soon, but thank you so much, Nova. I really appreciate you being with me on this.'

'Always, my soul friend.'

'Miss you.'

A noise from behind made James jump. He turned to see Frank silhouetted in the light from the kitchen. 'Hey, was that you crashing around down here earlier?'

He almost told the truth, but then he remembered his dad's concerned expression earlier. 'Yeah, sorry, did I disturb you? Just a late-night workout.'

His dad shook his head. 'You maniac! Try and keep it down, will you? I'm back in the office early.'

'Of course, sorry! Sleep well.'

'Night!' Frank withdrew, closing the door behind him.

James lifted the phone back to his ear. 'Did you hear that?'

'Not exact words, just enough to recognise who it was. How is your dad dealing with this? Or does he think you're behind everything?'

'Denial is the path he's chosen. He's blaming freak drafts and me being noisy. But then, he hasn't actually seen anything.'

Nova laughed. 'And how long are you going to take the blame if things escalate?'

'I'm hoping they won't. What with everything with Mum and the new job, he doesn't need this any more than I do.'

'How very selfless of you.'

'Don't take the piss; you know I'm right.'

'Of course. Look, I'd better let you go charge your phone. Besides, I can't really talk anymore – it's late, and Mum's going to start shouting at me soon. But we can carry on talking over messages if you need to?'

'It's alright; I really am OK. Thank you again. And I'm sorry we didn't get to catch up on your news today.'

'Ha! Nothing as interesting as you've got going on; my day was very average. Keep me updated, won't you?'

'Of course. Thanks again!'

'Night!'

When she hung up, James sat in silence for a few minutes. It was cold, but he didn't want to go back inside just yet. He sent Will a check-in message asking about his day and saying how much he was looking forward to seeing him and then stared blankly at the night sky for a few minutes. It was strikingly beautiful. There was no light pollution at all; it was a clear night without cloud cover, revealing masses of stars. When his fingers began to sting and his jaw to clench, he reluctantly got up and went back inside.

He yawned as the relative warmth of the house enveloped him and then froze in his tracks; all of the kitchen cupboard doors were open.

'Oh, come on!' he said out loud. 'Why did you do that?'

Silence was his only answer, so he closed them all and went up to his room.

Nathaniel

The euphoria of being visible to James was still generating a powerful hum of warmth within Nathaniel long after James's footsteps had grown distant.

They had connected in a very real way. The satisfaction of seeing his reflection was nothing compared to this: the experience of being seen by another being. A broad, uncontrollable smile broke out on his face for the first time in over a century. The significance of this was immense. It was a step forward, a new beginning. Joy washed over him at this sudden change in his fortunes.

James was very special. He was able to *see* Nathaniel, and despite the way their encounter had ended – with what seemed like shock – Nathaniel was hopeful he could show James over time that he was nothing to be alarmed by. He would do it right this time! It would be a gradual process that wouldn't cause any screaming, panicking, incense waving or frantic bag packing. He hugged himself, the certainty that his existence was changing for the better consuming him. A hesitant voice in his mind offered caution, the concern that his sudden optimism was misplaced, but he pushed it away. He was sure the shock of his presence would fade. James would stay, becoming accustomed to him, maybe even considering him a friend, a part of his everyday life. Nathaniel wanted that so badly, to be a part of James's world. To belong.

He reached out. James's energy was more peaceful now; he was outside the house, but Nathaniel could still sense him. He scanned the building, picking up on the other energies present. James's father, sleeping. And the one who had woken, the seeping darkness, was clearly detectible as it roamed downstairs. The joy from his interaction was momentarily spoilt by the spike of fear Nathaniel felt when he picked up that energy once more. He gritted his teeth and forced himself to tune into it, monitoring its energy levels as he used to have to do long ago before it had been bound. It was deeply unpleasant tasting that malevolence again, but it would have to be done for James's safety. Not to mention Nathaniel couldn't bear it if the entity drove his possible new friend away before they even had a chance to get to know one another. No, he would not let that vile creature take anyone else from him.

He shuddered, remembering the day it had shattered all of the twins' glassware and lovely Arthur had been covered in tiny cuts. The blood dripping onto the tiled floor, the absence of his usual cheerful smile and the wincing when Agatha had applied salt water. Nathaniel had looked on, feeling powerless and entirely useless. His only contribution was being able to warn them when the entity's energy levels were recovered after an attack and it was likely to cause more trouble.

He sighed. That day had been the beginning of the end of his wonderful time with the twins.

He thought back to when the twins had arrived, Agatha, Arthur and their friends who often joined them around the table with their candles and hand-holding. Nathaniel had watched them, confused at first. In the century-and-a-half between his death and their arrival, no-one had actively sought contact with him before. He had drifted through the house, lost and confused, noticed by no-one, barely even aware of himself.

At first, he had been suspicious – did they mean him harm, perhaps? Arthur had an open, friendly face, but Agatha he'd found a little intimidating with her severe bun and tightly buttoned black dress.

Then, cautiously, he had started to speak to them, little by little. At first pushing things around to indicate his presence, spelling out words and rapping on wood, playing with the candles as they requested. But as time went on, he realised that when they sat in their circles, they fed him with light, and it reminded him who he was; he felt wanted and heard when he had been asleep for so long. The twins had been so powerful, their energy lifting him, calling him back into himself and enabling him to communicate, and they had been kind. So very kind.

It had all seemed so wonderful, but in the years since, he had wondered if it was his encouragement of their connection and activities that led to what later transpired. If, perhaps, the terrible way it had ended hadn't all been his fault.

Spurred on by their contact with him, their obsession had grown over time, their occult circles growing larger and more elaborate. Then one dark night in 1870, *it* had joined them: the dark entity that refused to leave.

He moved to the desk and looked down at the watch. *A.G.* Just the sight of those initials pressed on the old wound in his heart. He cast his mind back to its original owner, concentrating as more detail returned to his memories.

Dear Arthur, with his piercing green eyes and easy laugh every time Nathaniel had pulled his hair or flipped his tarot cards. Arthur, who reminded him so much of his older brother. Except Arthur had accepted him for who he was without question. If Arthur had been his older brother in life, Nathaniel was sure he would have protected him. He would never have let his parents do what they did; he would have come back from boarding school and fought for him. Arthur had cared for him so much. He had told him of his longing for the garden one day, and the following week, Arthur had filled the drawing room with plants and flowers, setting up a picnic basket and proclaiming that if Nathaniel couldn't reach the garden, he would bring it inside. Nathaniel had been so touched by that gesture, by all the summer afternoons when the twins would open the windows and doors and sit inside in patches of sunlight instead of leaving him alone indoors. Arthur had done so much for him, and in the end, Nathaniel had failed him.

Nathaniel felt the old shame and guilt as he recalled the awful night it had all ended, how he had looked on and then fled but not done anything to help. Too scared to step in, in case he'd be influenced or absorbed by that dark energy. It was so strong, so persuasive. It would have been too easy to just surrender and relinquish the light he held onto, his shred of humanity.

Caspian Faye

Perhaps if he could have helped, things would not have gone the way they had. Arthur might not have met that awful fate, and Agatha might not have suffered the pain in the months that followed. He remembered how she would sit holding that very watch and staring into space, as if it would somehow bring him back or change the past. How she had eventually made a little shrine to Arthur, the watch at the centre.

Nathaniel felt the weight of the sorrow prickling at him, but it was too late now; he couldn't fix it. He had been too weak and afraid – no amount of dwelling on it would change the disgust he felt towards himself.

He looked up at the spot above the bedroom door where Agatha had placed strong magic to protect him, magic that still held to this day. He had gone to sleep for a long time after she passed, her health failing less than a year after that terrible night. Nathaniel had spent many weeks at her bedside, wishing he could do more to comfort her as she suffered spasms of coughing, but it seemed to him that her body gave up, her heart irrevocably broken by the loss of her brother.

He knew that to deliberately linger in the house once she had passed carried many risks for her soul, but a selfish, lonely part of him had still hoped she would. That despite her desire to be reunited with loved ones, to find peace and be safe, that she would choose Nathaniel. That he would be prioritised, just once.

However, when her body finally failed, he watched her slip away into a light that formed on the landing. For a moment, he'd been curious about what it would have felt like, if perhaps he could have followed her into it – but she'd looked back at him and shaken her head, her expression knowing.

Somehow, she seemed to know he needed to remain here for some reason, and he felt it too. That he wasn't done yet, despite the deep weariness often permeating his being these days. Or at least, that's what he chose to believe. In his darker moments, though, a fearful voice in his heart would whisper that perhaps the light was just not for him, that he would never be chosen to find peace.

The door opened behind him, and James walked in, snapping Nathaniel out of his reminiscence.

He watched James as he entered the room looking around cautiously, his expression guarded. Nathaniel hated to see him on edge, especially knowing he was partly the cause of it. James went to his bed and sat down, plugging his phone back in and leaning over it. Nathaniel stared at the defined lines of his back, studying every muscle, watching his hands moving on the screen. Every movement of his seemed fluid, poetic. Nathaniel loved the way he moved; he felt he could watch him do the most mundane things for year upon year and never get tired of it, always wanting more.

He wanted that future, but he knew for that, he needed to focus, needed to have a plan. He tuned in to the energy downstairs; the entity was weak enough after its earlier activity that Nathaniel wasn't immediately concerned for James's safety. He would be alright for a few days at least – but after that? Nathaniel paced, his agitation building to a level he hadn't felt in years.

It seemed so desperately unfair that the entity should be awoken again just as a human came into his life who could see him. The timing was absurdly cruel.

Or maybe this was it: he was here because of this beautiful being. It was all part of a bigger plan, a chance to get it right this time, to be brave. He was meant to meet James, to protect him somehow. To make this house safe, to create a home where he could be happy.

Nathaniel sat with the thought for a moment. It felt right. James had seen him; there had to be a reason for that, a deeper meaning.

James

The salt was down, and James settled into bed, hoping for a peaceful night's sleep.

'Please don't do anything tonight, I'm really tired,' he said out loud to the empty room, hoping the ghost was listening and could be reasoned with. He switched the light off and lay there conjuring a protective visualisation in his mind's eye until he drifted off.

He was deep in a dream – a penalty shoot-out in an important final, back on his old team with Will cheering him on from the sidelines as he stepped up to the mark – when he woke with a jolt. Annoyed at being woken from such an exciting dream and finding himself back in this reality, he swore to himself and sat up. His room was as he had left it, and he had no idea why he'd woken up so suddenly, when he heard it: a loud knock on the bedroom wall. He got out of bed quickly. The sound was coming from the dividing wall between his room and one of the empty spare rooms.

'Hello?' he said out loud.

Silence followed and then another knock, this time louder. James moved closer to the wall. It was definitely coming from the other side and not from within his room. He put his ear to the wall, his heart racing, and heard a muffled dragging sound. There was something very jarring about it, reminding him of nails on a blackboard.

He stepped back. He was going to have to investigate. He pulled on his socks against the cold floorboards, threw his dressing gown on and opened his bedroom door. The moment he stepped out onto the landing, the temperature dropped, but he reassured himself that it was normal, just an old house thing. He padded down the landing, passed his dad's room and paused for a moment. He could hear soft snoring, so the noise wasn't Frank.

He continued on, swearing as he snagged a sock on a loose nail, passed the spare room that was silent and then turned the corner into the corridor that led to the other two bedrooms. He ignored the first one and made for the second, the one that was adjacent to his room and shared a wall. As he stood on the landing outside, he could still hear noises coming from inside: a strange shuffling that set his teeth on edge. All of his instincts were telling him to run, but he ignored them. He must be brave; he wasn't going to give this ghost the satisfaction of seeing his fear.

He rested his hand on the door handle for a moment, gathering his courage and then pushing it open quickly.

Complete silence fell; nothing in the room moved.

'Very funny!' James said out loud, trying to sound bolder than he felt.

The moonlight pouring in through the large curtainless windows illuminated the room, and he stepped in without touching the light switch. His dad had asked the movers to deposit the bulk of the boxes and miscellaneous furniture in here, out of the way until he got the house in order, and James recalled them doing so neatly. When he'd done his initial walkthrough of the house on arrival, he'd been in here. He remembered noticing the masses of dead flies on the dusty windowsill and the peeling wallpaper. All the furniture and boxes had been stacked against the wall then, but now…he gazed around at the chaos with a growing sense of unease.

Whatever had done this was very determined. The boxes were scattered all over the room, stacked in bizarre configurations; the old dining table was in the middle of the room with half the chairs around it; and the doors of the wardrobe were hanging open. He looked around as the hair rose on the back of his neck. Whatever had done this was likely still in here with him. The thought returned that perhaps there was someone sneaking into their house somehow – an old resident with a key or perhaps somebody hiding somewhere like the attic – and he decided he needed to leave, quickly. He spun and ran for the door, not even caring that he was showing fear now. He snatched the key out of the door with a shaking hand and locked the room from the outside, just to be sure.

He set off back to his room at a smart pace, feeling better when the door was closed behind him. He sat on the edge of his bed and took a few deep breaths, telling himself he was safe and that he'd just seen too many horror films.

'It'll seem better in the morning,' he whispered a few times as a mantra before he got back into bed, pulling the edge of the covers up over his head.

'If you can hear me,' he ventured, 'this isn't exactly what I had in mind! Please let me sleep.'

He closed his eyes, started doing the protective visualisation again, and the next thing he heard was his morning alarm. He sat up quickly, bracing himself for a mess, but after scanning his room for any sign of mischief, he realised all was as he had left it. He had an odd recollection of a dream last night: the forlorn boy he'd seen, standing at the foot of his bed, watching him. But it wasn't frightening; if anything, it was a calming image, which seemed odd considering the events of the night before.

Dismissing it as a bizarre reaction from his subconscious, he rolled over and picked up his phone, only to be greeted with several notifications from Nova.

So, I couldn't sleep in the end after our convo and ended up researching the history of your house. Check THIS out. X

James lay back on his pillows and opened up the screenshots Nova had attached in the following flurry of messages. Some were from an ancestry site she was a member of, some were census records and some were old newspaper articles. James looked at one, a report on a Victorian séance gone awry that resulted in the death of one of the participants. An Arthur Gadsby had a sudden heart attack during a particularly intense session and passed away aged only twenty-three.

James continued looking at what she'd sent and then saw it: the address of the deceased was recorded as—

'Oh, shit,' he said out loud as it all sunk in – the séance had taken place in his house, and this man had died here. It all added up: the ghost, the lingering energy and the disturbances escalating since they discovered the watch. *A.G.* It was clearly Arthur's, and uncovering it had stirred up the activity.

He looked at Nova's next message.

So, the era Arthur is from doesn't really match the description of your ghost, but maybe he was a fan of fanciful clothing? We need to find old family pictures to be sure. No other deaths that I can find linked to your address BUT looks to be a possible missing person case. Someone from the Birch family, a Natalie born 1695, disappeared aged 17, date of death unknown. It was concluded she ran away as she was apparently 'troubled' so may have lived a happy life elsewhere? X

A few more screenshots to show her sources and then Nova finished with, *Gruesome murder in your area in the 1700s though! Horrible reading but here it is. X*

James looked at the source. A local man had been decapitated and the body parts burnt in an apparent satanic ritual, but no one was ever caught in connection with the murder. With his heart racing, James flicked through the remaining information to double check that this particular man had no direct link to his address and breathed a sigh of relief.

'OK, so you're Arthur?' he asked out loud. Nothing but silence. 'Maybe not, then? I am trying to understand,' he added. 'I'd like to find a way for us to co-exist peacefully, y'know?'

When there was no response, he went downstairs to get breakfast. His dad had already left for work, his shoes and coat gone from the hall. James picked up the post and continued on into the kitchen where he stopped dead. All the cupboards were open again.

'This isn't funny!' he burst out. 'I don't know why you're doing this, but you have my attention, okay? You don't need to keep doing stupid childish shit like this, it's just annoying, and it's going to spook my dad!'

He made his way around the kitchen, closing the doors. 'He's not as good with this stuff as I am, alright? And you don't want to mess with me; I have a witch friend, and she will make you regret it.'

James stuck the kettle on to make a coffee, feeling satisfied he had made himself clear.

He found the coffee and set it out on the counter before he went rooting for a spoon and the cafetiere. When he turned back around, the coffee was gone.

'This is not helping! Do not get between me and my coffee. You do not want me to be caffeine deprived, especially after all that nonsense last night!'

James looked around the room, grateful for the anger and frustration that was currently completely outweighing his fear. After a moment, he spotted the coffee sitting on the windowsill. He marched over and grabbed it. It was cold to the touch, and he shivered involuntarily.

Shaking off his unease, he brewed his coffee, made some peanut butter on toast and, without lingering, took it back up to his room. For some reason, his room felt like a better place to be than the kitchen. He sat in a patch of sunlight by the window and ate his breakfast, contemplating the morning ahead. A curious part of him considered going back to the spare room and unlocking the door to see if anything had moved since last night, but he dismissed it. There was likely no good to come from encouraging this ghost by giving him and his pranks too much attention.

When he'd finished his food, he brushed the crumbs from his hands, set about unpacking the last few boxes and then settled to get a few hours of pre-reading done for his course work. Half an hour in, his phone went off with an update from his dad and the news that Posey would be arriving between midday and 2pm.

Putting his reading aside, James decided to set all her things up for when she arrived to help her settle in. He went down to the garage and connected his speakers, bringing in the boxes stacked in the hallway marked *Cat Stuff* by his mum.

He found his current favourite playlist and pressed play as he opened up the first box and started re-assembling her cat tree.

He was only halfway through when the song changed to one that reminded him powerfully of Will. He stopped, dropping to his knees as he recalled the night they'd danced to it at a beach barbeque, the taste of salt on Will's lips and the sand under their feet. He could feel the sadness creeping in, the very air in front of him seeming extra empty, as though Will not being in his arms was creating a vacuum of some kind. He sighed and stood up, trying to shake it off. He was going to see Will soon; it would be okay. He just needed to stick to his routine, take it one day at a time and keep working towards his goals. He skipped the song, took a deep breath and told himself that the change would get easier, even if it felt like crap now.

He went back to the cat tree, focusing on the meditative nature of constructing with his hands, and was getting into a much better frame of mind when the music coming from the speaker began to crackle.

With a groan of frustration, James walked over to the speaker to check it, but as he reached it, the crackling stopped.

It looked fine – it hadn't got damp – so he went back to the boxes. The moment he reached them, the crackling started again, only this time, it became progressively and rapidly worse, completely obscuring the music.

James stood up and marched back towards it, fighting the urge to hurl it out the window. He bent down to turn it off, but before his hand touched it, it sputtered out completely with an odd hiss.

He picked it up, switching it off and on again, but it didn't respond. He sighed with frustration and put it back down, digging in his pockets for his earbuds.

As he straightened up, he sensed something and turned quickly, expecting to see the boy behind him. There was no one there, just that uncomfortable skin-crawling feeling of being stared at again. It suddenly struck him that he really didn't want to be there anymore and, abandoning the cat tree, he found himself leaping up the stairs to his room two at a time.

When he reached his room and shut the door behind him, he felt some relief. It was odd, he thought, that the room in which he had actually *seen* the ghost was the room he felt safest in.

Irritated with himself for being spooked but still unable to find the will to go back downstairs, he stayed in his room and did a bit more reading instead, although his concentration was weak. It was a relief when the doorbell finally went off, and he ran down the stairs to get Posey.

As he opened the front door, the courier in overalls was unloading Posey's crate from the back of the van parked in the driveway. She looked up and smiled. 'She's been good as gold!'

She lifted out the familiar cat carrier, and James stepped out onto the gravel to take it from her, regretting his lazy decision to not put shoes on when his socks became instantly damp. Posey's black fur was visible through the cracks, and when he clicked his tongue, she peered up through the carrier and gave a soft meow.

'Hey, baby! Missed you; how are you doing?'

She meowed a little louder, her green eyes bright and alert.

'I'll take that as "good,"' he said.

He lifted the carrier inside the house and set it down in the hallway by the radiator, placing her bowls just outside it with some kibble and water, and then opened the carrier door to let her slowly acclimatise.

'You come out when you feel ready, okay, baby?' he whispered, expecting her to take a while to feel safe in the new surroundings. There was already a cat flap installed on the kitchen door from a previous owner, but he wondered if he might need to get her a litter tray until she felt safe enough in the new place to venture out. He sent Nova a picture of Posey crouched in her carrier. *The Queen has arrived. X*

He almost sent the picture to Will but then stopped. Will didn't really 'get' animals. He'd made the mistake of calling Posey his 'fur baby' once in front of him and been mocked mercilessly for a good five minutes.

He put his phone away and crouched down. 'Okay, when am I getting a snuggle?' he asked.

Posey moved forward daintily to the door of the carrier, her little nose twitching and her mouth open as she took in the scents of her new territory.

Just as she stepped over the edge of the carrier, she froze. Her eyes went wide, fixed on something over James' shoulder for a few seconds, then she bolted sideways up the hallway and shot into the sitting room.

James looked over his shoulder, suddenly feeling nervous in the hall. It could very well just be cats being cats – she had often been erratic in his last house and occasionally seemed to be looking at something he couldn't see – but with everything that had happened so far, it was unsettling behaviour.

He followed her into the sitting room and found her furiously sniffing the couch. He sat down, waiting for her to hop onto his lap and snuggle up for a bit as she usually would, but she paced instead. James waited patiently, but she was showing no sign of settling.

'Okay, shall we go up to my room?' he suggested, scooping her up. Her eyes remained wild as he walked through the hall and up the stairs, but she didn't attempt to jump from his arms. Once he reached his room, he let her hop off onto his bed, where she circled a few times and sat down, licking a paw.

'You're happier in here too, eh?'

A sudden crashing from downstairs made him flinch. He opened the door again and peered at the top of the stairs. The noise was hideous. He had no idea what was going on, but everything in him wanted to stay right where he was. He felt a sense of duty to investigate, but the fear was keeping him rooted to the spot. Posey was on edge again, up on her feet, fur bristling and staring at the door.

He took a step forward and, for a moment, it felt like someone was tugging on his arm, pulling him back into his bedroom. He shook it off and propelled himself halfway down the stairs. The hall was a mess: coats strewn across the floor, the shoe rack upended and shoes scattered everywhere. The cat bowls were turned over, kibble and water spread across the mat, and the cat carrier was upside down. James stood on the stairs for a moment, exasperation rising.

'I don't know if this is your idea of funny, but it's getting really boring! I'm not scared of you! I don't understand why you're doing this.'

When there was no response, James went down, against his better judgement, and began to pick everything up. As he bent over to gather his dad's slippers, he felt a sudden, tangible presence in the hall, the familiar sensation as the hairs went up on the back of his neck and fear spiked within him. A shadow flashed in the corner of his eye, and he tried to move but wasn't quick enough. A hard shove to his back caught him off balance, sending him face-first into the wall. He threw out his hands in time to avoid injury, but the moment he had stabilised himself, he turned and ran back upstairs, crashing into his room and slamming the door behind him. He had had enough. He stood, his heart racing as a cold sweat broke out all over his body, suddenly knowing something for sure: it was unlikely the forlorn-looking boy he'd seen in his room could possibly be behind this.

With that shove, he had felt true malice, deep, malevolent intent. It was a hard shove, demonstrating strength along with the clear intention of causing him harm. There was no other way to interpret it. James liked to think he was pretty good at reading energy and judging character, and while the boy in his room might be capable of playing with cupboards, he didn't seem the sort to be violent. Which meant there was more than one ghost in the house, and one of them definitely wasn't the friendly kind. The poltergeist activity took on a different tone in retrospect. It was not mischievous and silly; it had been calculated and intended to intimidate. James ran his hands over his torso, attempting to soothe himself. Whatever this presence was, it was dangerous, and he was truly scared now, despite wanting to put a brave face on it.

He sank onto the floor and pulled out his phone with shaking hands; the battery was dead, again. He plugged it in and waited for it to charge enough to call Nova.

Nathaniel

Nathaniel was restless. He'd had an anxious night, pulled from his wall by the horrible realisation that the entity was upstairs and passing by his sanctuary. He had felt it prowling, testing the warding on the room before it moved on. He had hoped it would retreat back downstairs, but instead, it circled the landing and then woke James, drawing him out of safety and into danger. He had stepped from the wall, pleading with James not to venture into the spare room, but James hadn't heard him, and he couldn't muster the courage to follow him yet. Even if he had, he couldn't think of anything helpful he could have done; he would only have been risking himself for nothing.

He had been so relieved when James had returned to his room unharmed, but this was still a dreadful turn of events that spelt future disaster, and Nathaniel was furious at his lack of a plan. Agitated to the verge of panic, Nathaniel had remained wakeful all night, his only recourse to watch over James as he slept. The dark presence was far stronger than it should be, and it was very worrying. Nathaniel could only guess that it had used its time while bound to rest and somehow strengthen itself. It had been destroying things downstairs all day, drawing James out of the room to investigate despite Nathaniel's desperate attempts to keep him away from it.

Unable to be heard, Nathaniel had tried to pull James back physically using willpower, but he lacked the energy to stop a living human, especially one as strong as him, from doing anything.

It was more frequently active than he recalled it being last time and seemingly regaining energy rapidly after every bout of activity, not to mention the fear now pouring from James that was going to feed it further. If James's dad also became terrified, things would get even worse. Two emotional human power sources for it to drain.

He looked at the cat where she sat on James's bed now, her fur illuminated by the sun; she remained poised, eyes locked on the open door, and he thought about how much more sense the feline seemed to have than its owner.

Nathaniel focused and scanned the house. The dark presence was full of gleeful energy, a twisted joy in the damage it was doing, and satisfaction with itself.

He tuned it out as best he could and concentrated on what he really cared about: James. Thankfully, he was returning to his room again, but as he burst through the door, it was evident that he was not okay. He ran his hands over his body, an automatic attempt to self-soothe that Nathaniel recognised. The powerful yearning to replace James's hands with his own and hold him until he felt safe was overwhelming.

James's energy was erratic: fear, excitement – an intense stress response. Nathaniel put aside his own longings and moved closer, projecting an energy of calm towards James where he sat on the floor, clutching his phone as though it were a lifeline.

He wasn't sure if it was wishful thinking, but James did seem to be affected by his energy. His breathing slowed, and he closed his eyes with a deep sigh.

A few moments later, he opened them and started doing something with his phone again. Nathaniel moved away to give him a bit of privacy, and then he heard the voice he recognised as James's friend Nova again.

'James, what's happened now?'

James's voice sounded a little strained when he spoke. 'It pushed me! It's been making a mess constantly, it woke me up last night, this morning it hid my coffee, and just now it bloody pushed me! Hard, too – I had to act quickly so I didn't smash into the wall face-first.'

A moment of silence and then Nova spoke in a much more sombre voice, 'That's not good. I mean, the coffee thing sounds kind of funny, but the pushing, not good at all. That's a serious escalation.'

'I disagree on that; hiding my coffee is never funny. There are three things I hold sacred—'

'Coffee, recovery lie-ins and snacks!' Nova supplied in a lighter tone.
James laughed. 'You know me too well.'

'Jokes aside, I need to get up there sooner rather than later. We have to sort this out. Forlorn boy lurking around your room has fast become an aggressive brat that has to go.'

At her words, Nathaniel stiffened and turned to look at James's face for his reaction. Every part of him willed James to know the belligerent entity wasn't him. He hoped more than anything that James could feel that. It was unbearable to think of James remembering his face, of associating these horrible events with him whenever the entity reared its head. Not to mention the implications if someone was brought in to exorcise the house and focused their attention on him. Would he be safe in the wall, or was it possible he would be banished somewhere unknown, torn from his home whilst the entity evaded detection and stayed behind in the house, able to hurt James without anyone remaining to look out for him? Nathaniel began to spiral into fearful scenarios before James spoke.

'I'm not sure…I think there might be two ghosts, Nova.'

Nathaniel's heart sang at those words; the relief was immense. James knew. He had looked into his eyes, however briefly, and he had seen him for what he was.

'The plot thickens! Go on…'

'Well, my room is the only place I feel safe in this stupid house, and my room is the only place I've heard or seen Forlorn Boy. It's also the first place Posey has even sat down since she got here. We need to come up with a better name than "Forlorn Boy" for him, by the way.'

'He's probably Arthur.'

'I don't think so. Not only is the clothing the wrong era, but when I recall his face…he looked younger than that, more like our age.'

'You could ask him his name?'

'What, like now?'

'I mean, yeah, but also there's a meditation I'll send you. If you really think he's innocent of all this, and you feel safe in your room, it should be OK for you to go into it, provided you take a few precautions. I'd rather be there with you, but I'm not sure you should wait that long to get to the bottom of this. You at least need to know that whatever is in your room isn't evil.'

'Noted. So yeah, my room feels fine, but everywhere else is a different story, and that's where the scary or annoying stuff has gone down. I can't say how I know, but it definitely feels like a different energy—shit, am I basically going mad? Is this all stress from the move and missing my old life? Maybe there's a gas leak here, or toxic mould or something?'

'Don't start on all that cliché sceptical crap, James; you know better than that.'

'Maybe, but there's a big difference between the theory and the reality.'

'I get it, I do, and I'm here for you. We'll get you through this, I promise.'

'Thanks, Nova. I really don't know what I'd do without you.'

Nova laughed. 'Fall prey to a scam medium or have to move again and live with your mum and her parasitic new man?'

'I think I prefer the ghosts to him. Also, I couldn't leave my dad alone here.'

'Fair. I'm so sorry, I have to go; my class starts in a few, but I'll send you what you need ASAP.'

'Okay, thanks, Nova; love you loads.'

Nathaniel watched James put down his phone, still feeling a warm glow from everything he'd said. James felt safe here in his room; he didn't dislike Nathaniel's presence. Nathaniel smiled; he had forgotten how nice it felt to know he wasn't unwanted here. But better than that, James really saw the young man he was; he'd seen him from the start.

James

James stared at the kettle, willing it to boil quicker so he could get back upstairs. He tapped his fingers on the worktop, hating how on edge he felt. He'd turned on all the lights in the kitchen against the overcast afternoon, but the dark shadows in the hall felt like they were more solid than they should be, a sense of something unimaginable lurking out there.

The kettle finally boiled, and James poured his tea immediately, trying not to let his imagination take over completely. He grabbed a protein bar out of the cupboard and a satsuma from the fridge and made for the stairs promptly.

By the time he got back upstairs, Nova had sent him over an audio recording, followed by a message.

Here you go. Remember to create a salt circle and stay within it while you do this. Light a candle if you have one and ask your spirit guides and/or ancestors to protect you while you're on this journey. Visualise yourself surrounded by a protective golden light before you go in, any issues or questions I'm here. X

He checked on Posey, who had settled down again. He'd set up a litter tray in the corner and brought up her water, food bowls and bed. She'd availed herself of all of them and then decided to sleep on his bed, but he didn't care as long as she was happy. She looked like she wasn't going to need anything for a while, so he could focus on what Nova had sent him.

James went rummaging in a drawer and found what he was looking for: the three half-burnt candles he had left from the last evening he'd had Will over before the move. One red, one white and one pink. Will had mocked him gently for being a hopeless romantic, but James was sure he had secretly appreciated the effort – if not James's attempt at making a lasagne. In the end, they'd had to order food in but had still had a special night. He smiled at the memory despite the constant ache of missing Will. They'd engraved their initials and the date on the side of the red candle, so James put that one back in his drawer, not wanting it to burn down. The white and pink ones he placed on the floor, and he found his lighter, along with the salt.

He took a deep breath, popped his headphones on and lay down on his rug, tuning in to the relaxing musical intro and the soothing, grounding voice.

He drifted off, following the instructions in the audio to picture a garden, the clear blue sky slowly forming above him as he concentrated. He looked down as he felt the dewy blades of grass underfoot, focusing on them as the sun's heat began to warm his skin. He sent out the intention that anyone who wanted to speak with him could join him here, in this space of safety and peace. He added that he would like to speak to the spirit he had seen in his room, if he would like to come forward.

He continued to walk in the garden, and as he gazed around, the details began to swim, reality breaking down, edges blurring, trees shrinking into the ground, regrowing in a different formation until it all settled into an almost exact replica of his new garden. He had only just registered that when he felt a presence behind him. He looked around, and there underneath the tree canopy up ahead was a figure. He moved towards the figure, hoping it was who he thought it was: the boy he had seen in his room.

As he drew closer, his hopes were confirmed – there he stood, but clearer and more lifelike. There was a solidity to him; the colour of his hair and skin were fully saturated; he looked real. He was gazing in awe at the canopy above, one hand gently resting on a tree trunk, but when James spoke, the boy immediately turned to him, his full attention captured.

'Welcome, are you…Arthur?' James asked.

'No…I'm…Nathaniel,' the boy said, a little hesitantly.

James nodded. 'It's so nice to meet you properly. And what a great name!'

The boy beamed. 'Thank you.'

Nathaniel

Nathaniel gazed around him, taking in his new surroundings. One moment, he had been in the bedroom, then the confining but safe walls had dissolved. For a moment, he'd been terrified, but once the haze of green had begun to take the shape of the place he most yearned to be, his anxiety had faded. It wasn't a memory; it wasn't a dream – his soul was here. But it wasn't the actual garden, he knew that. He could no longer go there; it was another version of it somehow. He looked at the canopy overhead, then he heard James's wonderful voice, and it all started to make more sense. He looked at James, at the garden around them that was a kind of hybrid between the garden as Nathaniel remembered it, and the way it was in the present moment.

Hearing his name out loud, spoken with such tenderness and conviction, in this beautiful garden he wanted to stay in forever, was so magical. Hearing James say it made it real, made him love it so much more. The name that in life he had spoken only in his heart or heard used in a cruel way by those who had mocked and eventually betrayed him. They had corrupted it, made it foul with their vicious tongues. But James saying it so sincerely, he cleansed it of their influence and made it new, made it right. He couldn't stop smiling; he hoped he didn't look like a fool, but James was still grinning back at him with such warmth that it was impossible not to.

'Is this real, or am I just imagining it?' James asked. 'Are you just an image my subconscious has generated?'

Nathaniel wasn't quite sure what the second part of the question meant, but the first he desperately wanted to answer. 'I am! I am real; I promise you that.'

'So, you're inside my mind somehow?' James asked him. 'I've invited you in here?'

'Maybe, but I don't think this is your mind, or mine, but a sacred third space, where souls can meet.' Nathaniel suggested. He gestured at their surroundings. 'It looks a lot like your garden, doesn't it? But see, there are some details you won't recognize – they're mine. My garden, or my version of it. So, it's…our garden.'

James nodded. 'That makes sense.'

Nathaniel was unable to break eye contact. He wished he could look into James's eyes for eternity. Here in this space, where only the two of them existed. All of James's focus was on him and him alone, and he never wanted it to stop.

'My garden—our garden, I mean. I miss it so much. I don't know how you've done this, brought me here, but it's wonderful. Thank you.'

James's gaze intensified, and Nathaniel looked down at the pathway beneath their feet. It was almost too much. Waves of emotion rolled over him at being in this space which had always felt so special to him, the sanctuary he had thought was lost to him forever.

To be here, and to be here with James no less, was magical but also overwhelming, like nothing he had experienced before. The connection he felt to him was like the pull of an ocean tide, dragging at him all the time. Deep, powerful and irresistible.

'I brought you here?' James asked, his tone tinged with awe. 'Wow, that's one powerful meditation.'

'I would theorise that the meditation was merely the means by which you focused,' Nathaniel ventured. 'It's your power, your strength of spirit that called me here.'

James gave him a thoughtful look but didn't comment. Instead, he stepped off the little pathway into the grass, plucking a flower from a nearby hedge and presented it to Nathaniel with a soft smile. 'Here, see if you can take this.'

Nathaniel reached a hand out and accepted the flower. It felt tangible and made him want to try and touch James, too, but he held himself back. The green hue of the carnation lying on his palm was so vivid, so beautiful. He wanted to ask James so many questions, learn everything he could about him, but in that moment, he had no idea where to begin.

James broke the silence. 'Nathaniel, not that it isn't really great to speak with you, but I need some information, if you don't mind?'

'Of course, anything,' Nathaniel replied and meant it. He trusted James completely and wondered when that had happened. Had it been instantaneous? An immediate decision based entirely on James's energy? All he knew was, terrifyingly, he would bare his soul for him without question.

James frowned. 'I don't know how much you know, or how much you see, but things have been really scary in the house that we both live—I mean, exist in.'

'It isn't me,' Nathaniel answered immediately. 'I would never do those things! I dwell in my—our—room, and I don't venture downstairs often. Our room is protected, but the rest of the house is not. There's an entity that you set loose. That's what pushed you earlier.'

'Wait, *I* set loose? How did I do that?'

'Oh, I don't mean that in a placing blame kind of way. It wasn't your fault; you weren't to know. But it was inside the watch.'

James sighed. 'I feel like you're telling me what I already suspected, which makes me think maybe I am just making all this up, to support my own pre-existing ideas.'

'No, James, I am real!' Nathaniel hated the frantic tone in his voice, how much he needed James to believe in him.

'But that's exactly what I would make you say,' James replied, his face downcast. Slowly, he began to fade away. Nathaniel leapt forward with sudden courage, trying to grab his hand and keep him grounded here in this space with him. He wanted so desperately to spend more time here, even if it were only a few more moments. Away from the confines of the house where he had been stuck for so long, here in this place where James could see him without effort on his part – but he couldn't make physical contact; his hand slipped right through James's.

'Wait, please, I can prove it to you!' he called out, but James had already gone, and with him, the garden began to dissolve, leaving

Nathaniel back in his room, watching James stretching and yawning on the floor as he woke.

He felt energised from the interaction, so he channelled that into manifesting himself; it came easier than ever before, and when James looked up, he gasped.

'Oh, Nathaniel?'

Nathaniel nodded, surprised at how easy this felt. For a few seconds, they stared at one another, a charged moment that helped him to sustain his presence.

'James, I can prove to you that I'm real.'

'I—I'm sorry I'm such a cynic; I just…it's hard to believe I'm not just losing my mind. The last few days—weeks—have been a lot.'

'I understand, but I can give you information that you don't currently have, something you could not have known otherwise!'

James nodded. 'Thank you. I'd really appreciate that.'

Nathaniel pointed at the top of the doorway. 'If you peel back the wallpaper there, underneath there's a protective spell hidden a long time ago by someone dear to me. An actual, physical, tangible thing. Look, you'll find it! Just be careful not to damage it, or you'll be putting yourself in danger – this room won't be safe anymore.'

James's eyes widened. 'Wow, thanks. I'll be careful. I don't want to piss my dad off, but I'll have a little look later.'

'And—'

Nathaniel hesitated. Should he share this with James, or would doing so ruin everything? James's energy felt so safe, so much like coming home. Was it an illusion, or could he trust it? He didn't want to risk another betrayal, but perhaps this was a chance to see once and for all if he really could trust him. Surely it was better to be hurt sooner rather than later.

James was staring expectantly at him, his beautiful eyes questioning, and Nathaniel made up his mind. If he really was a pure soul like he seemed, then he would receive this information with care and respect.

'I am Nathaniel; I have always been Nathaniel. But at birth, I was named Natalie. They always told me I was a girl, but I never felt it;

it wasn't right. I tried to live their lie, but I couldn't, and so I began to fight for my truth. But I didn't run away from home like they said. I have always been here. I never left.'

James's mouth dropped open. 'What happened to you? Did someone—' He gasped, covering his mouth with one hand. 'I'm sorry, that was intrusive. I don't want to bring up bad memories – only tell me what you're comfortable sharing; don't feel you have to.'

'I don't know,' Nathaniel said quietly. 'The memories are incomplete. I'm not sure I fully understand what happened. The last thing I remember was' – he thought for a moment – 'something burning, a strong smell, blood, voices…then they were gone. Then he was gone. Theodore, he left, and…' He unexpectedly choked up and trailed off. He couldn't fully recall what had happened. 'I'm sorry, I don't quite remember. I don't think I ever have; it's a bit of a blur.'

'Sometimes our minds do that to protect us,' James said quietly. 'Don't force it; it'll come back when you're ready, if it's supposed to.' He stepped closer. 'I'm sorry. I can't even imagine what you've been through.'

Nathaniel was captivated by the empathy radiating from him. He felt as though he were drinking it in, savouring it with gratitude. Such kindness after so long without it was immensely healing. He had forgotten what it felt like to be cared about. James's life energy was flowing into him; the power of his attention was strengthening his focus, his grasp on himself and with it, his memory.

'It was magic!' he burst out suddenly.

'Magic?'

'I was…it was my friends—no, I *thought* they were my friends. It was Theodore; he led them.' He paused as snippets of memory returned to him. 'He was—I trusted him, and he brought the others. We met them in the village a while beforehand. I would climb out the window, wearing my proper clothes—the right ones—and go into the village without my family knowing.'

As he spoke of it, Nathaniel recalled those moments again. His hand in Theodore's, slipping through the trees together, moving through the shadows undetected and then a dimly lit tavern, flashes of whispered conversations. How good it felt to have some friends his own age after being locked in his room for so long. The sense of belonging, of community. How much those stolen nights out meant to him after the horrible day when his mother turned that heavy key in the bedroom door and told everyone he had gone missing, that he was touched in the head, that he had run away.

'I—we had fun together. I thought I was one of them and they would help me. They said they had powers; they were magic workers.'

'But they lied? Why?'

Nathaniel thought back. He remembered giving them money, all the money he had, for supplies: books, ink, herbs and little glass bottles of powder. All the things Theodore had said they needed to work on the spell. 'Coin, perhaps, or curiosity, I think? A search for power and knowledge? Perhaps both.'

James frowned. 'Messing with forces beyond their control?'

Nathaniel nodded as it slowly came back to him in more and more detail. 'They were performing a ritual. It was supposed to make my body the way I needed it; make it match my soul.'

'But they murdered you?' James burst out.

Nathaniel shook his head. 'No…I don't think they did, not on purpose. The ritual went wrong somehow, I think. It was just a horrible mistake.'

'I'm so sorry,' James said quietly.

'Me too,' Nathaniel replied.

James reached out a hand, and it passed through Nathaniel's shoulder, only this time, there was a slight resistance. Nathaniel felt an energetic charge pass through him unlike anything he had felt before. It was like sucking the power from a device but a hundred times better.

James gasped, 'I can *almost* feel you, like the air feels thicker somehow!'

A sudden bang from downstairs broke their eye contact, James looking at the door with apprehension. 'Oh no, not *again*…'

'James, you home?'

James exhaled with relief when he heard Frank's voice, and gave Nathaniel an apologetic smile. 'I'd better go, but I'd like to talk to you again later, if that's OK?'

Nathaniel smiled back, unable to conceal his joy. 'Of course, anytime. I'm not going anywhere.'

James nodded and went to the door. 'Coming, Dad!'

A moment later, he was gone, but Nathaniel remained where he was in the middle of the room, one hand lingering on his shoulder where James's hand had passed through.

James

'What do you need, Dad?' James asked as he jumped down the last few stairs into the hall. Hopefully whatever it was wouldn't take long and he could get back up to Nathaniel.

Frank wiped some sweat from his brow with a forearm and gestured towards the driveway. 'Ah, slight car issue. Not ideal timing. I need you to give me a hand; I think I can probably fix it myself with a bit of luck.'

James followed him outside. The car's bonnet was open, and there were tools scattered on the ground.

'It was making a funny noise on the way home,' Frank explained, 'so I thought I'd have a little look at it, but just now the damn thing refused to start for me.' He checked his watch. 'What time does Will get here?'

James stopped dead. The events of the afternoon had completely driven thoughts of Will from his mind. Ignoring the prickle of guilt, he forced a smile. 'Not until eight.'

Frank passed him some tools. 'Okay, great, we should have more than enough time here, then.' He bent over and started fiddling under the hood. 'You know, back when I was your age, cars were so much simpler and easier to maintain. These days, they deliberately make them complex so it costs you every time you have an issue.'

He swore and put his hand out. James passed him what he wanted, his mind still not quite grounded in current reality.

'It's an absolute racket, isn't it?'

James realised he was waiting for a response. 'Oh, yeah, I agree. A racket.'

He tried to focus, especially as his dad began to narrate what he was doing so that James could 'learn for the future', but it was proving difficult to care about his dad's car tutorial when he'd just accessed a different reality and had a heart to heart with a ghost.

His relief was immense when Frank climbed into the driver's seat and tested the ignition and the car started up. 'Great, are we all done? I'd like to shower before we leave to get Will.'

Frank looked at his watch again. 'Are you planning to take a two-hour shower then?'

James unhooked the hot rods and slammed the bonnet closed. 'Not quite, but I'd better stick the boiler on!' he replied as he made a dash for the front door.

When he reached his room, he was disappointed that Nathaniel wasn't immediately visible. 'Hey Nathaniel? I'm back, if you're…around still?' he said out loud, feeling a bit silly.

He waited barely a minute before he grabbed his headphones off the floor and lay back down.

Nathaniel

Nathaniel's eyelids fluttered back open; James had spoken his name. He awoke still full of warmth from their last interaction, unable to believe his luck at being called on again so soon. Reflexively, he ran his hands down his torso, flattening his clothing that never wrinkled, one hand going to fix his hair that never really moved out of place, before he drifted out of the wall. James was lying on the floor, his eyes closed, and Nathaniel's heart leapt – another escape to the garden, perhaps?

He concentrated all his energy on James, and a moment later, an arch began to form in front of him. This time it was a slower but more detailed process, almost as if the garden was becoming more clearly defined. The wooden archway slowly grew vines, a golden light filling it and green grass just visible beyond. Nathaniel wanted to pause and take in its beauty, but the desire to get through to James and have as much time there as possible far outweighed that impulse. Joyfully, he stepped through into the garden. It was just as beautiful as last time. The blue skies were gone, but the sun was setting, casting an orange hue over everything, including James when he turned to face him.

He gasped. James was devastatingly handsome, the light catching his perfect features and reminding Nathaniel of the most striking paintings he had seen during his life.

'You came back!' James smiled. 'You heard me.'

'I will always hear you.' Nathaniel replied without thinking and then flushed. 'I, ah, how come you're back so soon?' he added quickly.

James gestured at a nearby bench. 'Shall we?'

Nathaniel followed him to the bench, excited at the implication that he meant to linger here a while.

'I really didn't want to leave last time,' James explained quietly, 'but my dad called me down to help him out with his car. You know what a car is, right?'

Nathaniel laughed. 'I do. They change a lot in between sleeps, but I am familiar enough now.'

'"Sleeps"? So, you sleep?'

'I mean, not in the way you do, but it's the best word I have to describe it. I sort of…I go back into the wall and drift into a dormant state, but when a human comes into my space, I wake up again.'

James's eyes widened. 'I woke you up?'

'You did.'

'I'm so sorry, I didn't mean to disturb you—'

'No! Don't apologize. I…it was the best thing that's—I mean, thank you.'

James stared at him then, his head cocked to one side and a questioning look on his face. Nathaniel met his gaze and managed not to look away this time. Emotions bubbled in him as he struggled to find the words to explain, but none came easily to his tongue.

After a moment, it was James who looked away, sucking in a deep breath. Nathaniel wished he knew what was going on for him in that moment, what had just passed between them. He could feel the danger of reading too much into it creeping up on him.

'Your father and you, you're close?' he asked, ending the silence. James turned back, seeming grateful for the abrupt change of topic.

'He's great,' he responded. 'He's always been there for me when I need him; I've always been able to talk to him about anything.'

Nathaniel contemplated that for a moment, about how different his life would have been if his father had been like that. 'You could talk to him about…anything?'

James nodded. 'Pretty much. He's cool. When I told him about my boyfriend, Will, he just asked what football team he supports.'

Nathaniel stared at him, aghast. 'What did you say?'

'Whichever one I play for, which my dad said was the correct answer. And then he said he was glad I'd found someone who makes me happy and asked if I could bring him for dinner.'

'Will.' Nathaniel said, testing the sound of his name out loud, pushing down the envy.

'Anyway, what was your family like, Nathaniel? I'm guessing not like my dad.'

Nathaniel shook his head. 'No. I had a little freedom when I was young. Father was distant, and Mother was tired a lot. She used to get headaches and take to her room every summer.'

He looked around the garden. 'When I got older and they started to pay more attention to me, I longed for those days.'

'I'm sorry you didn't have the support you needed,' James said. 'Not that me saying that changes anything, but still.'

'It does help. Thank you.'

Nathaniel looked at the pink tinge to the underside of the clouds as the sun dipped lower. 'And thank you for calling me into this magical space again. It's so nice to get out of the house, away from the confines of those walls.'

'You're always welcome here,' James replied. 'I'm very happy to be here too, you know.'

Nathaniel couldn't contain his smile of joy at that. 'I'm glad. It feels so safe, just us.'

James leant forward, resting his elbows on his knees, one leg brushing up against Nathaniel's. He froze, waiting for James to hastily withdraw it, ceasing contact, but he didn't. The energetic crackle continued.

Nathaniel never wanted to move; he was happier here than he could ever remember. The thought of being dragged back into the cold, grey house with the cloying heaviness of the entity roaming downstairs filled him with dread.

'So, you can't leave the house?' James asked gently.

'No, I can't.' Nathaniel replied, hating the reminder of how different they were.

'And the other thing, the entity I accidentally released, can that…?'

Nathaniel shuddered. 'No, it can't either. You're always safe in the garden.' He looked around, wanting to appreciate every moment he had in this liminal space with James. 'I used to sit out here – well, in the other garden, our garden – and write stories in my notebooks,' Nathaniel said suddenly, wanting to let James into his inner world, share his past in any way he could. 'Or read. When I got older and my governess made me do needlework inside, I would deliberately stab the needle points into my fingers and spoil the fabric with blood. Then I would claim the pain was too much and she would dismiss me, then I could hide in the trees with my books.'

'What kind of stories did you write?' James asked.

Nathaniel cast his mind back. 'Mostly adventure stories, tales of pirates and distant shores. I would live through my characters, and then it felt like I was free, not trapped here. I once dreamt up a privateer captain and gave him my name…he was as real to me, if not more real, than any living human. We were great friends.'

'I wish I could read them, your stories,' James said quietly. Nathaniel stayed silent, flattered by his interest and unsure how to respond.

James looked away into the greenery for a moment before he spoke again. 'Isn't it weird to think of me living in the house now, walking on the same floorboards as you did, looking at the same garden as you? Time just blows my mind when I think about it.'

'And here we are, talking about it. Even more peculiar! Imagine if someone had told me back then that I'd be here now…I wouldn't have believed a word.'

'I don't think many would.' James laughed. 'But seriously, Nathaniel, thank you for speaking with me, for being here with me. It's, um, a privilege.'

'The privilege is all mine. Thank *you*.' Nathaniel responded immediately.

'Perhaps, if it would be cool with you, we could do this regularly. Not that seeing you in the other reality isn't also great, but I, well, I really like seeing you like this.'

'Like this?' Nathaniel asked faintly, overwhelmed by James's words.

'Yeah, in colour, looking totally solid, y'know? And in a space that's ours.'

'*Ours.*' Nathaniel echoed.

Another moment of silence, James gazing at him while Nathaniel wished he knew what he was thinking. Then James cleared his throat. 'Right, I should go. I have to shower and sort myself out; Will arrives soon.'

James's words abruptly punctured the happy bubble Nathaniel had been floating in, and he came crashing back down to earth. 'Of course,' he replied automatically with forced cheerfulness.

'I, ah, before I go, can I ask…this entity…how much do you know about it, Nathaniel? Other than our bedroom is safe and it can't leave the house?'

'I know lots about it,' Nathaniel told him. 'I was here before it arrived. Call on me whenever you have time, and I'll tell you everything I remember.'

James stood up and extended a hand. 'Okay, well, see you soon, then!'

Nathaniel stood too, wishing he had the courage to try for an embrace, but he didn't. Instead, he accepted the handshake. His hand slid into James's like they were meant to be together and sent energy crackling through his palm. He noticed James look down and frown slightly right before he vanished. As before, the garden melted away around him in a blur of colour, leaving Nathaniel standing in the archway. For a moment, he wondered if he could stay here, but despite his efforts not to step through it, he felt forward momentum, and the golden light faded, leaving him back in the bedroom right where he started. He looked around, hoping for one more moment of connection with James, but he was already leaving the room. Nathaniel stared at his back as he stepped out onto the landing, the door shutting behind him.

James

'Do you want to drive, get some practice in?' Frank asked, gesturing at the driver's side of the car. James jumped in without hesitation and clipped his seatbelt in.

'Is this really about me getting practice, or is it because you had a long day at work?'

His dad laughed. 'A bit of column A and a bit of column B, but that's beside the point. Get reversing this car, Provisional Boy!'

James adjusted the driving seat, checked his wing mirrors and turned the key in the ignition. Thankfully, the car started.

'So, did you have a good day, get a lot of reading done?'

'Yeah, great. Very focused. Definitely made serious headway on that reading list. Got Posey settled in too; she seems to like the house,' James lied.

'Good lad! Did you fit a run in too?'

James backed the car out of the driveway. 'Nope, time got away from me. Maybe I'll make Will join me for one tomorrow!'

Frank laughed. 'You'd best be secure in his affections before you do that!'

'What?'

'Getting your boyfriend to travel down for a visit and then making him go for a run on a Saturday? Bold move.'

James snorted. 'He'll accept it as the price he pays for my wonderful company.'

Frank laughed again, and James grinned back as he drove slowly through the drizzle, the car lights on the wet road ahead making it glisten. He was doing his best to play along with his dad's banter – it was nice to see him showing signs of high spirits and his old self again, after the months of change and heartbreak – but it was hard when his own mind was spinning. The whole day had been so intense, and then the afternoon, the encounters with Nathaniel. *Nathaniel.*

Caspian Faye

It was hard to process, the things he'd found out, the energy he'd felt between them. The fact that he'd gone from being paranormal adjacent, a friend to a witch and an open-minded listener to anecdotes, to a full-on believer, to someone who had actually seen and spoken to a ghost and been attacked by another one—all in the space of mere days.

He realised his dad had said something about his day at work and mustered a smile and a 'Yeah,' as he grappled with his overwhelm. He needed to ground himself; he was about to see Will. He needed to put this aside for a moment and make sure Will felt welcome and loved.

He pulled up alongside the small train station as his dad checked the time. 'We've got at least fifteen minutes before he gets in. Do you want a coffee?'

'Sure. Oat latte, please.'

Frank hopped out of the car, and James leant back in the seat, closing his eyes for a moment, very grateful for the chance to be alone. He took a few deep breaths, and the garden came back into his mind's eye, Nathaniel's intense grey eyes staring into his. He wondered if they would have been close if he'd lived back in Nathaniel's time, if they'd met at some fancy dance or dinner. He pictured himself for a moment in the dress of Nathaniel's time, wandering around the garden with him, arm in arm, in the real world.

His phone buzzed, jolting him back into the present, and he opened his eyes to see a message from Will updating him on the annoying kids on his train. There was also another one from Nova asking if he'd done the meditation yet.

He wished he had time to call her and tell her everything, but it would have to wait. He sent back, *I did, sceptic brain kicked in but the ghost (Nathaniel) gave me proof I think (!) will check when Will has gone home on Sunday night. X*

Nova messaged back almost immediately, *Exciting! Have fun with the prince, hope he's in good form. X*

James rolled his eyes. Nova could never resist making little comments about Will. They seemed to get along well enough, but she didn't make a secret of the fact that she thought he was too high-maintenance. James acknowledged he could be a little bit of a diva, but that was part of his charm.

He bit his lip, anxiety around what might happen over the weekend gnawing at him. He needed the ghosts to stay quiet and out of sight while Will was around. He was fairly sure Nathaniel would read the proverbial room, but as for this nasty entity…that was a whole other kettle of fish. It clearly couldn't be reasoned with, so he'd settle for spending as little time as possible downstairs, clearing up any mess it made as quickly as possible and hoping for the best.

His phone went off. *I'm here!! Where are you baby? X*

James messaged back, *outside in my dad's car! X*

A moment later, Will emerged from the station, dragging an absurdly large suitcase behind him. James jumped out and opened the boot, waving him over. He looked up and gave James a smile that made his heart skip a beat.

'Well, I made it! Can't say my eardrums are still in one piece thanks to the screaming brats, but—'

James grabbed him and pulled him in for a kiss, the warmth of his lips a sharp contrast to the cold rain coming down on their faces.

A moment later, Will broke away. 'Romantic though this is, my suitcase is getting ruined, and some of those clothes are dry clean only.'

James hoisted his case into the boot, pulling it closed. 'There you go! Now come here.'

He pulled him in for another kiss, but the sound of his dad clearing his throat killed the mood.

'Got the coffees when you're ready! They didn't have oat milk, so I got soy for you both.'

Will turned sharply away from him. 'There's coffee?'

James gave up and got back in the car; clearly romance would have to wait.

***

'That was so great, thank you Frank!' Will said as he carried the dirty plates to the sink.

James's dad smiled. 'You're welcome. Glad you enjoyed it.'

James yawned and noted that having Will here made him feel a bit better. Things felt familiar; the kitchen felt safe now with all the lights on and food strewn everywhere, a world away from how it felt when he'd been here alone. He could almost convince himself that he'd overreacted, that things weren't nearly as bad as he'd thought earlier. He couldn't feel a trace of the entity; it was as if it had retreated. Maybe it had, he thought hopefully – the push was its biggest move, and he hadn't run screaming from the house in terror, so it had nothing left. Perhaps it would lose interest, give up, and everything would be fine.

Or perhaps it was just biding its time until it could isolate him again. He shivered, not wanting to contemplate that. He messaged Nova back as the others chatted away. *Will is in good form, charming my dad as always.*

He stood up and stretched, contemplating whether or not he'd eaten too many roast potatoes.

'Fancy a walk?' he asked Will.

Will pursed his lips. 'I suppose I could be persuaded, if it's stopped raining.'

James nodded. 'Looks like it, and I could do with the air.'

Frank grinned. 'You boys enjoy that. I've got some work to be catching up on and then I might watch a film if you want to join me. I'll make popcorn.'

'That sounds great, Frank; count us in!' Will answered with enthusiasm.

James grabbed his coat and pulled some boots on, then sat in the hall waiting while Will faffed around with lots of layers. When he was finally ready, James took his hand and led him out the back door into the night.

The rain had cleared and the cloud cover with it, revealing the stars and a bright waning moon.

'Wow, it's alright here. Cute,' Will commented, looking around at the trees and the sky above.

James nodded and squeezed his hand. 'Not much light pollution; makes for good views. If Nova was here, she could probably tell us where all the planets are.'

Will narrowed his eyes. 'And a good many other things we don't care about too!'

'Don't be a bitch,' James told him as he led the way down the path through the garden to the forest trail he'd run the other day.

'Have we met?' Will replied with a laugh.

'Luckily enough, yes,' James murmured back, squeezing his hand again. 'And most of the time you're funny, but I wish you'd be nicer when it comes to Nova. I don't know what I'd do without her.'

'Don't be so oversensitive! It's hardly my fault if she's obsessed with boring stuff.'

'Boring is subjective. And anyway, it's not just that! You're always making little comments about her; it's mean. I want you two to get along – you're both so important to me.'

'Over. Sensitive.'

'Says the guy who once complained for half an hour that I made his hot chocolate wrong!'

'Oh, don't bring that up again! You need to learn to take constructive feedback, James. You used the wrong kind of whisk, and the cacao was improperly blended, okay?'

James sighed. He didn't want to ruin the weekend with Will by going any further with the conversation, so he shrugged. 'If you say so.'

For a few moments, they walked in silence, their breath misting in the cold night air.

Then James tried again. 'I've really missed you. I know it hasn't been long, but it's felt like forever, not seeing you every day.'

'Me too,' Will said quietly.

'So, what's the news back home?' James asked.

'Not much,' Will answered. 'Taz got a hideous new haircut; it's giving bird's nest that's been run over by a bus—no, several buses, on a really rainy day.'

James laughed. 'Is it really that bad?'

'You'll have to judge for yourself when they post photos. What else? Rebecca and Liam had another one of their bi-monthly fights and are on a break again.'

'Does that even count as news?'

'Probably not…oh, and Stevie is playing your position on the team now. I've been going to watch practice still. It's been nice, helps me feel connected to you, I guess, and our old routine.'

James felt a pang in his heart at that, his mind flashing back to the flirty looks that had passed between him on the pitch and Will sitting in the stands, usually sipping an iced coffee and looking impossibly handsome.

He stepped around a large puddle in the pathway, catching Will's hand again on the other side. 'I hope my next team are as cool as them,' he said. 'Not that any team will ever replace them or that time, but I hope I can at least earn a spot in the starting line-up and fit in.'

'You will. You were the best player they had, my athlete jock star!'

James laughed. 'Shut up! You are so cringe sometimes.'

'Says you while wearing *that* coat and one of your signature cat-hair jumpers, yuck and yuck.'

'Posey's hair adds a touch of class, I'll have you know! And what's wrong with my coat?'

'Best not ask that question; I don't have all night.'

James turned and pushed him against a tree. 'That insult is going to cost you a kiss, I'm afraid.'

Will grinned, 'I'm OK with that.'

***

When they stumbled in through the back door, shaking the rain from their coats and the mud from their shoes, Frank was humming in the kitchen and making popcorn under Posey's watchful eyes. James was relieved to see she had ventured out of his bedroom and currently seemed comfortable enough on the windowsill.

'Got caught in the sudden downpour, then?' his dad asked.

'No, we're perfectly dry, actually,' James retorted as he peeled off his damp layers and watched Will fussing with his hair in the hall mirror.

'Sarcasm is the lowest form of wit,' Frank quoted.

'But the highest form of intelligence!' finished Will.

James laughed. 'When you two have finished quoting Wilde, what movie are we going to watch?'

His dad emerged with the popcorn and some drinks on a tray, Posey trotting behind him. 'I had a look already, picked out a horror that looks good.'

'I love a horror!' Will chimed in.

'I, ah, I feel more in a comedy mood actually, or action, maybe?' James suggested. The last thing he wanted to do was watch a horror or risk stirring up activity by having one on.

'Comedy, then, I think!' Will replied, dropping onto the couch and picking up the remote. 'Okay, what have we got here…'

Posey jumped up after him and attempted to climb onto his lap; he shifted away from her, with a shrill 'No, cat, no!'

'That's only going to make her more determined,' Frank advised. 'If you want to avoid her attention, act like you really want it.'

'Ew, cats literally make no sense.'

'Neither do you, baby!' James said as he settled beside him. 'And I don't mind which comedy we go for, so long as it's easy watching.'

His dad put the tray on the table and turned the lights down, settling into an armchair. 'Alright, then, we'll let you pick, as you're the guest, Will!' Posey hopped up onto his lap, and he shifted around to accommodate her. 'Well, hello there, nice to have you back with us!'

She responded by settling against his sweater and purring loudly.

Will flicked through options as James watched his face, studying the handsome features he loved so much. He wished they could spend every weekend together, but he knew that was unrealistic. It had taken him a few hours to get here, and the trains weren't cheap, either.

Will selected something and laid back into James's arms, who stared at the screen, only half paying attention to the film as it started. The sensation of Will against his chest and the familiar smell of his hair products and underneath that – his skin – was just too distracting. He really wanted to take Will up to his room for some privacy, but he knew his dad was lonely, so he turned his gaze back to the screen and settled in for the next couple of hours.

By the time the film finished, Frank had fallen asleep and was snoring softly. Will slowly uncurled himself from James's arms and stood up, stretching with a yawn.

James contemplated his dad. 'Do you think I should wake him?' he whispered. 'He's had a long week, obviously.'

'If he stays like that all night, I think he'll wake up with a sore neck,' Will pointed out.

James didn't say anything, but he was also concerned about the entity making itself known during the night. He tapped his dad gently. 'The film is over, Dad; we're going to go to bed.'

Frank started a little and blinked. 'I was just resting my eyes,' he said quickly, and Will laughed. Posey got up, looking disgruntled at the sudden movement, stretching her legs and rolling her back out before deciding to perch on the arm of the chair.

James went into the kitchen, making sure to switch the light on first, and threw some calming tea bags into mugs, setting the kettle to boil. He felt Will's arms wrapping around his waist and sighed happily at this welcome display of affection, leaning back into his touch, but something felt wrong.

A sudden gust of icy breath on his neck startled him and he turned quickly, confirming that Will was not in the kitchen. He surveyed the room, every hair on his body standing on end, but there was no sign of his boyfriend, and the sensation of physical contact had vanished.

He left the kettle boiling and ran back to the sitting room, his stomach flipping over. When he burst through the door, his dad and Will were still chatting. They both looked up.

'You alright?' Will asked. 'You look a bit pale, baby.'

'Yeah, uh, just tired. I'm making chamomile tea, either of you want sugar?' He knew it was a lame way to try and cover his panic, but neither of them seemed to be alarmed.

'No, thanks,' his dad answered as he got up.

'Me neither,' Will replied as he made his way across to James.

Feeling like a wimp but unable to deny he needed their company to return to the kitchen, James made his way back to pour the tea. Thankfully, it gave him an excuse to turn away from the others and their small talk. His hands had stopped shaking, but he couldn't stop thinking about the sensation of the pressure of those arms around him. The entity had made physical contact twice in one day – and this time with a disturbingly deceptive move. He shivered again, handed the mugs around and led the way out of the kitchen at the fastest pace he could without his behaviour seeming odd.

'Night, boys, sleep well!' his dad said as he stopped in the hallway to make sure the front door was locked.

'We will; you too, Frank!' Will replied.

'Night, Dad!' James called, slowing his pace on the stairs, lingering until his dad also began his ascent. He didn't want anyone downstairs alone for a moment at night, not after what he'd just experienced. It certainly seemed like the entity was targeting him, but better to be safe than sorry.

Posey trailed up the stairs after them, and Will frowned. 'She's not coming to bed with us, is she?'

James nodded. 'I think she'll want to sleep in my room.'

'Baby, this house is big enough; I don't think that's necessary.'

James ignored him, opening his bedroom door and letting the cat walk in ahead of them. She went straight to the bed and hopped up onto it, prompting Will to roll his eyes.

'Oh, come on…'

'It's a big change for her, too, y'know. This house is a new territory, and I want her to feel safe.' James picked her up. 'It's very important to me that she's happy here, and I wish that you would make the effort to understand that.' He crouched down and placed Posey gently in her own bed. 'There you go, you sleep there, okay?'

'As if she's going to stay there!' Will objected, as he looked around the room, taking in James's new space. "I'll be going home covered in cat hair!'

Nathaniel

Nathaniel had sensed the extra energy in the house. Not as vibrant as James or as gentle as his dad, but pleasant nonetheless. At times, this new soul felt conflicted somehow, but he couldn't quite get a clear read on that. When the door opened, Nathaniel saw who the energy belonged to: this was boyfriend Will, from the picture on the nightstand.

He could feel a change in James since they'd last been close. He tuned in and focused. James was frightened; something had happened. But he was also excited, happy, full of affection for his boyfriend. They were bickering playfully about James's cat, but Nathaniel could detect an edge of resentment underneath Will's words.

Will walked around the room, exploring it as James placed a suitcase on the floor and pointed out onto the landing.

'Upstairs bathroom is straight across the landing; should have given you the full tour earlier, really.'

Will laughed. 'You should have, but you were too busy being a dreadful host, making me walk places and getting us soaked in the rain! Still, there's always tomorrow.'

James made a face at him and pulled back the bed covers. 'Go on, then, hurry up and get yourself sorted.'

Will rummaged in the suitcase for a moment and pulled out a wash bag. 'Don't you dare fall asleep while I'm gone, or there will be consequences.'

James blew him a kiss. 'Don't take too long, then!'

He left, and Nathaniel watched as James fussed with the bed a little more, sipped some tea, stretched, brushed his hair and stripped down to his boxers.

As if he could feel his gaze, James looked around the room. 'I—I don't know if you're there, Nathaniel, I'm not sure how this works, but I'd appreciate it if you could be quiet this weekend, please. I don't want you spooking Will…and, ah, privacy would be nice too, thanks.'

Nathaniel didn't have enough energy remaining from earlier to be visible or form words, so he tried to project the energy of agreement towards James, a promise he would make himself scarce. He hoped James could feel it, that he would know Nathaniel only wanted him to be happy.

James seemed content that the matter was resolved and sat on the edge of the bed, patiently waiting for Will with his eyes on the door and his hands resting in his lap.

Nathaniel gazed at him for a minute longer, at James's beautiful hands, and wondered what it would feel like to be touched by him. What it felt like to be Will. To be solid and feel someone else's warm body, to know that they chose to connect with you over all the other possibilities. To feel special, to be wanted, to be held even for a moment, would be such a gift. The space where his heart used to sit ached, suddenly so painfully awake. A part of him waking after so long asleep that he had almost forgotten it was there. He *was* capable of feeling, still, of yearning for the love he never thought he could have, never thought he could ask for. Not after Theodore. He had shown Nathaniel that love like this was not for him.

And yet James was so unique, so magical, driving away the dull blanket of despair that Nathaniel had lingered underneath for so long. It was the most bewildering turn of events.

The joy of his emotional isolation ending was truly exquisite, but the agony of longing for what he could never have was equally intense. He lingered at the wall, feelings tearing through him and ripping into parts of him he never knew existed, until he couldn't stand it anymore, so he turned away and vanished into the dark.

James

Waking with Will in his arms again put an immediate smile on James's face; he nuzzled into his neck and enjoyed the uncomplicated closeness. Will murmured something that sounded like, 'Go back to sleep, baby.'

James smiled and propped himself up on one elbow, wondering what had woken him up. The light filtering through the curtains was still the soft grey kind, and the house seemed still. The gentle pitter-patter of rain on the window was the only sound in the room. He looked around, but nothing seemed out of place. Posey was curled up near his feet but fast asleep and completely motionless.

Then Will's phone lit up on the nightstand with a buzz. He reached over to see if it was anything urgent and saw the message that flashed up on the screen.

Have you told him yet?? X

He frowned; it was from Stevie. Perhaps he thought James would be jealous he'd taken his spot on the team. He knew Will's unlock pin, but he didn't want to seem untrusting, so he dropped Will's phone back where he'd found it and snuggled back down. When Will was fully awake later – and hopefully in a good mood – he'd bring it up. Or maybe Will would explain it without him having to.

He fidgeted, and Will sighed. 'Go back to sleep; it's so early.'

James stilled; his arms settled back around Will, but his mind was racing. There was an odd feeling in his stomach. He told himself he was probably being irrational and paranoid, but now that he really thought about it, maybe something had felt off the last few days. And he'd missed it because of all of the ghost stuff he'd been dealing with. Will had definitely messaged less than he normally would, and while they had had a great time last night, there were moments that James had felt Will seemed a little disconnected, as though he wasn't quite there in the way he had been before. But then, it could just be Will adjusting to this new situation and environment, and perhaps he'd been busy this week. James didn't want to seem like he was making something out of nothing.

He lay still, running it all over in his mind until he eventually drifted back off into a light doze, and when he awoke, Will was sitting on the edge of the bed with his back turned.

James stretched out a hand and tugged the back of his T-shirt. 'Morning, baby…'

Will jumped slightly and turned quickly. James didn't miss the way he flipped his phone over in his hand, the screen now facing down.

'Morning!' Will gave him one of his charming smiles. 'Sleep well?'

'I did. Surprising, considering you left your phone on vibrate.'

'Oh, sorry! I forgot about that, what with last night being so, so amazing.' He leant over and gave James a gentle kiss. 'I hope it didn't disturb you?'

'Only earlier when it woke me…'

Will gave him another kiss. 'Sorry, baby. What do you want to do this morning?'

'I was thinking maybe we could go out for breakfast; there's a local coffee shop I could take you to.'

Will grinned. 'Sounds good. Hopefully it will be better than the station coffee was, ugh!'

He hopped out of bed, taking his phone with him. James hated the suspicious part of him that was suddenly noticing these things.

They dressed quickly, motivated by the prospect of breakfast. The brisk, lengthy walk only increased their appetites, and by the time they reached the coffee shop, James was starving. He ordered their coffees and some breakfast bowls as Will found seats in a cosy booth.

He slid in opposite Will, taking a moment to appreciate how his eyes shone in the low light, and suddenly realising the glow reminded him of the shine in Nathaniel's eyes when they'd met in the garden.

'What?'

'Just thinking how incredibly handsome you are,' James replied quickly.

Will looked down, a little flushed. 'Uh, thanks.' He reached for his coffee and ran his index finger around the rim of the cup, licking the foam off it. 'And so are you, gorgeous,' he replied, but he didn't make eye contact.

James took his hands. 'I wish you didn't have to go home tomorrow.'

'Two breakfast bowls?' asked the server in a cheery voice.

'Yes, thanks.' James released Will's hands and leant back so she could put the food on the table.

Will grabbed a spoon and dug in, something in his enthusiasm seeming a little forced. James ate his breakfast much slower, forcing it down past the lump that had unexpectedly formed in his throat.

Will finished long before he did and sipped his coffee, his gaze remaining on the street outside. His posture seemed relaxed at first glance, but James noticed a slight jitter: one of his knees was bouncing under the table.

'Are you OK?'

Will smiled quickly. 'Absolutely! That was great, and the caffeine is really kicking in. What would you like to do today? Let's make a plan!'

'I don't really mind as long as I get to spend time with you. I haven't really explored the town properly yet, so we could do that, wander around a bit. I think there's a little museum and a cinema we could check out too?'

Will nodded. 'Sounds good! Any decent gay bars around here?'

James snorted. 'I don't think there's any decent bars at all, sorry.'

'And here I am, bringing all my best looks with me.'

'Like that means anything. You pack for college like you're going to fashion week.'

'Okay, so dancing all night will have to wait until you visit me, then.'

James sipped his coffee and steeled himself for what he was about to bring up. 'Will…I want to talk to you about something, but before I say anything, I want to tell you how much I love you.'

Will looked up, his eyes wide. 'Well, that's a really dramatic way to start off! What on earth are you about to say?'

'No, it's nothing really, I hope. But I have to ask…okay, I trust you. I do…but…this morning, when your phone went off, I saw the message that came up on the screen. I didn't unlock it or snoop, but it was clear it was from Stevie.'

Will swallowed. 'Right. What message was that?'

'It just said, "Have you told him yet??" and there was a kiss after.'

Will nodded slowly. 'And that made you think what, exactly?'

'Well…you know what that looks like?'

'No, actually, I don't! I think you'll have to communicate more clearly with me, as I don't have trust issues, baby. I get that your mum cheating has probably made you paranoid, but I thought what we have is stronger than that.'

James grabbed his hands. 'Will! Don't get all prickly on me. I'm asking because I need reassurance. Maybe I am paranoid, but…is there something between you and Stevie?'

'You need reassurance? So, you *don't* trust me?' Will demanded.

'All the articles I read on long distance relationships said that it's really important to communicate honestly and directly and say what you need and for us to hold space for each other and—'

'Oh, spare me the random articles you read, James! As if any of that actually means anything compared to real-life experience. I know I'm your first serious relationship, so I do try to be patient with you, but I'm not going to sit here and listen to you preaching some pop psychology someone put online for clicks.'

James took a deep breath and tried to hide how much Will's dismissal stung. 'It's not—Will, I read this stuff because I really want us to work! And I need you to be honest with me, please.'

'I don't want to talk about this now, not in here. Ask me later.'

'So, there is something to talk about?' James asked, his stomach twisting horribly.

'If you want to talk, we'll talk. But you asked for it, remember that.'

'That isn't really an answer.'

'Oh my God, James, why do you have to be so exhausting?'

'"Exhausting"? I just asked you a question about Stevie, that's all.'

Will knocked back the remainder of his coffee and got up. 'I'll meet you outside.'

James stayed where he was, slightly stunned, as Will exited the café abruptly, pulled his collar up and leant against the glass window. Without glancing back at James, he pulled out a cigarette and lit up. James turned away and finished his coffee, refusing to watch Will smoke. It felt like a pointed gesture – Will knew how much he hated it, and it had been a long time since he'd smoked around him.

He picked at the edge of a napkin, hating how vindictively poisonous Will could be when he was riled up. He wished for once they could have time together that wasn't hovering on a knife's edge of drama. Peaceful moments that were calming, not stressful. That he could feel safe saying whatever was on his mind, the way he could when he spoke with Nathaniel.

He sighed. His life was ridiculous. There was no way he was sitting here wishing his living, breathing, boyfriend was a bit more like the ghost haunting his new house. He pushed the train of thought away and looked back out the window at Will's moody face. He was still pouting over his cigarette, and it annoyed James how hot he looked.

He tried to sort out the feelings swirling inside him. He loved Will, he was sure of it…but right now he felt so disrespected and hurt. As if his feelings weren't important to Will at all, just an inconvenience. If he was honest with himself, he'd felt this way before but put it aside for the sake of their relationship and to create harmony between them. He hated fighting with Will, and he didn't want to now, either, but he knew from Will's behaviour that it was too late; he was already in a mood, and there was no putting that aside. He would have to apologize and grovel for a bit if he wanted his charming Will back, or tolerate his bad humour, put up with some passive aggressiveness and wait until it levelled out again – but their time together now was so limited, he really didn't want to waste it.

He sat there considering a new option: he could confront this now and continue to press for a resolution. He knew it would be an unpleasant confrontation, but then, lots of things had been unpleasant lately – ghosts thinking he was an easy haunt, Will leaning into his attitude problem from the moment he got off the train, and his dad plastering a smiley face on top of all the damage his mum had inflicted. It was all getting a bit much, and he was sick of it.

He took a deep breath and got up. He would deal with this now, head on.

Will was still smoking when he stepped out onto the pavement. He squinted at James. 'You ready to go?'

James nodded. 'Look, this weekend is supposed to be fun – I need it to be fun. I've had enough shit going on lately, and I'm not in the mood to ruin this. I don't want to fight.'

Will shrugged. 'So don't. It's all your choice – make a big deal about nothing or don't.'

'"Make a big deal about nothing"?' James repeated, struggling to maintain his calm.

Will started walking. 'Yeah. That's what it looks like from where I'm standing.'

'Will, please just be straight with me?'

'James, baby, I'm not straight with anyone,' Will quipped back.

'Don't make jokes! I need to have a proper conversation with you, okay? That message I saw this morning, what was it about?'

Will finally slowed his pace, stopping to stub his cigarette out and toss it in a bin. When he looked up, his expression was resigned.

'Okay, fine, but it's not my fault if you don't like it.'

'So you're not going to take responsibility for your actions?'

Will rolled his eyes. 'You're sounding like some kind of wannabe therapist influencer again. But whatever. Stevie thinks I should tell you about this one little thing that happened at his party, and he's being a real pain about it.'

'What happened?'

'Stop interrupting; I'm getting there. It wasn't much – we just kissed when we were really drunk. I told him after it didn't mean anything to me. It was just a bit of fun, but he's been going on and on like a right drama queen, as if we killed someone or something. He keeps saying that I owe it to you to tell you about it, like it *matters*.'

James just stared at him. His legs had gone weak, and he felt lightheaded. 'You didn't want to tell me?'

Will pulled another cigarette from an inside pocket and lit it. 'No, I knew you'd be dramatic about it too, and honestly, we never actually said we're exclusive anyway. Especially with you moving away, I think we should probably open things up, y'know? I'm only nineteen; I don't want to feel trapped by a relationship that really only exists every few weekends. I think we'd probably both be happier if we were a bit more fluid about our commitment.'

James shook his head. 'I—this is too much.'

Will exhaled a plume of smoke. 'I was going to have this conversation tomorrow in a mature and calm way before I left, but you just kept pushing.'

'Pushing?' James asked faintly.

'Yeah, pushing. Endless questions, taking everything so seriously, as usual.'

James took a deep breath to steady himself and regretted it when cigarette smoke hit his lungs and triggered a cough. 'Taking things so seriously? How do you suggest I should take things, Will? Our relationship matters to me!'

Will looked amused. 'Well, I suggest you relax a bit. We can both be chill about this, and then we'll be happy.'

'Do you…you and Stevie, is there something between you?'

'No! We're just friends. Stevie isn't my type. I mean, he's hot, but I'm not dating him.'

'You're contradicting yourself. Do you like him like that or not? Did you enjoy kissing him?'

Will shrugged. 'I mean, it just kind of happened…and I guess I did. And he did, but I'm with you. It's not like…well, I don't know. We can open things up and then I guess it's possible something might happen with him again. I know he wants that, but I need to think about it.'

James swallowed and fought back tears; he couldn't believe they were having this conversation.

'Will, I don't want to open things up. I love you; I don't want to think about you with someone else. Even the thought, knowing you and Stevie kissed…I feel sick.'

Will stared at him for a moment, 'I hear what you're saying. It's been so wonderful James, it really has, but I think we've run our course, haven't we?'

'What—are you breaking up with me?'

'I think it's for the best. I don't think we're on the same page anymore. You're a hopeless romantic, and I'm a bit more realistic about things. You think you want this now, but months from now, you'll feel just as trapped by this long-distance thing as I do.'

'No, I won't! You're everything to me, Will.'

'Don't be emotionally manipulative, James! We want different things; I believe if you really love someone, you can set them free. Unconditional love is not possession.'

'What? This really hurts, Will. You're breaking up with me so you can do what? Hook up with Stevie?! I thought he was my friend! He played at my side.'

'Don't be silly; it's about much more than just Stevie!'

'Fine then, hook up with loads of random guys? That's worth more than what you feel for me?'

'Freedom, James, I want *freedom*. It's not about Stevie or random guys; it's about me and what I want.'

'I thought you were happy with me…I thought we were happy together. What about last night?'

Will shrugged. 'Last night, I wanted you. That doesn't mean that's all I ever want.'

James nodded; there was nothing more to be said. Will's words were echoing around his mind, pulses of shock and heartbreak alternating in a dizzying fashion. Everything looked shiny and unreal.

'I—I'm going to go home.'

'I'll come with you; I need to get my stuff.'

Will put his cigarette between his lips, pulled his phone out and started typing. James deliberately kept a stride ahead of him so he wouldn't see who he was talking to. A moment later, Will made an approving noise. 'There's a train in thirty-four minutes; should be enough time. Mind giving me a lift back to the station?'

Nathaniel

'We're friends, aren't we?' Nathaniel asked as he dangled a shoelace for the cat to swat.

He took her enthusiastic participation in their game as confirmation of mutual agreement. It had been a long time since anyone had brought a furry companion into the house, and Nathaniel realised how much he enjoyed their company. It was so much simpler than interacting with humans: they could see him without him having to expend any extra energy, they took him at face value and they didn't ask questions. He didn't have to prove himself; they just seemed to know he meant well.

He hoped she would spend most of her time in the bedroom with him; it would make his life so much less lonely to have a regular friend – and to keep her safe from the entity. He was confident she wouldn't take any risks, cats being so much cleverer than humans about these things, but the entity could be so fast and so vicious.

The cat pounced, timed it well and captured the shoelace, Nathaniel let her chew triumphantly on it and drifted to the window.

He could sense James was almost home and knew something was wrong. As he approached the house, the waves of emotional distress emanating from him were so strong Nathaniel felt each pulse like physical blows to his stomach. He watched him march up to the front door, Will trailing behind.

Instead of closing off, Nathaniel tuned in, wanting to decipher what was going on. At first, it was a swirling mess of powerful feelings, then he began to find threads – anger at first, then underneath the anger, intense sadness. A deep pain that spoke to him of love turned sour, spoiled through betrayal, twisted and polluted, ultimately lost. It was a familiar blend; Nathaniel remembered it, and it pained him to know James was feeling it now. He wished he could have somehow shielded him from ever knowing such an emotional state.

James's feelings were so overwhelming that his energy was frightening, affecting Nathaniel so badly he felt like he was drowning alongside him. He staggered under the weight of it, Theodore's face flashing into his mind's eye. The night he had climbed out his bedroom window and they had sat together in the moonlight, the shadows of the trees playing across his face. Theodore taking his hands in his.

'I promise you, Nathaniel, I will love you forever, for eternity.'

The vision of a bright future that he had painted and Nathaniel had wholeheartedly believed in. Theodore's gentle hand on his face.

'Once we do the ritual, the world is ours. And we will be each other's…we can leave this place, this pathetic small town. Never mind your family; you won't need them anymore – what they think of you won't matter. You'll always have me, forever.'

Tears rose in Nathaniel's eyes again, old pain raised to the surface by James's turmoil.

He wanted to withdraw, retreat into the wall, but he also knew James needed someone above all else now. Whatever had happened, he didn't want to leave him alone with it; he simply couldn't. He decided then and there that even if James didn't know Nathaniel was here for him, he always would be.

He heard the key in the front door, then it slamming shut. Footsteps came stomping up the stairs, the door was thrown open and James burst in. He glanced around the room, seized the suitcase from the floor and turned quickly. He almost collided with Will as he followed him in.

'Steady on.'

'What are you doing creeping up behind me?' James snapped.

'Getting my stuff, if that's okay with you. Or would you like to fling it theatrically from the window? Perhaps you could burn it while playing angry music?'

'Don't you dare make jokes, not now, not—' James choked up and fell silent. He looked down, his confrontational air fading into defeat.

'I'm sorry, it's…just my way of coping. I'm really sorry things have gone this way,' Will said, his tone contrite. It was convincing to

Nathaniel's ears, but the read he was getting on Will's energy didn't quite match it.

James looked back at him, hope in his eyes. 'Really? So maybe we…can we work this out? I mean, come on Will! This is insane; it's *us*! I'd really like to try. I love you so much; I don't want to break up.'

Will nodded. 'I do love you too.'

They stared into one another's eyes for a moment, and Nathaniel felt a surge of hope in James. He leant in, one of his hands cupping Will's face, as he drew him into a gentle kiss. Will went with it, and the moment looked so tender Nathaniel began to fade back into the wall, his eyes averted. Just as he was settling back into the familiar darkness and the numbing safety of his comforting nothingness, he felt a jolt in James that pulled him back into the room.

Will had pulled back, creating distance between them.

'That was a beautiful goodbye, thank you.'

'Goodbye?'

Tears were welling in James's eyes. Will's expression was pained, but he remained dry-eyed.

'I think it has to be. We want different things; there's no talking our way around that.'

'You don't want to be friends?' James asked in a plaintive tone.

Will sighed. 'I think it's a bit too early for *that* conversation.'

Nathaniel tuned into his energy again out of curiosity. Will was much calmer; he felt disappointed in some way, perhaps a touch of guilt, but ultimately content. Nathaniel peered at him, confused by how someone could have captured the interest and heart of someone like James and apparently not even remotely appreciate what they had. That Will would have done anything to jeopardise his connection with him in the first place was desperately confusing, but to choose to throw it away altogether…it defied comprehension.

James deserved so much more. He deserved someone who could really see how incredible he was, who would cherish him, protect his heart and keep him safe. Someone who wouldn't lie and use him to get what he wanted and then abandon him without so much as a second thought. Nathaniel could feel anger building in him at how unjust this was, at how wrong it was that James was being treated in such a way. Watching Will was turning Nathaniel's stomach; he was charming like Theodore had been, a charming, deceptive liar who cared only for himself and was utterly callous, selfish, repellent and—

The lightbulb in the lamp on the bedside table exploded in a sudden shower of glass, making both James and Will jump. For a split second, James's pain was interrupted by shock as they both turned to look at it.

'Great, just what I need! Another mess for me to clear up when I get back!'

His tone was bitter and stung Nathaniel, especially as he wasn't sure if it was his or James's feelings that were responsible for the explosion. It was hard to tell when he couldn't decipher whether he was feeling his own feelings or James's anymore; assigning an owner or origin to the energetic turmoil swirling around them was impossible.

'Have you got everything, then?' James asked Will, his tone suddenly flat and cold. 'We need to get a move on.'

Will glanced around and fiddled with his suitcase, picking a few items up off the desk. 'Yeah, I'm ready.'

James gave one last look around the room and then addressed thin air. 'Okay, Nathaniel, try not to do any more damage while I'm gone. Don't worry, Will is leaving so there'll be no more arguments or anything else disturbing your peace!'

Will gaped at him like he'd lost his mind. 'James, are you feeling alright?'

'Of course I'm not! But it's no concern of yours anymore, is it? Let's go.'

'Who the hell is Nathaniel?'

'He's no-one; it's not important. Stop pretending to care and get in the car.'

Nathaniel remained where he was long after they'd gone back downstairs and he'd heard the front door close behind them.

Now that James was gone, he could discern his own emotions again, the hurt stinging like salt in a fresh wound. The crushing disappointment that James would think him capable of doing damage out of spite or call him *no-one, not important.* He sighed. He felt very heavy again, very tired.

He had been so foolish to believe he and James had a meaningful connection. Of course it was a one-sided situation. He had exaggerated everything in his heart because he was lonely and pathetic. He had allowed his feelings to gallop away from him after those special moments in the garden and over-romanticised everything. He was a mere shadow to James, just a curiosity and a source of information, not someone of significance like his solid, real boyfriend – or ex-boyfriend, as the case may be.

He was always nothing in the end. It didn't matter what he wanted or what people said – it was all wishful thinking, and he was a damn fool to have made this mistake again. After all the nights he had wasted staring into the shadows for the slightest sign of movement, every bat or bird rustling in the trees giving him hope, until the day he'd realised Theodore was never going to return. After all their time together, leaving Nathaniel had been easy. It didn't matter how much of his heart he gave someone; it was never going to be enough because *he* wasn't enough.

He took one last look out the window at the garden; he would leave his time with James behind there too. They may have been fleeting moments, but those conversations had felt like everything to him, a euphoric revelation that he wouldn't trade for anything in the world. Yet he had to accept the end of the fantasy. This was not the beginning of something beautiful; it was the delusion of a sad little ghost. He drifted back into the wall and felt the darkness blanket him. It was time to go back to sleep.

James

'Did you have a nice breakfast?' Frank appeared out of the kitchen, a piece of toast in one hand. He looked slightly puzzled. 'Where's Will?'

James forced a smile. 'Oh, he had to go home a day early – drama with his sister. It'll be alright, though.'

'That's a shame, such a short trip. What's going on with his sister?'

'I'm not sure yet,' James lied, wondering how long he could keep this pretence up. He wasn't exactly sure why he couldn't bear to tell his dad the truth. Was it his own pride? That saying it out loud would make it real? Or was he protecting him as he dealt with the fresh pain of his own divorce? Perhaps a bit of everything.

'I just made some coffee if you want it,' Frank said as he turned back into the kitchen. 'You got some post, too, by the way.'

James followed his dad in and picked up the jiffy bag off the counter. He tore it open without thinking, and something wrapped in bubble wrap tumbled out, followed by several bits of wood, a few small candles and a note.

Frank chuckled at the assortment on the counter. 'I know who that's from.'

James peeled off the bubble wrap to reveal a little glass bottle stoppered with a cork. He held it up to the light. It was filled with dried plant flakes and salt and had been sealed with wax with a sigil engraved on it.

'I'll take that coffee, actually, thanks, Dad,' James said, unwrapping the note when Frank's back was turned. He sat at the table contemplating his options. The delivery had reminded him he couldn't afford to wallow in his feelings about Will forever. He needed to talk to Nathaniel again soon and find out what he could about the entity. He rolled the bottle between his fingers. In one way, he wanted to do it now – the idea of seeing Nathaniel lifted his mood a little – but on the other hand, he wanted to choose not feeling anything, to switch his mind off for a while and give himself a rest. He looked at Nova's note.

Jamesy…the bottle is to be carried on you and either worn or kept under your pillow at night. The spell I cast should serve as full protection for now. I'm going to come as soon as I can and I promise we'll do further research and get to the bottom of this. In the meantime, probably best to lay low and avoid 'feeding' anything, if you can. LOVE YOU X

He rolled the note up and put it with everything else, pulled out his phone and messaged Nova.

Package arrived today, thank you so much. Would love to talk when you have time, more has happened with haunting, getting very uncomfortable. X

Frank put his coffee in front of him and sat back down, his eyes on the garden. 'I might try and cut the lawn today if the weather stays dry.'

'That's a good idea,' James said absently, his eyes on his phone.

Nova replied almost immediately. *Of course, I can talk when I get home later? But are you sure you don't want to wait until lover boy goes home tomorrow night? X*

It took everything James had to maintain a normal demeanour reading those words. He took a deep breath, put his phone face-down for a moment and had a sip of his coffee. Then he sent back, *He's gone. Talk later. X*

He collected the bits Nova had sent off the table and put them back in the jiffy bag, making a decision. 'I think I'm going to go for a run, see you in a bit.'

Frank nodded, his eyes still on the garden. 'Enjoy!'

Nathaniel

James sat down heavily at his desk with his hair damp from a shower, switched on his larger device and sipped a drink. He had deposited a package on the table, and Nathaniel watched him take items out and examine them, opening a drawer and rummaging around until he pulled out a chain.

Nathaniel felt like a puppet, and he hated it. Despite the sleep he had chosen and surrendered to, James's strong emotions had pulled him from his restful state. That irresistible magnetism again, dragging him from his peace and into awareness, James's feelings returning to join his in an unbearable cacophony.

James fiddled with the chain, and Nathaniel drew closer, curious to see what he was doing. He pulled something off and tossed it into the drawer, then threaded the chain through the metal loop fixed into a cork in a small bottle. Nathaniel moved to stand at his shoulder, looking at the device all lit up and glowing. He reached out and drained it. It would give him the energy to manifest and clear his name, make sure James knew he hadn't done any deliberate bulb-exploding. Maybe then he would feel more positive towards Nathaniel, and they could have another conversation in the garden. He knew he was courting pain again, but he couldn't resist trying anyway. Not to mention the overwhelming urge to want to comfort James in some way. If he couldn't sleep, then he was going to need a distraction – and a challenge would do just fine. James was going to have to cheer up so Nathaniel could get some rest. He'd had quite enough of *feelings*; it was time to resolve this.

He laid a palm on the device and felt the steady flow of energy, then pulled it towards him. Despite the events of the last few days, it felt good to recharge energetically, irrespective of his emotions.

He watched James's face, eagerly anticipating the moment when he became visible to him. It was hard not to hope that maybe he'd smile; perhaps his eyes would light up a little. Either of those would make Nathaniel's day, ease the hurt from earlier. He knew chasing that validation was likely to end ultimately with disappointment, but here he was all the same, indulging the impulse.

James was still looking down, undoing the catch on his chain. He placed it around his neck, settling the tiny bottle into place against his muscled chest. As his fingers let go and the bottle settled, a sudden sensation hit Nathaniel. He gasped and looked around. There was nothing to account for the momentary feeling – it felt like a door being slammed in his face. But it was just a feeling in the air; nothing physical had occurred. It wasn't the entity's evildoing, as it was currently still dormant downstairs.

Puzzled but growing less alarmed as nothing further happened, he returned his focus to the device and drew power from it. James swore and plugged it in, allowing Nathaniel to completely fill himself with power, enough to manifest for a long time.

He focused and brought himself into the room, moving from behind James to beside him, waiting for him to notice his presence.

James continued to stare at his device, even though Nathaniel was right in his eyeline; it was confusing. He moved, waving gently and finally placed his hand in front of the screen.

'James?' he spoke out loud, but there was no reaction whatsoever. It was as if he had ceased to exist, and as his eyes scanned James's face and landed on his chest, he suddenly understood. It was so much worse than being unimportant to James – James didn't want any contact at all; he didn't want to see or hear him anymore.

He stayed where he was for a long time, gazing at the little bottle on the chain. Clear, tangible evidence that he was not welcome here. An excruciating feeling of rawness tore through him. There was no denying now he had made a grave mistake, allowing himself to be drawn in by someone so wonderful arriving into his world – but this was the worst mistake he'd made since Theodore, and Theodore was the biggest mistake of his mortal existence. He'd been so sure he would never, *ever* allow himself to be hurt that way again. Yet here he was. Despite his best intentions to keep his feelings under control, he had betrayed his promise to himself to keep his heart safe.

His failure to extinguish the last kindling of hope long ago had allowed it to spark up again and, fed by their connection, it had become a wildfire before Nathaniel had even had a chance to realise what was happening.

Perhaps a fire he would never gain control of again. He would have no choice but to let it burn what was left of his heart to ruins. James wasn't going to leave; he was going to stay, but Nathaniel would be forever shut out. Now he must go back to being silenced and invisible, after a taste of what it felt like to not be. There was no way he could forget that taste; it was far too late.

Regardless of how much it hurt, he knew he had to respect and honour the message that bottle sent, so he turned away and drifted back towards the wall, hoping the despair he felt would help him to rest. He couldn't bear it anymore – these intense emotional highs and lows that he had no control over, the power he had accidentally given to this human to influence his emotional state with even a minor interaction.

Before he stepped into the darkness, he looked back at James, allowing himself one last look, one last high, and reflected on how good it had felt to have hope again, to feel so alive, to have those wonderful moments of connection even for a short time. Maybe it was worth the inevitable pain. That was the price of wanting what you could never have. And perhaps he should be gentle with himself; perhaps he never stood a chance at all, considering the circumstances.

As he settled back into the wall, he heard the device start up, James's voice and the voice of his friend becoming audible. He reminded himself that James had a busy life and people who cared for him; he didn't need Nathaniel, and Nathaniel had made a promise to himself a long time ago that he would stop going where he wasn't wanted and chasing people who didn't value him anymore. He cast his mind back to the moment in his human life when he had set those intentions, feeling so determined to be strong in the face of rejection by those he had loved so dearly.

It had felt good at first, a sense of sudden power and self-worth and a lessening of the agony of heartbreak. He didn't need anyone else; he could be strong and reject them right back. But as time passed, and his loneliness had grown, his resolve had weakened. It seemed rather meaningless to insist he wouldn't settle for anything less than someone choosing him when no-one ever did.

It was hard not to reach out and desperately crave love from those who withheld it when the alternative was nothing. Even crumbs felt better than that. Crumbs were sometimes enough to stop you starving altogether, enough to keep you clinging on. He was crying again, uncontrollable non-corporeal tears welling up and pouring down his cheeks.

The intensity of his feelings was shocking, overwhelmingly beautiful and horrible all at once. Part of him wished James had never set foot in this house, and part of him was more grateful than he could ever have described that he had.

He let the tears flow as he settled within the wall, the sound of James's voice still audible. He allowed himself to listen for a moment longer, and then with effort, he blocked him out, focusing on putting up energetic walls around himself before he tried to sleep.

James

'Hey!' Nova waved. 'Ooh, the bottle arrived safely; looks good on you! But then, everything looks good on you. Jamesy, what's wrong?'

James never could hide his feelings from Nova; she would see through any front he put up with her razor-sharp perception.

'I…well…' He paused to gather himself, then gave up and let his voice shake. 'Will, he broke up with me. When I said he's gone, I meant…'

'He's gone, gone?'

James swallowed hard, unable to form words for a few moments.

'James, I'm so sorry. Let it out; feel those feelings. Feel it to heal it, remember?'

He nodded miserably. 'I—I keep hoping that maybe this is all a weird nightmare and I'm going to wake up back home and none of this happened. No move, no creepy old house, no breakup. It hurts so badly, the things he said…but I still want him. I still want more than anything for him to call and say he's sorry and he made a mistake and he wants me back. I hate that, I do, but it's what I want. I'd take him back in a heartbeat, and it feels so…weak.'

Nova shook her head. 'James! It's not even been a full day yet; will you please go easy on yourself? I'm so sorry. But these things take time, and you'll go back and forth – some days will be easier than others and some harder. It's totally normal to feel like you want the person back and things to be like they were. You still love him; you can't just stop loving him instantly because he treated you horribly.'

James nodded. 'Thank you.'

'I'm here for you, and if I can get anything from my shitty breakup with Aquarius last year, hopefully it's being able to help you through yours. Now, what did he say to you?'

James wiped his eyes on his sleeve and repeated everything as best he could. The moment he finished relaying the morning's conversation to Nova, she launched into an angry tirade.

'Wow…I mean, wow! I always knew he was a bit shady, to be honest, and definitely not worthy of your love, but James, he really is the worst!'

James nodded. 'I know you feel you have to say that, but—'

'Don't you start that! I mean it, every word! You know I always thought he wasn't good enough for you, and now I can say it outright. He wasn't and isn't.'

'But Nova, I know you think that, but that's because you don't know him like I do; you don't—'

'James, please! I know this hurts badly right now, I do, and I know you love him, but in time, you'll see him for what he really is: a selfish, manipulative user.'

James sighed. 'Maybe he's not perfect – he can be really mean and harsh – but he can also be so amazing. Nova, I can't believe he broke up with me, and I can't imagine there being a time when it feels okay that we aren't together. I can't imagine *ever* feeling okay that he's not my boyfriend, and honestly, the thought of him and Stevie—'

'Try not to think about that right now.'

'How can I possibly *not* think about it?!'

'Yeah, fair, that was a stupid thing to say. I'm sorry.'

'It's going to haunt me, Nova! I can see them together in my mind on a loop, and my imagination just generates all the things I don't want to think about…' James trailed off miserably.

'Oh, Jamesy, I'm so, so sorry. Look, I'm going to come and visit as soon as I can; I'll talk to my mum tonight and look at my schedule. I'm here for you. I know it feels awful now, but it will get better.'

'Will it? Or is that just something people say?'

'It really does, in a way. You just get used to life without them, and you look back at the relationship with clearer eyes and see the ways that they were actually shitty to you. Maybe also chat to your dad about this? My mum was so helpful during my breakup, weird though that sounds.'

James shook his head. 'I can't! He's got enough of his own stuff going on; I need to seem fine so he doesn't worry.'

'Your mum?'

James considered for a moment. 'My mum…no chance. She did a Will when you think about it.'

'But maybe she'll have insight? I just think you need all the support you can get right now, James; I get that I'm probably the only one you can talk to about the haunting, but at least consider sharing your heartbreak.'

James started sniggering, the whole situation suddenly striking him as absurdly funny when she said it out loud. The sniggering became unhinged laughter as Nova stared at him, her bemused expression becoming tentative amusement, and then she allowed herself a giggle too.

It felt good at first, but then James realised his laughter was verging on more tears, and he stopped, his eyes watering and his face aching.

'Sorry, Nova…I just…it's not funny at all, really, but it's just so ridiculous that it also kind of is.'

'I know what you mean. So, things are getting worse with the ghosts, too?'

'Yeah, another bit of actual physical contact. Something…' He shuddered thinking about it. 'Something actually put what felt like arms around me in the kitchen last night. I thought it was Will, but it wasn't. He and my dad were in the sitting room; I was totally alone, and when I turned, I saw nothing there.'

Nova shook her head. 'This is beyond anything I've ever experienced. I don't like the way it keeps escalating, and in such a short time, too.'

A sudden shout from downstairs made James jump and quickly brought him back to the pressing realities of the moment. He opened the bedroom door. 'Dad?'

'Are you upstairs James?' Frank called back; his voice shaky.

'Yes! Just talking to Nova. Are you alright?'

'I…I'm fine, don't worry about me.'

James turned back to his laptop. 'I need to go and check on him; I don't believe he's okay at all.'

Nova nodded. 'Of course. I'll drop you a message later about coming up there to see you and sorting this paranormal mess out. Keep me updated on your dad!'

She ended the call, and James ran onto the cold landing, noticing the sudden drop in temperature as he descended the stairs. His dad was in the kitchen, sweeping up uncooked rice and shards of glass.

'What happened?' James asked.

Frank looked up; his face uncharacteristically pale. 'I, uh, I think there must have somehow been a build-up of pressure in the rice jar. I must have overfilled it and maybe there was too much heat in the cupboard…I don't know. Nothing to worry about.'

James frowned at him. 'So, it exploded?'

'I think so. I took it out and put it on the counter, and when I turned my back, it somehow shattered everywhere.'

Frank looked away, as if he didn't want to make eye contact with James. 'Oh, by the way, I was talking to your mum earlier. She would love you to come and stay for a bit; she really misses you.'

'Now isn't really a good time though, is it?'

'I'm sure the first few days at college will just be introductory stuff anyway, nothing to worry about. Family time is much more important anyway, isn't it? I'll call them tomorrow, I'm sure they'll understand.' His tone was unnaturally cheery as he finished sweeping up the last bit of the mess and dumped it into the bin. 'You can take Posey with you; it'll be fun! What do you say?'

'No, I'm not going. Dad, you're not really making sense. What's going on?'

'Your mum will be very disappointed. I think you—'

He broke off, the rumbling sound coming from the garage ending his sentence. His eyes widened. 'Shall we go out for a bit? Now?'

James heard the shrill edge to his voice and knew he was terrified; his dad already knew something wasn't right with the house.

'Just a minute, Dad,' he turned and walked towards the sound, hoping the bottle around his neck would do its thing.

As he entered the garage, he saw the source of the noise: his dumbbells were being flipped across the floor, the heavier ones producing a rumble and the lighter ones being dragged, creating a cacophony of grating noises.

'Stop it!' He entered the room with confidence he didn't feel but projected as much authority as he could into his posture and voice. For a moment, he felt pushback, a charge in the atmosphere like static and the sensation of something rushing toward him. He stood his ground as it reached him, all the hairs on his body standing on end. Then it stopped; the feeling of a protective shield around him was palpable as a calm descended.

Frank entered the garage behind him, his gaze on the scattered equipment on the floor. 'You didn't leave those there, did you?' His tone made it clear he already knew the answer.

James shook his head. 'I think maybe it might be good to have a chat. Perhaps we should go out first, though.'

Frank glanced at the door. 'Before we go, we'd better take Posey's things out to the shed.'

'What?'

He gestured for James to follow as he went back to the kitchen, pulling out the cat food and filling her bowl. 'Is her bed in your room?'

James nodded. 'Yes, but why?'

'She won't come back in,' Frank said, looking sheepish. 'She was watching something very intently in the living room earlier and seemed a bit on edge already, but then she followed me in here, reacted weirdly and ran outside. Probably about half an hour before the jar incident.'

'Reacted weirdly?'

'Jumped around a lot, did an impression of a hissing toilet brush and then sprinted away.'

James opened the back door, clicking his tongue. 'So, we'll get her back in. She can stay in my room; she likes it there.'

Frank shook his head. 'She won't enter the house this evening; trust me, I tried. I called, I bribed her with treats, then I tried to carry her in…' He held his hands up and displayed the scratches all over them.

'Dad! That's not like her at all; she's never done that!'

Frank nodded. 'I know. Then she hightailed it off to the shed and isn't interested in coming back out.'

'I guess we have to accept that, then, for now, anyway. I'll get her stuff and take it out,' James replied, resigned to his cat abandoning the house. As he carried her bed back down the stairs, he decided it was probably for the best – at least he wouldn't have to worry about her, and she'd be out of the way until whatever this was got resolved.

'You take that out and then join me in the car, then,' Frank said, picking up the keys. 'Hopefully this is just a period of adjustment for her and she'll come back into the house soon, on her own terms.'

James couldn't resist giving him a sceptical look. 'I think we both know what the issue is.'

Frank swallowed hard, dropping his voice. 'Best leave that conversation for when we're outside, I think.'

***

'So…there's obviously something going on,' Frank began. 'I was hoping you wouldn't notice or have to deal with it, but I think maybe it's too late for that.'

James dipped a biscuit in his coffee and nodded. 'It is. I think I might have noticed before you did, and, as I keep telling you, I'm not a kid anymore, Dad. You don't have to protect me.'

'I can't help it; it's a parent thing.'

James snorted. 'Right, well, funny thing is, I didn't want *you* to notice. I was hoping to deal with it myself – well, with Nova's help – and then you wouldn't have to be worried or anything.'

Frank laughed. 'What a pair we are!'

James sipped his coffee as they fell into silence.

'Who's going to actually say it?' he finally asked.

Frank sighed. 'I will. I've never been much for ghost stories but…things have been happening that I can't really explain away anymore. I thought maybe I was going mad, but you're witnessing them too and, well, what do you think?'

'The house is definitely haunted.'

Frank managed a smile. 'It's a relief I'm not losing my mind. I did wonder; I thought maybe it was stress. Or the sleeping pills I've needed since…well, you know.'

'I get that. I've asked myself similar questions. But then I spoke to Nova, and she gave me some tips and things to try – she's even done some research. And I did this meditation type thing, and I spoke to one of the ghosts—well, I actually saw him in real life a few times, too—'

'"One of"?!'

James nodded. 'There's at least two, hopefully just two.'

Frank's mouth fell open.

'I spoke to Nova earlier. She's going to come up here and help as soon as she can, but for now, she's given me this.' James held up the bottle. 'It's a personal protection spell. I think it's why the activity in the garage ceased when I stood my ground earlier; it'll stop things attacking me again.'

'Attacking you *again*?' Frank queried faintly.

James nodded. 'I've been shoved and sort of…hugged. How about you?'

His phone lit up, and he glanced down; it was Nova. 'Two seconds, Dad.'

He opened the message; it was an old, cracked photograph of a dapper, cheerful-looking young man he didn't recognise, from one of her ancestry sites. Nova had written, *This is Arthur Gadsby!*

James messaged back, *Interesting, haven't seen him…yet anyway,* X and put his phone in his pocket.

'Right, what have you experienced, Dad?'

Frank put his drink down. 'I think maybe we should both start at the beginning and share every experience we've had; then we'll have a better idea of what's gone on.'

Half an hour later, James had given his dad an outline of everything he had experienced but found himself holding back the details of his conversations with Nathaniel a bit, focusing more on the entity. He had also learnt his dad had been hearing strange noises from downstairs, clearing up debris from recurring poltergeist activity, been feeling watched, seeing shadows from the corners of his eyes, and most worrying of all, had heard footsteps on the stairs at night that had been getting progressively closer to his bedroom.

'I…I thought it was you sleepwalking or staying up late at first,' Frank explained, 'but last night, they were on the landing, and when I yanked my bedroom door open, there was no one there. The steps stopped, and your room was in darkness.' He sighed. 'I put it down to my sleeping pills giving me auditory hallucinations, but all of these things together, it's just…I can't explain it away anymore. I've started researching paranormal phenomena, the different types and the possible causes or triggers, and I admit I considered the theory about adolescents and their emotions quite a bit. Especially considering your current circumstances, with all the upheaval and change.'

'Meaning what? This is somehow my fault?'

Frank fiddled with the edge of a placemat. 'Well, no, it wouldn't be your fault – more a consequence of you being in the house. The theory is that adolescence is such an emotionally intense and powerfully charged time that teenagers can sort of create energetic disturbances in their surroundings. That their feelings give off waves of energy that make things move in the physical world. Fascinating stuff to consider, really!' He paused for a moment. 'And…I…um, well…as I said, you're going through an emotional time at the moment – understandably, with the move and everything, so…'

'Oh, so *that's* why you wanted to send me off to stay at Mum's?'

Frank shrugged. 'Partly. I thought it might be interesting to see if it stopped while you were away, but also so I'd know you're safe.'

Frank paused and winced slightly as he spoke again. 'Also, well, I'm afraid I have to go away on business Monday afternoon, and I won't be back until the following day. It's a regional office meet-up with an evening conference, and it's compulsory. They've already booked my hotel; I wasn't exactly asked first.'

'So, you don't want me alone at the house?'

His dad smiled apologetically. 'Exactly. I thought if you went to your mum's place for a few nights that firstly, you'd be safe while I'm away, and also maybe secondly, before you got back, I could get a priest in, and you'd never have to know about any of this.'

'But if it was me and my incredible teenage angst creating energetic disturbances, what was a priest going to do?'

Frank shrugged. 'Not much, admittedly. But I wasn't sure; I'm still not. I think it's worth a try though, especially if you're sure it's a spirit. Or spirits.'

James sighed. 'I am completely sure, but still not really keen on that plan – the whole priest thing.'

'Me neither, but have you got better ideas?'

'Actually, yes. I've been making my own plans to get rid of the ghosts without you having to be involved.'

He pulled out his phone and sent Nova a message. *Okay, so, turns out my dad is aware of the haunting situation. Also, he's going away Monday afternoon and doesn't want me to be alone…no pressure, but could you come up? Might be a good time for us to try and get to the bottom of this XX*

She called back immediately.

'Hey! Can you pass me over to your dad? I'd like to hear his experiences firsthand if that's okay. I've made notes on everything you've told me, and I'd like to add his to my file too. I'm going to meet up with some pretty knowledgeable folk this weekend and get their advice.'

'Of course; here you go.'

James passed his phone to his dad, sat back and enjoyed finishing his coffee while Frank repeated his account to Nova. He reflected on how much relief he felt now he wasn't trying to hide the ghostly activity from him, and he also realised he hadn't thought about Will for at least a minute. The thought brought the pain back again in a fresh surge, and he wrapped an arm around his torso reflexively. The pain felt almost physical; being distracted was blissful, but when it hit him again, it was excruciating.

Frank passed the phone back, and it brought him back into the present moment.

'So, what do you reckon?' he asked Nova.

'I can be at yours Monday lunchtime.'

'Are you sure? I mean, I won't lie, it would be really great. I definitely don't want to go to my mum's, and as much as I want to be brave, I don't really want to be in that house alone.'

'I agree – I don't think you should be; I don't think anyone should be. And you won't; I'll be there.'

'Thanks, Nova.'

'Don't thank me; I'm just being your friend. Coming up and being with you is the least I can do, what with the way things have escalated the last few days…and now you're hurting from the breakup with Will. That kind of emotional pain around a spirit that feeds on darkness, you're a walking snack.'

'I've always said so.'

'I'm not joking.'

'Right, sorry. Just trying to make this seem a bit less…'

'Terrifying?'

'That's the one.'

'Then there's Frank; I don't like that one bit. This thing is aware of both of you, and now you're wearing the bottle, your dad is potentially more vulnerable.'

'I could give it to him; my room is apparently protected.'

'No! Don't do that. I don't trust the word of this spirit you spoke to.'

James felt a spike of indignation. 'His name is Nathaniel, remember? And he's not just some spirit. I can trust him. I can just feel it!' James paused, certain of his accurate instincts on Nathaniel's moral fibre. 'I haven't actually checked out what he told me, though. I'll do it later so you have proof.'

'No, please leave it alone, James, leave everything alone until I get there. If you tamper with a ward and it's genuine, you could accidentally ruin it.'

'Okay. Nova, are you really sure you can handle this?'

'Can we ever be sure of anything? But you know I've been practicing in the realms of the unseen since I was a little kid.'

'What a weirdo.'

'Totally, and proud of it.'

'I love you, Nova, you know that.'

'Love you too. Just hang on, okay? I'll see you soon; I'll text you when I'm on the train.'

James hung up and realised he may as well come clean on everything.

'Dad, Will and I…we broke up.'

Frank's eyes widened. 'What? This weekend? Is that why he left?'

James nodded. 'Yeah.'

'I'm sorry to hear that, truly. What happened?'

'We…wanted different things. Well, he did. It wasn't working for him, the idea of long distance, or I guess, being serious.'

His dad reached across the table and put a hand on top of his. 'I'm sorry son. I remember how it is the very first time you get your heart broken. All the feelings you didn't even know you were capable of feeling until that moment, the intensity – it's so hard. A revelation in the worst way.'

James nodded, too choked up for words.

'I'm here for you, okay? I've been there, a few times now. More than I'd like.' He sighed. 'There's nothing I can say right now to make it better; I know that. Only that I'll do whatever I can to help, and time will heal it.'

'How does that actually work, though, Dad? I mean, Nova said it too, but it just doesn't feel possible that it can get better unless I somehow get Will back.'

Frank paused for a moment. 'Well, day after day, you slowly get more used to just being without them, and eventually, the ache fades, and it doesn't sting when you think about them being with someone else. They just seem…less important than they used to. You build a new life without them being a central part of it.'

His dad stared off into the distance for a moment. 'It takes time. But it does happen, even though it always feels impossible at first. It always feels like this time is worse, this time is the exception…but you really can get over anyone. I promise you that: even if part of you will always miss them, always care about them, you'll move on.'

James nodded. 'Thank you. I'm always here if you need to talk about Mum. You know that, right?'

'I appreciate that, but I don't want you feeling caught in the middle; that's not fair.'

'You talking about how you feel or how you're doing isn't me being caught in the middle.'

Frank gave him a small smile. 'Alright, noted. Anyway, we were talking about you and Will, not me and your mother. Listen, the fact that we've moved here might seem awful now, but the silver lining is that it's going to be so much easier for you to move on. You'll be meeting a new group of friends soon, a new team, building a new life. Maybe you'll even meet a cute new boyfriend at college.'

'Bit soon to be thinking about *that*, thanks Dad,' James answered reflexively, but an image of a sweet-looking boy with grey eyes and a curious expression sprang to mind nonetheless.

His dad finished his coffee and pushed the mug to the side. 'Right. Best you take some time for yourself. And I suppose we should sort out our little ghost infestation first.'

'Speaking of, shall we go home?' James suggested.

Frank shook his head. 'No, I think we should have dinner out, and then maybe we could go and see something at the cinema.'

'Is this you just trying to avoid the house for as long as possible?' James asked.

Frank sighed. 'Maybe a little bit, yes. But also, I don't feel like cooking, and I think we could both do with a nice evening. Let's have a look and see what's on.'

James

The downside of their evening out was that by the time they arrived home, the house was in pitch darkness and looked very unwelcoming. James's dad switched the ignition off, and they both sat in the car, staring at the front door.

Frank rested a hand on the car door handle. 'Better get a move on, then.'

It was still another few seconds before he actually moved, though. James got out after him, breathing in the chilly night air and looking up at the stars in the cloudless sky. 'The night skies here really are great, aren't they, Dad?'

Frank paused and looked up. 'They are indeed. One advantage to moving out to the middle of nowhere, I suppose!'

It was still odd to think Nathaniel had once looked up at the same stars, once walked through the same front door and called the same walls *home*. James ran a hand along the doorframe as he followed his dad into the hall. The physical contact with the house made him feel connected to Nathaniel somehow.

'Penny for your thoughts?' His dad broke into his musing.

'Nothing much really, just zoned out.'

They wasted no time in flicking on all the available lights.

'It's bloody freezing in here!' Frank commented, 'Thermostat hasn't kicked in yet, though. Odd.'

James frowned. 'Unexplained coldness is textbook haunting sign number one, isn't it?'

Frank shuddered. 'Right. Cup of tea and up to bed, then?'

James continued down the hallway, 'Sounds like the best plan.'

They made their way into the kitchen together, an unspoken agreement to not leave each other alone in action. While his dad filled the kettle, James scanned the room. Nothing was out of place since they'd left, which was something, at least.

'Film was good, wasn't it?'

'Yeah,' James replied absently; he had only half been paying attention. An action movie had been a good choice, though: visually distracting and nothing spooky or romantic that would press on current concerns or fresh wounds.

'Do you really think Nova can handle all this? The goings on here?' Frank asked suddenly, abandoning the attempt at small talk.

'I hope so. I think so,' James replied. 'And if not, she'll know who to call for reinforcements. We're going to be fine, Dad.'

'I'm supposed to be the one saying that to you!' Frank said. 'Sorry, I'm a bit out of my depth on this one.'

James accepted the freshly poured cup of tea. 'Most people would be.'

He opened the cupboard and took out the container of salt, pouring some into a mug and then sliding the container along the counter. 'Here, you make a circle around your bed, and it'll keep you safe. One of Nova's tips.'

Frank raised an eyebrow. 'Or stick to my feet when I get into bed.'

James snorted, 'Probably, but I'll take grit in my sheets if I'm protected from...y'know.'

His dad picked up his tea and the container of salt as he left the kitchen. 'True, it's a fair trade off – and anything for a good night's sleep!'

James tried not to run up the stairs to his room, but there was a heaviness in the air downstairs creating an uneasy sense of foreboding that wore on him, a strange sense of tension building and something ominous in store.

As he reached his bedroom and stepped over the threshold, he felt his muscles relax and exhaled fully for the first time since he'd gotten home.

He switched his bedside lamp on and cast a fresh circle of salt from the mug, making sure not to put it down near his tea, while he waited for his dad to finish up in the bathroom. Without thinking, he idly scrolled through social media on his phone, watching a short video on sports nutrition and another one on lifting technique. He heard the bathroom door open and was about to put it down and get ready for bed when his friend Taz's photo dump caught his eye. It was a collection of recent 'good times', and the very first picture had Will in the background, smiling at someone off-camera. Knowing he shouldn't but unable to stop himself, he scrolled through. Sure enough, in a later photo he saw that someone was Stevie. He kept going and saw them laughing together in a group but standing suspiciously close. He stared, unable to stop himself imagining that night at the party all over again, their lips meeting and Will's heart changing allegiance.

'Night!' Frank stuck his head around the bedroom door with a cheery wave.

James jumped, dropping his phone on the bed. 'Night, Dad!'

Frank pulled an apologetic face. 'Sorry, didn't mean to startle you, especially at the moment.'

James forced a grin. 'I'm alright. Sleep well!'

His dad carried on down the landing to his room, and James let the grin fall.

He made his way to the bathroom, tense with repressed emotions. James cleaned his teeth slowly, glaring at himself in the mirror while considering a long, hard run the following morning.

After returning to the bedroom, he moved his phone to his desk, determined not to go online again and look at anything else he didn't want to see – but then realised there was no alarm set for the morning and picked it up again.

He considered the reading he wanted to get done and then allowed extra time for a run, setting an early alarm. Then Nova messaged over her travel confirmation details for Monday, so he messaged back to let her know he'd noted them.

Thank you, can't tell you how much I need to see you XX

She messaged back, *Same, ghosts aside I miss you so much. X.* Then she added, *(also, I think you should avoid socials for now. I'll mute a few people for you when I see you if you give me your phone.)*

James could feel his heart beating furiously in his chest. Obviously, the smartest thing to do was follow her advice; there was clearly something worse than what he'd seen earlier for her to warn him like that, and once he'd seen it, he couldn't unsee it. He should leave well alone and go to sleep, but he opened up his socials again nevertheless. He searched for Stevie's page before he knew what he was doing, clicking on his latest post.

The first photo was two hands intertwined. He would know one of those hands anywhere, the perfectly manicured nails and elegant fingers – Will.

He kept scrolling, and confirmed it was exactly what it looked like: shot after shot of them together. Will laughing over burgers, coffees, Will dancing with a milkshake under a streetlight. Nights out, nights in, and the final shot, a shaky kissing selfie. He stared, unable to look away, even though looking felt like being repeatedly punched in the stomach.

He took in every detail, looked at the caption, and felt his stomach turn over.

Stevie had written, *Whirlwind…when u know, u just know. My world. X* He'd tagged Will in the post, and Will had commented with a line of hearts.

James scrolled through comments from people he had thought were his friends too, but here they all were saying things like, *OMG so happy for you both*; *Congrats gorgeous guys*; *FINALLY*; *Meant to be*; *The power couple this town needs*; and *True love, couple goals!!*

The extent to which Will had misrepresented the truth felt like the worst part of it all, how he could have lied, come to stay and pretended he still cared for James when all this was happening. He had a replacement boyfriend lined up and ready to go, and it looked as if Stevie had wasted no time at all moving in on everything that used to be James's. He'd stolen his old life and the only thing he'd thought he had left of it: Will.

James scrolled back through the photos, looking for clues on how long this had been going on. He reread the comments again. It seemed highly unlikely this hadn't started long before he had even left. Stevie could call it a 'whirlwind' all he liked; it didn't quite ring true.

Maybe they hadn't been going on official dates before he moved, but they must have been aware of their feelings, of a growing attraction, way before that. He wondered how many times Will had kissed him and thought of Stevie or been in his arms but imagining Stevie's instead. If maybe they had discussed it and decided to avoid unnecessary drama by waiting until James moved away.

If Will could hide all this, then he was probably lying about everything else as well. James sucked a breath in against the tightness in his chest. The intensity of the betrayal was too much. It made him feel like a complete idiot. How could he ever trust his judgement again? Before he knew what he was doing, he had fired off an angry message to Will.

So how is that freedom thing going for you? Single but also announcing your new relationship to the world?? Did you ever actually love me? Or was I just convenient? Something about footballers maybe?

He stared at his phone. He could see Will was online, but his message remained unread.

He messaged Nova through the hot tears that were welling up in his eyes. *Too late. See you soon. X*

He looked at his message to Will again and saw that he'd read it, but there was no response. Then, as he watched, Will's status changed to offline.

James tossed his phone back onto the desk and threw himself onto the bed, rolling over as if turning his back on it would help him to get the images out of his head. But his favourite photo of him and Will was right in his eyeline. He sat up and opened the frame, pulling it out with shaking hands. He stared at Will's smiling face and tore into it, ripping the photo into four pieces and flinging it on the floor. It didn't really help; in fact, if anything, it made him feel worse. That night in the photo had been one of the best of his life, and now the memory was tainted forever.

The tears ran down his face faster than he could wipe them away, guttural crying that doubled him over, raw noises scraping from his throat as he curled into a ball, nothing in that moment mattering but the uncontrollable need to vent what had built up in his heart.

Nathaniel

Nathaniel stood silently and looked upon James's agony, frustrated once more by his helplessness. It struck him as profoundly wrong that James was still suffering so much pain. How had the idiotic Will not begged James for another chance yet? He couldn't fathom it. In his opinion, anyone who was lucky enough to call James their boyfriend was the luckiest man alive. Will was a fool, and Nathaniel knew James was better off in the long run, even if he didn't feel that way now. He deserved someone who fully saw his worth.

Nathaniel wanted so badly to stay away, but he just couldn't sleep with the waves of feeling still echoing through the fabric of the house, drawing him out of the wall to witness this.

Despite James's rejection of all contact with Nathaniel, he still wished with all his bruised heart that there was something he could do to take away the heartbreak, but he knew there wasn't. No-one had that kind of power.

There was no way he could ease James's pain, no words of comfort he could speak, nor could he soothe him with a touch. The only one who could help was Will – and even then, apologies could only go so far. Nathaniel knew some words could never be unsaid and never be forgotten. The damage was permanent.

Nathaniel contemplated his situation. The spell prevented all communication, locked him away from James forever, but there was one small thing he could do.

He moved to the side of James's bed and picked up the pieces of the image James had torn apart. He knew James would likely regret destroying it, so he carefully placed the pieces together on the desk for when James was ready to look at them again.

He was still curled up and crying, those awful wracking sobs. An inhuman song of agony. Nathaniel knew it well, knew how soul-deep such sounds came from, the wounding that was necessary to provoke such a noise. Drawn back despite himself, he drifted closer to James's bedside and looked down at him in the moonlight, closing his eyes and focusing on the soul in front of him. He could feel the intensity, the disruption to James's normal aura. The spell was there, a wall preventing him from manifesting or speaking, but he could still feel James's energy, and he could still control his own.

Slightly heartened, he put aside his pain at being shut out and honed in on feelings of pure, unconditional love, of peace and calm, timelessness, infinity. He placed a hand that James would never feel on his shoulder and projected those feelings out into the room, aiming to surround him with soothing energy as he finally fell asleep.

Nathaniel blinked, and suddenly he was outside, standing on manicured grass. He looked around. There were crowds of people watching him, sitting on tiered platforms. Brightly-coloured banners fluttered in the breeze as the sun beat down from overhead. A split second later, he felt an impact and went flying through the air, landing hard on the ground. The grass was wet underneath his palms, his hands resting on a white line of paint. He looked up in time to see a crowd of boys thundering past and rolled to the side to avoid being trampled – it seemed like they couldn't see him at all. Confused, he scrambled to his feet, looking around for a reference point, something familiar to make sense of this.

Then he saw him: James. He was standing on the edge of the field, wearing the same blue clothing as the running boys. He stepped forward as if to join them, but as Nathaniel looked on, the sun and the crowds vanished as it suddenly became night. The tiered stands sat empty, full of shadows, as James stood alone under the large lights. A man in purple appeared in front of him and blew a whistle in his face. 'You're late, James!'

James shook his head. 'No, the game—my team, they need me! I have to—'

'You missed it. Too late. No-one needs you now!'

The man in purple vanished, and James let out a yell of frustration. A cat ran past, and he turned. 'Posey! No, come back!' He ran after her as she hightailed it across the pitch, and Nathaniel ran towards them both. 'James? James!'

James stopped dead, but it wasn't because of him. It was because of Will, who had just materialised in his path. Nathaniel froze.

'Will!' James gasped. 'Do you want me back? Have you changed your mind?'

Will smiled slowly, flicking an expensive-looking scarf over one shoulder with a flourish. 'What did you say? I didn't hear you.'

James opened his mouth, but no words came out, just a rivulet of blood. Nathaniel gasped as James put a hand to his mouth and it came away with teeth in it.

Will looked at the teeth crumbling out of James's mouth with impassive curiosity, then shrugged and walked away.

James sank to his knees, frantically clutching at his face as teeth dropped onto the bloodstained grass. He groaned, and Nathaniel stepped closer. He wasn't sure if James could hear him, but he spoke aloud anyway.

'I'm so sorry. You deserve better, and you will one day have it, I'm sure. Will didn't know what he had, the utter fool.'

James's groans lessened in intensity, and the heaving of his back slowed. Unsure if it was a coincidence but encouraged anyway, Nathaniel continued. 'You're...I think you're dreaming, and somehow, I'm here too. But I'm real. I'm really here.'

James looked up at him. 'Nathaniel?'

He got to his feet, the blood vanishing from his face and his teeth back where they belonged. Their surroundings flickered and reformed; now they were in some kind of restaurant. Nathaniel looked around. The light was low and the decorations colourful and garish.

James pointed at a corner booth. 'We had our first date there.'

Another flicker, and Nathaniel saw them: James and Will laughing together and sharing a plate of chips. Another glitch, and he was sitting opposite James in the booth. James was reaching out, taking Nathaniel's hand. 'I knew you wanted me, still want me—'

Nathaniel pulled his hand away in a flustered panic. 'No, no, stop! Please, I mean I do, I—God, I do, but not—I'm not Will, I'm—'

James's face fell, and he dropped his head into his hands. The crying started again. Nathaniel took a second to curse this whole situation;

being inside someone else's dream was the most bewildering experience to navigate.

'James, listen! I didn't mean to be here, but I am. So please listen to me. You will emerge from this pain; you will be loved; you *are* loved. I am always here for you, even if you don't know it. You have me, for what that's worth. My endless support. Always.'

James's sobs slowly petered out, and he let out a deep sigh. The restaurant began to fade away, replaced instead by a beach. A breeze rustled through the reeds on the sand dunes behind them as soft waves crashed on the shore. Gentle moonlight fell on James where he sat on a towel. He looked at Nathaniel, and it felt as though he truly registered his presence for the first time. He reached out a hand, and Nathaniel took it. His heart skipped; here, in this dream, not only did the touch feel real, but this time, maybe James meant it for him.

'It's beautiful here,' James whispered.

'It is. Where are we?'

James smiled. 'My very favourite holiday.'

He sighed and lay back on the towel, pulling Nathaniel down beside him. As they lay shoulder to shoulder, Nathaniel knew if he was mortal, he would have stopped breathing at such closeness. He said nothing, not wanting to spoil this moment. No matter what happened, even if James blocked him out forevermore, he would always have this. The faint sound of the waves, their shoulders touching, the stars reflected in James's endless eyes.

As he watched James, his breathing slowed, and his eyelids began to flicker. Nathaniel could sense the relief of true rest approaching, so he stayed where he was, giving James's hand a tender squeeze and sending him all the loving energy he could, until he saw those beautiful eyelids finally close. He felt his heart rate slow and knew that, for tonight at least, James would know some measure of peace.

Only when he was satisfied that he could do no more did Nathaniel let his own head fall back onto the sand. He turned his head so he could admire James's profile and watch the gentle rise and fall of his chest. Nathaniel looked down at their interlocked hands. It would be so easy to let the peace of this place lull him, and yet he didn't want to miss a single moment of this night. If this was to be his last time with James, he would make sure it could last him for eternity. He lay still, settling into a trance of contentment, the bliss of timelessness after centuries of experiencing every second.

Then Nathaniel blinked again, and he was back standing beside James's bed. His heart wrenched, and his hand went reflexively to his shoulder, remembering the gentle pressure of James lying alongside him. He watched as James rolled over and stared at the ceiling for a moment, and Nathaniel extended a hand, waving it right in front of his face.

James didn't react. The dream had changed nothing. Back in this reality, the spell bottle was still doing its work.

Nathaniel stared at him for a moment more, his heart aching. Why hadn't James taken it off? He had welcomed him in his dream, pulled him down to lie with him in the sand – surely that meant something? But then, dreams weren't reality, he told himself firmly. James's guard was down, and he was grieving Will. Nathaniel had just been a distraction in a moment when he couldn't bear to be alone with his pain. It wasn't about him, and he *had* to stop hoping it was.

He jumped when the hideous alarm sounded, once again wishing he could destroy the horrible phone emitting it. Then James's dad called from outside the door, and Nathaniel side-stepped as James climbed out of bed, not wanting to be walked through. He doubted James would feel it, but he hated the sensation – it was a horribly visceral reminder of his situation.

He watched James pull his dressing gown on, tighten the drawstring on his pyjama pants and shuffle out of the room. Nathaniel listened to their footsteps fading away down the stairs and scanned the house for the entity, checking its whereabouts. It was currently dormant, so he drifted back into the wall.

James

When James's alarm went off, he opened his eyes with difficulty. They ached from crying and felt both dried out and damp at the same time. He rubbed them and sat up, then felt the headache that had settled in sometime in the night. He silenced his alarm, threw his phone back on the bedside table and curled into a ball, pulling a blanket over his head.

He didn't want to come back to this reality. Last night had been a wonderful reprieve from the emotional turmoil of his feelings. He lay still, revisiting it. He couldn't recall all the details, except for the beach. It was so vivid, it almost felt more real than the bed he lay on now. The moonlight, the sand underneath his fingertips, and best of all, Nathaniel. He recalled his kind eyes and gentle touch; the Nathaniel of his dreams was good company. He'd lifted his spirits and made James feel like everything was going to work out somehow. He closed his eyes – maybe if he drifted back off, he could get back there – but his dad's voice jolted him out of his attempt to revisit last night's dreamscape.

'James, you awake?'

At least he had told his dad about Will, so he wouldn't be too worried or surprised by a change in James's behaviour. He lay there, trying to summon the energy to get up. He knew in theory the best thing for him would be to face reality, drink a lot of water and go for a run. Accomplishing something would make him feel better, but the more he lay there, the more he realised he just didn't have it in him. It felt like all his energy had drained out of him with last night's tears.

'James, are you okay in there?' his dad called through the door again, and he mustered the energy to drag himself out of bed.

'Yeah, but don't ask me to get dressed or do anything.'

'Does eating some of the pancakes I made count as doing anything?'

'Nope, and I think I can manage that,' he shouted back.

He pulled his dressing gown on and followed Frank downstairs, giving himself permission to do nothing but eat the delicious smelling brunch and crash in front of the TV for the day.

As plans went, it worked. He rewatched so many episodes of one of his favourite series that time slipped by without him noticing, and he felt pleasantly detached from current reality. His dad joined him, only getting up to fetch food or tea, and kept what little conversation they did have very light. James left his phone upstairs and felt much better for it; the images he'd seen the night before threatened to creep back into his mind's eye if he didn't keep himself away from it. There might even be more comments by now, more posts – but he wasn't going to see them. He didn't need to see all his old friends welcoming his replacement without second thoughts, discarding James now that he wasn't right in front of them. Taking Will's side. He hated how Will used charisma to win people over. *Weak* people, he told himself. Easily swayed sycophants.

He only had to get through one more night and Nova would be here. He could always count on her loyalty. She had his back no matter what, and he knew being around her again would make him feel better, although the comfortable numbness that had settled over him was quite restful in its own way.

When his dad made a comment about the time and got up to switch a light on, James realised the sun had set, and an entire day had passed without any paranormal activity.

The sitting room did feel the safest after his bedroom, but he also considered if it might be the spell bottle doing its thing, or if his current disengaged emotional state was helping – if perhaps there was nothing for the poltergeist to feed on. That was a definite positive, but then he realised he was disappointed Nathaniel also hadn't been more active lately. It hurt a little that he hadn't seen him around his room, but maybe there was a reason for that. Perhaps he needed help to manifest, or an invitation?

The day in front of the TV had been restful, but he wondered if maybe a garden meditation before bed might be nice. His stomach flipped a little at the thought, and he paused, wondering what on Earth that was about. Was he nervous about having another chat with the shy ghost? It was absurd; Nathaniel was long dead and existed solely on the spiritual plane. He shook his head. Heartbreak was doing odd things to his psyche, for sure.

He got up and went to the kitchen for more snacks, deciding Nathaniel merely made him feel comforted somehow. He provided perspective, reminding James that ultimately, reality was more complicated and more expansive than break-ups and bitchy, cheating boyfriends.

As he rifled through the cupboards, he hoped Nathaniel would put in an appearance soon, even if it was just in his dreams.

Nathaniel

Nathaniel tried to sleep again, but it was all in vain. His mind wouldn't stop racing; after the night on the beach, he felt James's absence all the more. He wished he could join him and his father in the kitchen for pancakes – he didn't know what pancakes were, but they sounded nice. He tried to recall the taste of cake and couldn't quite manage it, but he remembered liking it. But more than the pancakes, he wanted the company. He wanted to share silly jokes and idle conversation. He cast his mind back to the happy early days with Theodore; he hadn't realised how much he would miss those seemingly insignificant little interactions until they were gone forever.

Giving up on the attempt to rest, he drifted back out into the room and found the loose floorboard. It usually took him a long time to summon the energy to open it, but today, it lifted easily. Pleased with himself, he rifled through his little hoard of treasures. He ran his fingers through his collection of odd pens and pencils from his friend Emily, the old paintbrush, the scarf covered in lurid flowers from the musical people, and settled on his prized possession: the book Agatha had given him. It was an effort, but he could usually lift it and turn a few pages at a time before he ran out of energy.

He took a pen out; perhaps he could leave James a little note. No, that was too much. Maybe a little drawing instead. Then there was the book; today was a good day for that. He drifted to the window and settled in a patch of light, laying the book on the floor where he could flip pages. It was in good condition still; he had been so careful with it. A little mildew on the edge of the pages, but no damage to the spine or cover.

He turned the first page and settled down. He was a chapter in before he realised he had company. He looked around and spotted her: Posey had sneaked back in and was watching him from under the bed, wide-eyed.

'At least you can still see me.'

She inched forward a little when he spoke.

'Too cold and lonely outside?' Nathaniel asked her, and she blinked, her expression knowing. 'Oh, of course, silly me! You can tell when that evil thing is dormant too, can't you? Clever girl.'

He clicked at her, tapping the floor, and she ran over, pouncing on the page he was turning. He tried to turn it again, and she swatted it back.

'No more reading for me, then.' He closed the book to protect it from damage and rolled his pen across the floor. 'Shall we make some art instead?'

She chased the pen enthusiastically, batting it around while Nathaniel went through James's books on the desk in search of some paper. He found a few sheets and returned to the floor.

'What shall we sketch?' he asked Posey. When she made no suggestions, he decided on a flower resembling the carnation James had given to him on their first meeting in the garden. After that, he drew Posey, sitting on the floor, lying in the sun and napping on the bed. He realised as he completed the last sketch that the sun had gone down, so he left his work on the desk where James would hopefully find it and settled on the windowsill.

James

James yawned and stretched, picking up the empty wrappers from the snacks he'd demolished. 'I think I'm going to have to go to bed.'

'Not in the mood for one more episode?' Frank suggested with a grin.

'You're a bad influence!' James told him. 'I'm tempted, but I also should get up tomorrow and get a run in. I've skipped so many lately.'

'That's okay, you know that?' Frank said. 'You have to be softer with yourself at times like these.'

'I get that, but I know getting back into my routine will make me feel better. More like myself again. I just need to find the motivation somehow.'

It crossed his mind that improving his fitness might impress Nathaniel, that thought providing a sudden, surprising spark of motivation. Then he wondered why he was bothered what a ghost thought about him beating his personal bests, or if it was even likely that he would care. What would be impressive to a guy from the 1700s, anyway?

He realised his dad was smiling at him, a distant look in his eyes. 'What?' James asked.

'I'm so proud of you; I really am. You're going to do alright.'

James snorted to hide how touched he was. 'Okay, Dad, it's just a run though.'

Frank shook his head. 'No, it's about much more than that.'

James stood up and picked up his mug. 'Yeah, I know. Thanks. And I'm proud of you too.'

Frank grabbed the remote and settled back in his chair. 'Night then, sleep well.'

'Night, Dad!'

James nipped into the kitchen, made a quick cup of fresh tea without lingering and took it up to his room. He decided he would return to the garden for a chat with Nathaniel and put his tea down on the bedside table. He lit a candle and some incense, cast a fresh salt circle and lay down, closing his eyes eagerly. As before, he dropped into an altered state of consciousness, drifting off into a moonlit garden that bore a strong resemblance to the one just outside the window. He settled, taking a moment to appreciate the stars overhead and the soft grass underfoot. He looked around. 'Nathaniel? Will you join me?'

He waited as trees rustled in the breeze. A few wispy clouds drifted past the moon, but there was no sign of the ghost. James started walking, looking around in all directions, but he was still alone.

'Nathaniel?' he asked again, more hesitant this time.

He took a few deep breaths, scanning the horizon for a distant figure, but no one appeared.

A strange little tug at his heart and suddenly, he was staring at his ceiling again; he was back in the bedroom. It was irrational to feel rejected by Nathaniel not showing up; he knew that. He wasn't beholden to James's whims, and yet his absence hurt. He got up with a sigh and extinguished the candle. He was just being oversensitive about everything because of the breakup.

James stubbed out the incense and flicked the bedside lamp on, a dark patch on the floor near the bay window catching his eye. He moved closer and felt a spike of anger. A floorboard had been taken up, leaving a hole in his floor.

'What the hell? Nathaniel! Did you do that—'

He stopped himself. Being unfriendly wasn't going to entice Nathaniel to put in another appearance. He crouched and peered into the space in the small underfloor cavity, wondering how many more secrets this house was hiding.

He poked around at the items in there. At first, they just looked like a lot of random rubbish, but as he rifled through the contents, he realised it was a hiding place. There was quite a collection, clearly hoarded over a long period of time. He found old stationary, broken household items and trinkets, some dating back mere decades and others looking much older. He picked up a dirty scarf with a hideous pattern on it and dropped it swiftly. Bemused by Nathaniel's tastes, he lowered the floorboard back into place and straightened up, wiping his dusty hands on his dressing gown. Then something else caught his eye: a book lay on the floor in the corner. He walked over and picked it up.

'Wuthering Heights, eh?' he said out loud. 'Great choice, I have a copy of this—' He flicked it open. 'Shit! A first edition. Mine isn't a first edition.' He paused, turning the book over in his hands as his mind raced. Surely this was worth a fortune…it might solve a lot of his dad's financial worries. Maybe they could even afford to move to a house that wasn't falling apart, haunted and in the middle of nowhere.

He flipped to the next page, where a faded message had been written in fountain pen.

Dearest Nathaniel,
I wish you many happy hours at your window reading. May this keep you company when I am gone.
All my love,
Agatha X

Feeling sick with guilt, James hurriedly closed the book and put it back where he found it. Clearly Nathaniel was still very much around, even if he was choosing not to interact. He supposed he couldn't blame him, really.

James went to clean his teeth, staring at his red eyes in the harsh bathroom lighting. He mustn't be giving off a nice energy right now; no doubt he was as repellent to Nathaniel as he was to Will. He made his way back to his room, fighting the urge to check his phone. It was hard; the voice tempting him was getting louder, telling him the only way to have peace was to make sure there were no new posts. He didn't want to look – he knew it was bad for his mental health – and yet the urge persisted. He sat down on his bed and stared at the phone on his bedside table.

He reached for it and heard a soft rustling sound from behind him. He turned quickly, his heart lifting slightly; perhaps Nathaniel was back to visit him after all.

There was no sign of the ghost, but a few sheets of paper had floated off his desk and landed on the floor. He clambered over the bed and picked them up. One of them was his class schedule. Confused, he went to put it back where it belonged, and then he noticed the sketch on the other side: a flower, a fine-line drawing with intricate detail.

'That's beautiful, thank you,' he said out loud, in case Nathaniel was listening.

He picked up the other sheets to see several sketches of Posey, each one rendered in detail with obvious study.

'Wow…these are incredible,' he murmured, leafing through them. He couldn't deny how touched he was by Nathaniel's gift; he might not want to talk, but the art was a meaningful gesture.

James considered a moment. His behaviour was a little confusing, but then again, perhaps it was unrealistic to expect a ghost from the 1700s to behave the same way a modern human would. Either way, it was nice to know Posey had come back into the house and approved of Nathaniel. The idea of her lounging in here with him drawing her made him smile.

He got up and found some pins in his desk drawer, pinning each one of the sketches to the cork board he had yet to mount on the wall. Then he had a quick look around the room for his cat, but there was no sign of her anymore, so he climbed into bed and switched off the light. This time, he didn't even check his phone.

Nathaniel

Nathaniel watched James switch the light off and remained slumped against the wall in the dark, feeling many things at once. He was still trying to recover from earlier; he had no idea what had happened, but when James lay down on the floor and closed his eyes, Nathaniel had been hit by some kind of energetic impact. Whatever it was, it felt like being pushed and pulled at the same time. Bewildering flashes of gold had dazzled him; the sensation of a door being slammed in his face had disorientated him. He thought he'd glimpsed the garden he had come to think of as theirs amongst the onslaught on his senses, but he wasn't certain. The experience had left him energetically winded. The thought that James had gone there and shut Nathaniel out was unbearable – but just as he was processing that possible loss, James had come back, handled his book so tenderly and shown appreciation for his artwork.

The glow from James admiring his sketches wasn't going to lessen anytime soon. He looked at the corkboard leant against the desk, his art pinned to it, and smiled with pride. James might have shut him out for now, but he could still find ways to cheer him up and distract him.

He watched him settle in bed and contemplated his next move. He couldn't deny he was sorely tempted to try and join James in his dreams again – but it also seemed a bit immoral now. Last night had been the best night of Nathaniel's life, but it was also an accident born of the need to help somehow – and perhaps James's need for comfort dragging him in. But to do it deliberately was different. It seemed to Nathaniel to be something of a violation; he knew he would hate it if James could see into his innermost dreams and fantasies, so he turned away and drifted back into the wall to sleep alone.

He wasn't sure how long he had been unaware, but he came back to consciousness very suddenly. Something was wrong. It was just before dawn, and James was sleeping peacefully, so it wasn't an emotional disturbance that had woken Nathaniel.

He tuned in, and a wave of terror froze him where he was, instantly alert. He could feel the darkness, and it was far too close, and stronger than it had been since the terrible night Arthur had perished. He could hear a strange shuffling noise growing closer and closer until it was at the bedroom door.

He reached out, trying to understand what was happening, but the confusing mixture of energies didn't help throw light on the matter.

The bedroom door clicked open, and Nathaniel knew he had to do something. The entity was in James's room somehow. And yet…not quite. Its influence was in James's room, but the entity itself was still out on the landing.

Every part of him wanted to stay where he was, hiding, trying to stay safe, but he couldn't leave James unprotected. Steeling himself, he left the wall and surveyed the room. The sight that met his eyes filled him with horror.

It was James's dad – only it wasn't. He was staggering, his limbs spasming, his movements jerky and erratic. His eyes were open, but they were devoid of light, his eyeballs filmy and black. It was his body moving, but not his mind controlling it. He was being manipulated. Nathaniel had seen something similar before, all those years ago, and he could identify it instantly: the odd mismatch of energies and forms mixed together, fighting for control. A human body being operated like a puppet on a string. He remembered his terror the very first time the entity had forced its way into Arthur's mind, tearing down his psychic barriers and gaining a foothold where it didn't belong.

Frank continued lurching forward, his movements growing smoother as the entity grew accustomed to controlling him. Nathaniel waited, unsure of what its intent was, and then he realised: he was reaching up to the hiding place over the doorway, something glistening in his hand. The entity was going to force Frank to remove the protection on the room, leaving James—and Nathaniel—vulnerable.

He moved first to James's dad, tried to push him, hold him back from the door, but yet again, he found it was futile to try to stop a human, never mind one with the added strength and determination of the entity driving him. Frank merely staggered back a step for a moment and then carried on, his blank eyes seeing nothing. Nathaniel screamed in his face, but to no avail. He heard a deep, low laugh from the outside the room; the entity was amused; it could hear him. He peered into the dark landing and saw the corner where the shadows were that bit thicker and denser. There it waited to gain entry, its eyes glowing faintly red.

He stumbled backwards, away from the door. He couldn't be perceived by that *thing,* that murderous, evil thing. Every impulse made him want to flee straight back into the wall, but he knew he couldn't. He went to James's side, screaming again because he couldn't stop himself, not because he thought it would do any good. James slumbered on.

Nathaniel put a hand on his back and projected the opposite to what he had sent him before: agitation, unease, fear. Nothing happened.

Frank was making headway with finding the ward; he had torn the wallpaper above the door into strips, reached up and was blindly groping around for the little space where it was hidden. His hand closed on it and drew it down, but it remained intact.

Desperately, Nathaniel went for James's phone and sucked every last bit of power out of it. Then he did the only thing left that he could think of: he seized the half-drunk mug of tea from James's bedside table and flung it with all his might against the wall.

The mug shattered, cold tea splattering all over the wall as James's dad crushed what was in his hand, a shower of glass, wax and herbs scattering across the floor, the only remnants of Agatha's powerful magic. James sat bolt upright with a yell and groped for his lamp, switching it on. He gasped in horror at his dad, standing amongst the mess, blinking in confusion at the blood dripping from his hand and the glass around his feet.

Nathaniel took one last look at James's face, staring into those warm brown eyes a final time, before the entity swept into the room and dragged him away into darkness.

James

James leapt out of bed, running to where his dad still stood, staring at his bloody hands in the dawn light.

'Dad, what...?'

Frank looked up, his eyes full of fear. 'I…I don't know what happened! I went to bed and…I woke up here…what on earth happened?'

James flicked the main light on, and they both blinked in the sudden brightness. He pointed at the mess on the wall and the floor. 'I woke up to things being smashed and you standing in here, like this—' He stopped as he realised the debris on the floor was very similar to the contents of the spell bottle around his neck. He looked up above the door, his worst fear confirmed by the torn wallpaper.

'Shit, Dad, look!'

Frank followed the direction he was pointing in. 'Oh dear.' He swallowed. 'I did that? While sleepwalking somehow?'

James frowned. 'Exactly what do you remember?'

His dad paused for thought. 'Last night…I heard the shuffling again. It was closer this time, inside my room, and I'll be honest, I pulled the duvet over my head like a little kid. I told myself it couldn't hurt me, so I shouldn't allow it to scare me. Admittedly, that seems to be very flawed logic, as I think it clearly *can* hurt us.'

'And then what?'

'I don't remember much after that; I lay there for a while and then…nothing.'

'So, you fell asleep?'

He nodded. 'I must have. And then…'

An involuntary shiver ran down James's spine. 'You got possessed. Something has used you to destroy the protection spell.'

Frank swallowed. 'This is…you can't stay here tonight. Not now.'

James shook his head. 'Never mind that; it'll be fine.'

'Excuse me? If you think you're staying here in this—this horror film waiting to happen all on your own—'

'I won't be alone – remember, I'll have Nova! And I'm protected, Dad. We'll be fine. We'll get rid of the ghosts, and you can come back home to a phantom-free house after your work trip.'

Frank shook his head as if trying to clear it. 'No, it's not an option. We'll discuss a different plan over breakfast. Come on, let's get out of here. Again. You know, this ghost should really be picking up the extortionate cost of all these meals out.'

James mustered a weak grin at his dad's shaky attempt to be humorous about their situation. 'Okay, but I think you should get dressed first and sort out your bleeding hand. I think people might talk otherwise.'

He looked down. 'Oh…yes. Pyjamas probably also not the best coffee shop attire. Wait, you've given me a thought.'

'I have?'

Frank nodded. 'Yes. Right, hurry along and meet me at the car in five to ten minutes.'

James grabbed some clothes from the end of his bed and threw them on, cleaned his teeth and went straight out to the car. The glass and mess on his bedroom floor could wait for later; there was no way he wanted to hang around inside. The atmosphere in his room already felt different – less comfortable and more exposed somehow. Even with the bottle resting against his chest, he didn't want to tempt fate. He leant against the car, huddled into his hoodie while he waited for his dad.

He couldn't deny he was frightened. The entity being able to control a human was an absolutely terrifying new development, and he was worried for his dad. He'd spoken a big game about him and Nova fixing the situation, but what if they couldn't? What happened if there was no way to get rid of the ghosts? His dad couldn't afford to move; he knew that.

The front door opened, and Frank appeared, a tea towel wrapped around his hand and his laptop bag over one shoulder. He tossed the keys to James. 'You're driving.'

James hopped in and started the car; Frank climbed into the passenger seat and pulled an antiseptic wipe and a bundle of plasters out of his coat pocket. 'I'll sort this on the way. Usual place?'

James grinned. 'We're quickly becoming regulars.'

'Just goes to show, all you need to "get out more" is a good old-fashioned haunting!'

James forced a laugh this time, trying once again to be supportive and see the darkly funny side of all this.

By the time they reached their coffee spot, Frank had patched himself up and was ready to eat. They settled into a booth, and James watched his dad visibly relax.

'So, what I was thinking,' he began, 'is that we need to talk to more locals about our house. Interview them, maybe. Someone must know something helpful; it can't just be dreadfully haunted and no one else has ever noticed or said anything about it. That kind of thing gets around, doesn't it?'

James nodded, recalling the restaurant server's reaction to their new address the night they'd arrived. 'It does…but we'd need to ask the right questions to the right people; otherwise, they'll just think we're weird. And then what gets around will be gossip about *us*.'

'Hmm, good point, delicate subject matter.'

'Besides, I don't know what local rumours and gossip will really help with. I don't think it'll tell us more than Nova's research did.'

'What time does Nova get here?'

'About four hours from now,' James replied, suddenly distracted when his phone screen lit up with a message from Will. He grabbed it, noticing his hands were shaking as he unlocked the screen and opened the message.

I'm sorry that you're hurting James, I really am. But I have to do what's best for me. Your feelings are not my problem and if you're going to keep sending me aggressive childish messages, I will block you. You've been warned.

James stared, rereading the cold, formal words from Will and feeling as though they were written by a stranger. He wished he hadn't opened the message now; his emotions were in turmoil again, and he didn't want his dad to notice.

'James, did you hear anything I just said?' It was too late; his dad was giving him that searching look.

'Oh, yeah! Sorry, got distracted. Can you repeat it?'

Frank nodded. 'Okay, well, I was supposed to be working from home this morning and then driving to the conference, but I think I'll work from here instead. Then Nova can join us when she gets in, and we can talk though what the plan is before I have to leave. Do you need to go back to the house for anything before then?'

James considered a moment. 'Not really. I've still got a few books on my reading list that I haven't picked up, so I'll do that and bring them here. I was going to go for a run…but I can skip that today. Again. You know, I think sabotaging my cardio has become a joint effort between the ghosts and Will.'

He got up and went for their order, noting how the events of the morning had at least distracted him momentarily from the events of the night before. Until he'd read that message, he hadn't been feeling too sad. As he picked up the coffees, he glanced over at the window booth, remembering his breakfast in here with Will before everything had changed. It was so odd that things could shift so suddenly, that he could have gone from his illusion of a happy, strong relationship to his heart being crushed beyond repair in a matter of minutes. The intense sadness rose up his throat again, but he swallowed it back down. He had to be strong for his dad, so he plastered a smile on his face, forced a spring into his step and returned to their booth.

Nathaniel

Nathaniel was drowning. It was dark and cold; the disorientation was complete. He was spinning; there was nothing he could grasp onto, nothing that made sense. He was falling, endlessly. Then came the impact, a hard surface. He felt its solidity in a way he wasn't accustomed to. He was sure his eyes were open, but he could see nothing. He remained where he was, lying on the freezing surface, trying to draw breath into his noncorporeal lungs. Trying to regain his sense of calm.

The entity had breached James's room. For decades, he had been safe in there, but no longer. He recalled those last few moments, held James's face in his mind's eye, felt the warmth in his heart that followed. Was James safe? He needed to find out. But first, he needed to know where he was.

He stirred. Perhaps he could stand up and move, understand what was happening. Then he heard it: a shuffling sound. There was something here with him.

He looked around in the darkness, and finally, his eyes adjusted, picking out an area of shadow that was darker than the rest – and coming closer.

The sense of dread grew as it drew nearer, but he stood up, facing it despite the overwhelming urge to flee, to be anywhere else but here.

When it spoke, its voice was raspy. 'Welcome back, Nathaniel.'

Nathaniel shuddered. 'Who are you?'

He asked the question, though he already knew the answer; he was looking at the face of the darkness, the entity that had lurked on the edge of his world for so long, the constant threat in his mind.

'All these years and you behave as though we are strangers, you rude little creature.'

'I don't mean to be rude, I just…we've never exactly been acquainted.'

'And whose fault was that, might I ask?'

Nathaniel opened his mouth to reply but never got the chance. A flash of red light caught his attention a moment before he felt a searing pain in his heart. He doubled over, previously unaware that he was capable of feeling such agony in his present state.

The entity laughed. 'Just like old times!'

'What?' Nathaniel gasped out.

'You'll see. Even a little idiot like you will catch on eventually. Now that I have you.'

'Have me?'

It drew even closer, its red eyes glowering at him, its rotting, putrid scent turning his stomach. Another flash of light; this time it was more orange in hue, and Nathaniel felt it like a punch to the gut. He looked down and saw an orange thread trailing out from his midsection, intertwining with the red one coming from his heart. The entity jerked, and the tug sent him stumbling forward against his will. He realised with horror that he was somehow tethered to it now. It laughed with glee.

'Yes, the witch's spell is broken; there is nothing to protect you. You know you won't be saved; accept it. No one thinks you worthy of saving; no one cares about you now. So you'll stay here with me and help; you have no choice.'

'Help? Help with what?'

Another impact, this time a flash of blue before an icy touch wrapped around his throat, and it took everything he had not to cry out. It was so cold it almost felt hot, the sense of corruption remaining with him even after the entity drew back, leaving another cord of light behind. He felt polluted and dirty, as if his energy would never be the same again.

'Yes, help. It is the way of things, two freaks such as us, not of the living. We must fight together; we are natural comrades in arms. You understand? It is nature's way.'

'We are nothing alike!' Nathaniel shot back, defying it despite his fear.

'We are *exactly* alike. Both of us linger here on this plane of existence, tied to this reality, unable to rest.' The entity moved closer. 'Unable to move on. But we do not belong, we have no place…unless we claim it for ourselves. And we must.'

Nathaniel tried to back away, straining against the bonds. 'No, that's not right. We have a place here; we can be peaceful and co-exist alongside the living.'

The entity laughed, a harsh, grating sound. 'No, we cannot. They seek to rid themselves of us; they always do! We're a curiosity at first, a parlour game, a fun diversion to be talked about and played with – but then they tire of us. Want us gone.'

'No!' Nathaniel drew strength from his anger, struggling and testing the cords. 'They only want *you* gone because you're evil!'

A flash of purple, and more cords attached themselves to Nathaniel's wrists and ankles, burrowing into his being and flooding him with a strange desire to submit.

The entity laughed again. 'You talk like a child! Such immature, oversimplistic notions, good and evil. Nonsense, all of it. They want us both gone; the boy has shut you out, same as me.'

The entity's words stung, and unable to argue with that fact, Nathaniel remained quiet as it continued.

'So you will join me, fight back and take what we need. I've spent years bound and waiting, my strength growing, and now, my determination knows no limit. I shall not be denied.'

Nathaniel looked up into those red eyes. There was something so familiar about the glowing orbs staring back at him, something that went far beyond appearance.

'Denied what?' he asked the entity. 'What do we need?'

He could feel it smiling; he had pleased it with his questions. There was a sense of gloating in every syrupy syllable when it replied, 'Life…mortal bodies.'

Nathaniel let out a gasp, and the entity chuckled. 'Don't act as though you haven't thought about it: having physical form again. And a fine one too. I'll let you have the boy.'

Nathaniel recoiled. 'No, we can't! That would be impossible.'

'We can. I've already controlled the father once. With your help, I can inhabit him completely and make it permanent. And with my help, you can claim the boy for yourself. Think about it…a new life and true freedom await you.'

James

James opened his arms, and Nova flung herself at him. He pulled her into a tight hug, and for a moment, everything felt as if it was going to be alright.

'I missed you so much,' he mumbled into her hair, inhaling the familiar scent of coconut conditioner.

'Same!' She pulled back, her eyes shining. 'And here you are getting yourself severely haunted without me!'

'Well, I didn't do it on purpose!' James told her as she picked up her rucksack. 'I would have waited until you visited, ideally, but sadly, these ghosts are running on their own schedule.'

'Just rude of them, really.' She grinned. 'Where's your dad, then?'

'In a coffee shop waiting for us…um, also, thought I'd save it for in person, but there's been some new developments,' he explained as he led the way through the dead leaves and puddles towards the main street.

Nova raised an eyebrow. 'What's happened now?'

'I was woken up this morning by my dad apparently possessed and breaking the ward on my room. It was very dramatic, and it's made quite a mess.'

Nova stopped in her tracks. 'What? James, this is…well, it's not good.'

'Funnily enough, I worked that out myself.'

'Right, your dad – he's still going to be away tonight?'

'I don't know. He had to start working right after breakfast but promised to take a lunch break when you got here so we can talk through everything properly.'

'Got it. Best get a move on, then. I've got a lot of questions.'

When they arrived, Frank shut his laptop with a snap and beamed. 'Nova, so nice to see you!'

Nova settled into the booth. 'You too, Frank! Sorry to hear about your ghost problem. And your divorce.'

James went to the counter and picked up an iced latte for Nova and joined them as his dad was asking about her course. She had Frank laughing about one of her quirkier tutors as he settled beside her.

'Right, now that James is back, shall we talk about your house?'

'Direct to the point,' his dad commented. 'What's your take on all this?'

Nova sipped her drink. 'It's hard to give you a detailed take without having actually been in the house yet, but I think it's clear you've got a pretty serious haunting going on. Usually in this situation, people call in paranormal investigators, but I think that would be a waste of time. They'd just faff about and confirm what you already know.'

'I see. So, what would you suggest?' Frank asked.

'It kind of depends on what you actually want to do about the haunting. I mean, you could get a psychic medium to connect and communicate with the spirits, to tell you who they are, what they want and why they're there, help them find peace, closure and so on. Maybe find a way for you to all co-exist together. Sometimes spirits can seem aggressive when they're actually just scared, confused or disorientated.'

His dad frowned. 'And you know someone who does this kind of psychic medium thing genuinely? I'm not keen on some shawl-wearing scam artist extorting me for money and not actually helping.'

Nova nudged James with an elbow. 'James has some talent, actually. He hasn't developed it, but it's there. And that's why I'm here too. But if we can't handle it, then I have mentors and friends I can call.'

James cleared his throat. 'Anyway, the plan is, Dad, you go and focus on your work thing tonight; me and Nova will investigate and then figure out whatever is needed to make the house safe again.'

Nova nodded. 'In the meantime, I'll prepare some protections for you, Frank, but it'll be a little bit trickier now that one of the entities has a taste for you. Once they've been inside you, it complicates things a bit.'

James stared at his shoes and tried to keep a serious face at Nova's earnest words; now was not the time to snigger at double meanings. Luckily, his dad's attention was firmly on her.

'It's not that I don't trust you – or before you start protesting, "still see you as kids" – but I don't like this plan at all. I'm not going to abandon you to deal with this alone. I can't get out of the work conference, unfortunately; it would put my fledgling new job at risk, and I just can't afford that right now. But your mum is more than happy for you both to come and stay tonight.'

James sighed. 'Come on, Dad, don't start that again. You aren't abandoning us, and I totally get the new job thing. You've got to be all committed and stuff. Besides, you being away, and therefore safe, is one less thing for us to worry about. You're the one who got possessed; this will all go much easier and safer if you're out of the picture.'

'Well, this whole thing will go even easier if you and Nova would just get on the train and go and stay with your mum tonight!'

'I don't want to go and stay with Mum! And have to see—' James stopped, realising he was speaking far louder than was necessary and not wanting to say her new boyfriend's name out loud. Frank winced before he plastered a fixed smile back on, and James realised the damage was already done.

He continued in a much calmer tone, 'And how are we supposed to investigate anything if we just go away for the night anyway? It defeats the whole point of Nova coming all the way here.'

His dad took a moment, his eyes on James, before he sighed. 'Yes, I understand. Okay, I will allow this on one condition: if things start to get remotely dangerous again, you will leave the house immediately and get on that train, even if you'd rather not. Promise me.'

Nova smiled. 'We will, Frank, I promise! I won't let James do anything silly.'

'Alright, then. But this is insane,' Frank said, adjusting his glasses. 'The entire situation is utterly insane. Honestly, if you'd told me a few months ago that this would be my life…' He shook his head. 'But I can't deny what I've experienced. Thank God you're here too, James, or I would have checked myself into a psychiatric institute by now.'

Nova nodded. 'Being a sceptic can be hard like that.'

James elbowed her. 'And how would you know?'

'I've met enough of them!'

Frank stood up. 'Well, thank you so much for coming down, Nova. I really appreciate what a good friend you are to James.' He pulled his coat on. 'I'm going to use the rest of my lunchbreak to pick up a few things I need – rather left the house in a hurry this morning without my toothbrush and such – but keep me updated when you can, won't you?'

'Of course, Dad, try and have a nice trip.'

'I'm sure I will, in the zero-point-five seconds when I forget to worry about you two.'

Nathaniel

'But how would I do it?' Nathaniel asked hesitantly. 'I've never possessed anyone before…'

He could feel the entity's satisfaction at his line of questioning; it clearly took it as a sign it had won Nathaniel over to its plan.

'The way in differs from human to human. The father is easy because he is hurting; an open wound like that is as good as an unguarded doorway. All I had to do was feed on that delicious pain, grow stronger and then walk through it.'

'Are you suggesting that focusing on James's pain would allow me to possess him?'

'It's not quite that simple. First, you need to make the connection to his energetic field – I can tell you've done that already with the boy; good work. Then once that connection is made, you can strengthen it, really tasting his misery. Feel your way around it, explore the layers, the density. Press harder on the parts that really hurt, dig your claws into their soft, tender hearts, and when the pain flares, enjoy it, but make sure to force some of your energy back in too – create a two-way bond, a symbiotic connection. They never realise until it's too late.'

The entity gave a self-satisfied laugh, and Nathaniel could feel how proud it was. In fact, he could feel all of its feelings now, flowing through the cords binding them together in a constant hum.

'Rather like what I've done with you. Consider it a lesson. Bind yourself to your victim so they start to feel you as part of them, even become dependent on that connection without knowing it.'

'You did all this to James's father?' Nathaniel asked.

'I did, and then finally, I found my way in when he was unconscious. When they sleep, their defences are down; once you gain access to their dreams, you've already won. After that, it was easy to hold him long enough to do my bidding. It's the easiest pathway to manipulate and control.'

Nathaniel felt a chill pass through him at its words. He had already done that very thing: he had walked in James's dreamscape, indulged his cravings selfishly, allowed James's heartbreak and desperation to serve his own need for love. He felt sick. That night on the beach, he had framed it as a magical moment, but really, it was a violation. He should have been looking for a way out of James's dream, not trying to connect deeper – but he hadn't. It had never even occurred to him to do the honourable thing.

He looked at the entity. Perhaps he was more similar to the creature than he wanted to admit. He didn't deserve the things he wanted; he could only get them by evil means. Corrupt means to a selfish end, a corruption that clearly came naturally. Maybe the idea that he could ever be better than this was nothing more than another delusion; the entity was right.

'That doesn't seem sustainable,' Nathaniel said out loud, buying himself time to think. 'It's one thing controlling the sleeping, quite another to do it in waking hours, never mind completely taking over their bodies forever. I don't think we can do it.'

The entity moved closer to Nathaniel, and in its shifting features, he could see a leering mouth. 'You'd better hope we can do it, or it'll be all the worse for you.'

'What do you mean?'

'Either we succeed and take a human each, or we fail and I absorb your soul, harnessing *your* energy to try again.'

Nathaniel stumbled backwards but was unable to fall, the cords holding him in place.

'You can't escape me, Nathaniel, and you know it. You have no allies, no friends. No silly Victorian mystics to help you out this time.'

Nathaniel cast his mind back, and a thought struck him. 'Arthur…were you trying—'

'Clever boy. Yes, I was. Arthur was my first attempt to fully take a human form again. I shouldn't have chosen one so magically fortified; that was a foolish error. The bastard denied me again and again.'

'How, exactly?'

'He fought me valiantly, I'll give him that. Wouldn't let me take his body; then when it gave out under the strain, I absorbed his energy, but it wasn't enough to take Agatha, powerful witch that she was.'

Nathaniel paused for a moment, considering the horror of dear Arthur's essence being absorbed into the hideous entity and whether or not that was a worse fate than being possessed, trapped as a helpless observer while an evil force tore down your old life and rebuilt it to their taste.

'This time, though…this time will be different. A weak human with no skills in the occult; he'll put up no real resistance. Most importantly, he doesn't want to, not really.'

'What do you mean?' Nathaniel asked.

'Can't you sense it?' The entity paused for a cruel laugh. 'Of course not. Too enamoured with the son to even notice the father's state.'

Nathaniel curled in on himself with shame at the entity's words. 'I'm not enamoured…I—'

'Don't bother lying to me! Your obsession is clear, but I don't care; we can use that to our advantage.'

The entity moved, pulling Nathaniel with him. They moved slower this time, upwards through the darkness and then into the gloom of the garage. He knew where the entity dwelt now: the foundations underneath the house. It moved through the darkened room, its red eyes never looking away from Nathaniel for long.

'The father is tired…so weary, so heartbroken, so beaten down by life. He goes on, puts one foot in front of the other, day after day, but there is a part of him that *wants* to surrender, to give up, to rest. He didn't even bother to cast a fresh circle of salt last night…he practically *invited* me in.'

It came to a stop at the doorway, appearing to look out into the hallway. 'It will only take my strength of will, a little persuasion, the right ritual and the application of some energy to subdue him. The longer I hold him under, the less chance he will have of resurfacing.'

Nathaniel moved forwards. 'And what of James?'

'The boy may put up more of a fight than his father, and he is warded, but we'll break him.'

'How?'

The entity paused a moment. 'He exudes heartbreak. That alone is not enough – he is still too hopeful for the future – but his pain can be your fuel. Your will must be stronger than his; you must want his body more than he does.'

The entity glided through the hallway and up the stairs, Nathaniel dragged in its wake, its words echoing in his mind. They came to a stop on the landing, James's bedroom door left open.

Nathaniel looked at the bedside table and thought of the night he'd first gazed at the picture of Will and James together, of how that hunger had risen in him: envy, the deepest longing – he couldn't deny he had felt that way. That he craved the taste of such a blessed existence, thought of how wonderful it would be to be James, how it would feel to go through the world in his skin. How wonderful it would be to inhabit him, be inside him, the two of them fused together forever.

The entity was smiling, and Nathaniel realised it could feel some of what he was feeling through the cords. It knew it had struck a nerve.

Nathaniel turned away from its gaze. It made him feel naked and vulnerable; it saw too much and knew too much, things he had barely even admitted to himself.

'Is that why you stayed behind?' the entity asked, its tone almost kind, which was more unsettling than its usual spite-filled voice.

'What do you mean?' Nathaniel asked.

'You stayed behind, so that one day you could take the physical form you desire, the right one.' It gestured with what seemed to be an arm at the room, at James's belongings. 'This life, already laid out for you.'

'No…that's not it. Or at least, I don't think so. I never intended to take anything from anyone, I…' Nathaniel paused, trying to understand his own situation. 'I was just left behind. The light never appeared for me, in the end.'

Caspian Faye

'You were forgotten…little lost one. The higher powers forsake you. The responsibility rests with you now to show them the error of their ways, to take your own power and birthright.'

'What about you?' Nathaniel asked. 'Why are *you* here still?'

'You really haven't worked it out yet, have you?'

'Worked what out?' Nathaniel asked. 'How would I know why you're here when I don't even fully understand why I am?'

He was surprised when the entity appeared to give him an honest, sincere reply.

'The light appeared for me, but I could not go. For many reasons. In life, I did things that others would deem immoral and unforgivable, and I do not know what happens in the world beyond the light for those who have done such things, and why take the risk when I can stay here?'

Nathaniel was going to ask more questions, but before he could, the entity reverted to its usual mood with a disturbing laugh. 'No, I am meant for greater things. Someone such as me shouldn't be held back by the limits of mortal rules. It's much better to stay here and have the humans tremble before me, helpless as I take what I want and wreak havoc! You'll soon see…you get a taste for it. And the glory that is to come when I reach my full potential…just you wait.'

'But I don't like it when I scare people,' Nathaniel objected. 'I won't get a taste for pain; all these years, causing all that fear just makes me feel lonely.'

The entity moved closer to him, and he choked; it was like being surrounded by a dense cloud of cold, wet smoke that set every nerve on edge. He pulled futilely once again at the limits of the cords tethering him, and the red orbs in the midst of the darkness gleamed even brighter.

'Lean into that, boy, deep into it. Mine that loneliness. If you have to feel that way, why not make everyone feel that way? Why not relish what you do have: the power to cause fear and pain? Instead of pining for their friendship and approval, decide now that you are better than that. You don't need their paltry affections, just their delicious terror. Stop caring what they think and start enjoying how you can make them feel…the freedom in that is truly the greatest power of all.'

'But I don't want to!' Nathaniel managed to protest, although it felt like it took all of his energy to do so.

'Only for a short time, though, remember?' the entity switched tone again, its putrid scent turning sickly sweet. 'Wield fear to get what you want, and then you'll have it all, the perfect life you always should have had. You'll be James. You'll be loved; you'll shine; everyone will want to be around you, and you'll never be alone again.'

James

'Here we are, then,' James said, entirely unnecessarily.

Nova squinted as she peered up at the house from the driveway, pulling her coat a little tighter around herself. 'It's bigger than the pictures made it look, also way shabbier.'

'Yeah…we thought it was the extreme shabbiness that made it affordable for Dad, but actually, I guess it might have been the ghosts.'

'So really, you should be thanking them?'

James tried to laugh but couldn't quite summon the energy. 'Okay, ready to go in?'

Nova hoisted her backpack higher on her shoulder. 'Yep, let's do it.'

James pulled his keys out and mentally prepared for what awaited inside. The hallway was chillier than ever, noticeable as their breath began to mist in a way it hadn't outside.

Nova put her hand on James's shoulder, her fingers grasping a half-handful of his jacket. 'Oh, wow, there's so much energy here. I can feel it already… it's like nothing I've ever felt, even when I joined my mum's friends on investigations.'

'Didn't most of those places turn out to be "badly insulated drafty houses inhabited by people with overactive imaginations"? Also, why are we whispering?'

Nova shrugged. 'I may have said something like that. And…I don't know, instinct? I know it won't really help, but I don't want us to draw attention to ourselves.'

'Right, so what now?'

Nova considered for a moment. 'Could we have a hot drink in the safest spot in the house while we figure out a plan of action?'

James nodded. 'The safest spot is probably not *in* the house. I suggest the garden.'

'If we leave, I might not want to come back.'

James swallowed. 'Is it really that bad in here?'

'Honestly, yeah. It's one of those times I almost wish I didn't know what I do, that I wasn't so tuned in, and I could feel safe in my blissful ignorance.'

'You'd be fairly useless to me then, though, wouldn't you?'

'Fair, and it'd be worse in the long run. Okay, how about your bedroom? I know the ward is destroyed, but there might be some residual protection left. It seems like a good place to start, especially if we can make contact with the friendly one.'

'Nathaniel.'

James led Nova into the kitchen, and she walked around slowly, examining the cupboard doors while he made the tea.

'You ready?' he asked once it was poured. She straightened up and accepted a mug.

'Yeah, I was just looking for any residue, but there isn't anything I can see.'

'What does that mean?'

'That you're dealing with something old and powerful. Or that your dad has been doing lots of cleaning.'

James frowned. 'I think it's probably the former, unfortunately for us.'

They made their way upstairs carefully. A few of the stairs creaked despite their efforts, and James realised his heart was thundering in anticipation of the entity attacking at any moment. Once inside his room with the door closed, he felt safer, even if it was just an illusion at this point.

Nova sat down on the rug in the middle of the floor and started unpacking her backpack. 'Okay, so you're still wearing your protection spell, and I've got one on too. That's a start.' She pulled salt from her bag and cast a circle around the rug. 'Sit in the circle with me.'

James joined her, hands cupped around his mug for warmth.

She drew out a velvet bag, several books, a box of candles, a lighter and a container of herbs, setting them all to one side. These were followed by her laptop and several sigil-marked power banks.

'I have everything I think I need.' She swallowed. 'I'm going to start by reinstating the protection on this room; it won't take too long and gives us a safe space to return to if things get dangerous in the rest of the house.'

'Couldn't you just cast one for the whole house; wouldn't that just drive the evil thing out altogether?'

Nova shook her head. 'I wish, but no, it's not that simple. This thing is too powerful. Besides, a protection spell and banishing spell are entirely different things, and we need to do this gradually, in stages. I've watched people more experienced than me do this work, and if there's one thing I learnt, it's that trying to be too clever or over-extending too early is not a good idea.'

'Got it. I'll shut up and let you concentrate, then.'

Nova grinned. 'Not necessary yet; this part will be easy enough. Is that mess over there what remains of the last ward?'

'Yeah, that and my cup of tea from last night. Shame about that mug, got it on a trip to Brighton pier.'

'Can I see it?'

'I mean, it's shattered now, but it was a superhero—'

'Not the mug! The remains of the spell.'

'Oh, yeah.' James used a folder from his desk and a nearby book to sweep up the fragments of glass and pieces of the enchantment and bring it back to where Nova sat in the salt circle.

She poked at the mess that apparently made sense to her. 'Okay, thanks. I'm ready.'

James sat quietly while she lit candles and arranged herbs in a fresh glass bottle, drawing symbols in the air with her fingers and chanting softly under her breath. He had no idea what any of it meant, but the energetic charge as she finished was unmistakable.

'The room feels different again, like it used to…'

Nova smiled. 'That's the point. Put this up where the last one was, above the door.'

James reached up and did as she said, joining her afterwards at the window, where she sipped her tea. 'Okay, so phase one is complete.'

'What's phase two?'

'I think we should do a walkthrough of the entire house. I need you to point out exactly what happened and where so we can get an idea of the focal points of the activity to choose where to set up.'

James nodded. 'So we're going to focus where things are worst?'

Nova put her tea down on the windowsill and turned to him. 'Yes. Dig out the poison at the root, or at least try to.'

She looked around the room. 'You mostly saw Nathaniel in here?'

'I *only* saw him in here…but not for a while.'

Nova closed her eyes and held a hand up for silence. James finished his tea staring out the window, his heart giving a little jump as he imagined Nathaniel appearing again.

Nathaniel

'He's back…your boy. And he's brought a delicious companion… what fun,' the entity rasped.

Nathaniel could sense James's energy too, and an additional presence who he guessed was his friend, Nova. Her energy was familiar enough to him from all her calls with James and powerful enough to be distinctive. He knew immediately why she was here, and his heart sank. The pair were entering the house, talking in low voices. Nathaniel could sense their anxiety from upstairs, and he knew if he could, so could the entity.

'Come, boy!' it said as it turned in a haze of smoke and dragged him back down the stairs towards its favourite spot, the garage. As they passed the kitchen where James was, Nathaniel felt his noncorporeal heart scrambling inside his ribcage, desperate to cry out, to be heard, to get to James.

The entity could feel that too, and a spike of pleasure came through the cords, along with a sense of anticipation. It was so intrusive, the backwash through the connection.

'Humans are easy to manipulate,' the entity crowed. 'We'll break them tonight and be all the stronger for it. Are you looking forward to your new life? It's almost yours.'

Nathaniel looked away from those red eyes, staring instead at James's nearby weights. He moved over to them, running a finger along one, tasting for residual energy. Anything to do with James gave him something to hold onto, something powerful to grip against the relentless pull of the entity's influence.

'You're wasting your time,' the entity commented. 'Although your painfully pathetic yearning for him only feeds me, so by all means, do continue.'

Nathaniel withdrew his hand and lowered his head. Whatever he tried only seemed to play into the entity's plan.

'They're restoring the old spell!' the entity exclaimed. 'As if it will do them any good in the long run. I'll let them think they have a chance, lure them into a false sense of security. It'll be more fun that way.'

Nathaniel's hope leapt at that. If he could just get back to James's room, he could be safe for a while and hide again. Perhaps he would have enough time to figure out a solution to this awful situation.

The entity slid closer, perhaps suspecting the rising hope in him. 'Are you looking forward to what is to come?'

It occurred to Nathaniel that while the entity could sense his feelings, the reason for them remained unclear, so he forced himself to meet those red eyes. 'Yes, I—I'm so hopeful for my new life, even if I still feel guilt for taking it.'

The entity's eyes narrowed. 'Don't worry yourself; that guilt will soon pass. By tonight, you can be human again; by tonight, you can have the body you always dreamed of…imagine that.'

At a creak from upstairs, the entity's attention diverted, giving Nathaniel a reprieve from the awfulness of having its full attention on him – but not from the disturbing and conflicted direction of his own thoughts.

James

Nova's eyes snapped open. 'I've checked and double-checked; there is no-one in this room, or upstairs currently, apart from us.' She took a deep breath. 'It's as you expected: I sense there's two spirits present, and they're both downstairs. Come on.'

James followed her as she went to the bedroom door and pulled it open with a bravery he wished he felt. Her words were bothering him. 'They're both downstairs, but are they together?'

Nova pursed her lips. 'Impossible to tell at this range. I'll confirm after further investigation.'

James still didn't want to admit how hurt he was by the thought of Nathaniel joining forces with the other entity. He had felt something in their connection that really mattered to him, and the magnitude of that possible betrayal left him reeling.

'I guess I might not be the best judge of character then, eh?' He tried to pass it off as a light comment, but Nova reached out and took his hand, squeezing it.

'Will is a very charming guy; I get it, James. I get why you fell for him, even if I saw the red – maybe too harsh – orange flags.'

James sighed, the weight of his suppressed heartbreak threatening to hit him all over again.

'And as for Nathaniel, well, ghosts are tricky things. And you're new to this. It's no reflection on you if he turns out to not be what you thought he was.'

James squeezed her hand in return. 'Thanks.'

'Right, onwards!' she said.

James made a move towards the stairs, but she pulled him back. 'Not so fast. I need to have a quick look up here first, just to get a lay of the land.' She pointed at the bathroom. 'Anything weird in there?'

'Nothing other than the horrible tiles.'

Nova carried on down the hall, pausing outside Frank's room and placing her hand on the door. 'Ah, interesting. There's an energetic residue in your dad's room that matches the vileness downstairs…this ghost isn't lost or lashing out because its confused, I'm afraid. It's focused and nasty – it's made repeated visits to this room, spent time and energy here, which makes sense considering the whole "controlling your dad" turn of events.'

'Great news,' James muttered as Nova carried on down the corridor and turned the corner.

'Everything here feels quite stagnant, but I can tell without you saying anything that *that* is the spare room with activity?'

'Yeah, that's the one. I locked it and haven't been in there since.'

Nova turned the key and pushed the door open, James stared wordlessly at the total destruction within.

'I'm going to guess that you didn't leave it like this?' Nova asked in a hushed tone.

James stepped over the threshold and scanned the room. Nothing at all was how he remembered it. 'No…the entity had made a mess last time, but nothing like this. Is there anything left *in* a box? Or any piece of furniture that *isn't* broken?'

'Doesn't look like it.'

'So, unless my dad has been doing some very destructive sleepwalking…'

Nova put a hand on James's shoulder. 'Let's move on. It was just proving a point.'

'That locked doors don't stop it?'

'Among other things. Let's not give it too much attention for this; it'll only encourage it to wreck more of your stuff.'

James sighed. 'I don't have much stuff left at this point.' He followed her out of the room anyway, closing and locking the door behind them.

Nova remained silent as they walked back along the dusty corridor and turned back around the corner to the main landing. As they reached the top of the stairs, she pointed at the old dust sheets hanging on some of the windows. 'If I was your dad, I'd get proper curtains put in as soon as I could, or at least tear those down and let some more light in.'

Caspian Faye

The temperature dropped as they reached the ground floor, the fading daylight lending the house an oppressive gloom.

'The air feels thicker,' James whispered, and Nova nodded.

'It does…not uncommon when you get near to something malevolent.'

James pointed at the kitchen. 'We've done in there; there's the sitting room, which has mostly been OK.'

'Hmm, I need to check it out anyway,' Nova replied, walking in and doing a slow loop of the room, stopping only to switch the TV off at the wall.

'Is this a fire safety lesson now?'

She shook her head. 'Nope, just shutting off additional power sources for the entities to use. Might help us out later.'

'Nothing major has really happened in here, aside from Posey being weird, but that could just be her being her. The hallway, though—'

'Wait, James, give me a minute.' Nova held up her hand and moved to the middle of the room, looking around intently as though she could see something.

'What are you looking at? Is there something—'

'James! Shush, please.'

He did as he was told, but he was itching to ask more questions.

Nova beckoned to him, and he went to her. She took him by the elbow and backed away, leading them both into the corner of the room.

'Keep in physical contact with me,' she told him, hooking her arm around his. She was still looking at something in the middle of the room with narrowed eyes.

'Posey was doing that the other night,' James whispered, 'before she moved into the shed.'

Nova nodded. 'Cats *see.*'

James was about to ask her why they were standing here and what exactly she could see when he began to notice the shadows shifting in the room. He started deep breathing, trying to clear his mind and focus on what was in front of him, to be as open as possible with no judgement.

The faint sound of footsteps on hard wood floor were the first thing he noticed. He looked at Nova in surprise and gestured towards his ears; she nodded and pointed into the middle of the room, her expression questioning.

He stared at the space she was pointing at, and slowly, in the grey gloom, he was able to pick out shadows moving. They were just about recognisable as human shapes, milling about, forming a circle; and then slowly, they sank lower, as if they'd sat down. He wondered if they were an optical illusion in the poor light, or if his mind was generating random imagery based on the power of suggestion.

Nova stared for a few more moments and then blinked, turning to James. 'I need to check something.'

She let go of him, and as she did so, the shadows faded away from his perception.

Nova extended a hand. 'Give me your pen knife.'

James fished it out of his jeans pocket and handed it over. 'Be careful…'

He trailed off as she stepped forward, knelt down and slashed into the carpet.

'Nova! How is that being careful?!'

She looked up at him with a shrug. 'Sorry! But the carpet is vile anyway; your dad should chuck it.'

'Fun though your interior design tips are, he might not agree. You're here to help me with the ghosts, remember, not redecorate!'

'Don't be ungrateful; it's a bonus service.'

She turned back and carried on pulling at the edges of the cut she'd made, looking up at him triumphantly. 'Aha! Look!'

James peered down at the hole. 'What am I supposed to be looking at?'

'Don't be so dense; look – there's polished wooden floor under here! And'—she leant forward— 'there are little discoloured marks here. I'd bet if I ripped up all of this, then—'

'Please don't!'

'Stop fussing, James! I'm not going to, but if I did, I bet there would be matching ones that would line up perfectly with the table legs that once stood here.'

She stood up and handed him back the pen knife. 'What we just saw was the echo of the séances. They must have held them in this room. The table was there, and the footsteps we heard were from that time too.'

'Are you telling me that on top of everything else, the sitting room has an entire group of people and a *table* haunting it?!'

Nova snorted. 'No, this isn't a haunting in a sentient way, just an echo through time.'

'In plain English, not paranormal speak?'

'These aren't ghosts, just energetic echoes. They aren't aware, and they won't interact; nothing to worry about. Like…a replay or a recording of sorts that's linked to this space. It's stone tape theory – look it up at some stage when you've got some free time; makes for interesting reading.'

'Yeah, okay, I get it. But what does this tell you about the house?'

Nova gestured at the room. 'That this room is significant, the location of the séances and therefore the entry point for the entity that's been causing trouble, and maybe others. I'll know more later.'

She cast one last look around the room and then went back to the kitchen, switching off and unplugging the microwave and toaster as James trailed behind her.

'This is going to be a pain when we want dinner,' James commented, and Nova shrugged.

'We'll order a pizza, if we even have time…and an appetite. Okay, garage next.'

James noticed the tight feeling in his stomach intensifying at the thought of having to go into the garage. He led the way regardless, flicking the light on as he stepped into the darkness.

The light did nothing to banish the feeling of heaviness, of something threatening lurking just out of sight. Nova stepped in behind him and drew in a sharp breath.

'Coldest room so far. Could be physical reasons for that, but…' She looked around. 'I hate it in here. It feels like a battleground, like the calm after a storm and the calm before a new one all at once. Something is brewing…it's hard to put into words.'

'I know what you mean,' James replied and meant it. He pointed at the cavity in the wall. 'That's where we found the box with the watch in it.'

Nova stuck her hand into it, running a finger along the brickwork. 'I can feel the residue…hold onto me.'

She stretched out her other hand, and James took it.

'Why?' he asked, alarmed by what she might be planning.

'You might be able to see what I see like before if you concentrate.' She placed her palm flat on the bricks and gripped James's hand harder, closing her eyes and breathing deeply. He did the same. When he felt her turn around to face the centre of the room, he opened his eyes, did likewise and gasped. In the space in front of them he saw four people, clearer than the shadows they'd seen earlier. Clear enough to make out facial features and clothing.

A woman in a long cardigan and pleated skirt stood alongside a companion in flared jeans and a sweater. Behind them stood a couple holding hands and looking anxious, a woman in dungarees and a man in jeans and a tie-dyed T-shirt.

The couple were fidgeting, and the woman was biting her lip, but the two people in front of them appeared calm. The woman in the cardigan was holding something. James peered at it and realised with a jolt what it was: the box that had contained the watch. Her mouth began to move, but he couldn't hear what she was saying.

Nova frowned. 'These echoes are stronger, much more recent, but I really would like to hear what they're saying. I wonder if I can somehow amplify…' She paused, rummaging in her pockets and pulling out a quartz crystal. She held it out and took a deep breath to say something when a rumbling noise began.

Nova cocked her head. 'What is that? Are you in a flight path, or…'

Caspian Faye

It grew louder, the tools on the shelves beginning to rattle. She fumbled in her bag, pulling out her salt and casting a circle in front of them, then jumping into it. 'James, get in the circle, now!'

A hissing sound came from somewhere in the corner of the room as he joined her, trying his best not to show his fear. The hissing grew louder and slowly became a word: '*Sssssssstop!*'

James looked around and realised the figures were no longer visible, having faded away.

'Nova, what—'

Nova glanced behind them. 'The echoes are still here; we just can't see them because we aren't focused or calm anymore!'

'Can we maybe come back later and see or hear what you need?'

Nova opened her mouth to respond, but the loud crash from the hall drew their attention. 'Wait, what?'

James stepped out of the circle without thinking, reaching the door to the hallway in a few strides.

'James! Come back!'

'Two seconds; I need to just check out here.'

'James, get back in the circle!'

'Give me a minute!'

At first, he couldn't see anything that could explain the noise; then his eyes adjusted, and he realised the mirror had lifted off the wall and smashed on the hall floor. Large shards of it were scattered across the doormat, and the metal frame lay several feet away. He was contemplating the force required to destroy it so completely when Nova shouted for him again. 'James! The circle, now!'

He turned back into the garage, but just as he stepped across the threshold, the lightbulb overhead flickered and then crackled off.

He heard Nova say, 'Follow my voice; I'll find my torch!'

He took a step towards her and where he knew the circle to be, but before he could reach it, he stumbled. He almost recovered himself, but then something caught at his ankles, yanking his feet out from under him. His arms went wide as he reached out into the darkness for a way to save himself from falling, but they found only empty air.

He fell hard on the concrete floor, an impact to his chest driving the wind from his lungs with the accompanying crunching sound of breaking glass and the sensation of sudden sharpness. He gasped for breath as Nova's torch clicked to life and her hand seized his, pulling him to his feet and back into the circle.

'Shit, are you ok?'

He took a quick inventory. Bruises, no doubt, but the adrenaline was making it easy to ignore those for now. His knees were aching, his palms were scraped, and his chest hurt, but nothing was broken…except for the bottle on the chain around his neck. He stared at the glass shards in dismay; the protective ward was ruined.

He looked around in the torchlight for any signs of immediate danger and spotted one of his dumbbells in the middle of the floor. 'That's what I must have tripped on.'

'It wasn't there a minute ago!'

'I know.'

Nova's eyes were wide, scanning the room. Seeing nothing, she turned back to James. 'Oh no…you're bleeding.'

He looked down at his chest. Specks of blood were appearing on his T-shirt. He lifted it, and Nova swore again.

'Hold still; we need to sort this now.'

She unclasped the chain from his neck, carefully pulling what remained on it away from his body and dropping it into her bag. Sticking the torch between her teeth and pulling a tissue from her pocket, she peered at his chest, gently picking the little shards of glass from his skin and wrapping them carefully in the tissue. She put her torch on the floor and began to set out the candles from her bag.

'We can't spill any blood here,' she whispered, her face uncharacteristically pale.

'Why?' James whispered back.

'Best not go into that now. Try and stay calm; don't let them feed on your fear.'

'That's a lot easier said than done!' James retorted.

'Sit down with me and keep this tissue pressed on the cuts.'

James did as he was told as she lit the candles, their light improving the atmosphere in the garage only slightly. Nova moved quickly, tossing essential oils around the circle and setting out some small metal sigils.

'What are we doing?'

'Shh, James, just watch my back.'

She took his free hand and closed her eyes. James looked around the room, feeling a bit useless and wondering what exactly she meant by that. What was he supposed to be watching her back for, and what was he supposed to do if he saw something, anyway?

A few moments of silence and the candle flames began to flicker. Nova remained still.

The sound of low laughter rose, and James jumped. Nova squeezed his hand but said nothing. It was the nastiest laughter he had ever heard; he tried his best to ignore it, but it grew in volume, seeming to echo from everywhere all at once. He felt something on his head and jumped, looking up to see a few pieces of what looked like paper fluttering down from the ceiling.

They were fragments of something. He looked closer; it was the photograph of him and Will. The piece that had landed beside him showed half of Will's smile and one shining eye. His heart lurched, his throat tightening as he forced down his emotions. Looking at what he had lost, thinking of Stevie's lips now tasting the ones he knew so well. His hands roaming over the planes of Will's body that were so familiar, so special to him. Claiming his love and affection, taking everything James had once cherished, polluting all his happy memories with doubt.

All the painful questions began to surface on a loop: Did it mean anything? Had Will ever loved him? Or had it all been an act, Will settling until he could find the real deal, the guy he really wanted to be with? Did he compare them; was he mocking James to Stevie right now?

Nova's eyes opened. 'James, what are you—'

She never finished her sentence; the loud creaking at the garage door cut her off. With a sudden grating noise, the garage door swung up and back, letting the wind in. The candles blew out as a gust of wind and damp evening air flooded in, the salt of the protective circle scattering all over the floor.

Nova released his hands. 'Run!'

'Where?'

She grabbed her bag, leaving the extinguished candles where they lay, and shoved him towards the open garage door. 'Go!'

He hurdled the weight bench and made straight for the expanse of the unlit driveway, the feeling of something at his back the whole time, his heart pounding, expecting to be grabbed again, thrown, or dragged back into the darkness of the garage.

He put on a last burst of speed and felt the relief when his trainers hit the gravel, Nova skidding to a halt beside him a second later.

Nathaniel

'You see? You see how that gave me power?'

The entity stood in the doorway, smiling at Nathaniel. He could make out its features more clearly now; it seemed to be taking on more of a human form as time went on. Its eyes now appeared more bloodshot than red, and its face was more distinct in its lines rather than the previous swimming mass of shadows.

He nodded. 'I saw.' Nathaniel had felt it as well. The energy had surged from James like a pulse. He could feel the power in that pain; he understood how a creature such as the one in front of him could use it as nourishment. To Nathaniel, it had felt like the energetic equivalent of eating something poisonous: strong but incredibly nasty. He supposed if he surrendered to the darkness himself, that over time the taste of pain would become more palatable. Perhaps if he sunk to the vibrational frequency of the entity, it would even become sweet.

'That's your way in,' the entity told him softly. 'Remember, the cracks in his broken heart.'

Nathaniel moved to the threshold of the garage and reached out a hand, feeling the invisible barrier stopping him from entering the outside world. He was as limited as the entity was; he couldn't take another step forward. Couldn't project a calming energy to the humans that stood panting in the driveway, looking back with such fear.

He couldn't go to James's side, no matter how much he wanted to.

James

'So, what now?' James asked, after his breathing slowed and his heartrate almost returned to normal.

Nova frowned. 'We have to go back in.'

'Well, obviously; we can't stay out here forever.'

'No need to be snappy, James. I need to think. Let's walk; I don't want to be overheard.'

'Where?'

'Just around the garden will do. Come on.'

They skirted the house and made their way to the trees. Nova stopped by a particularly impressive one, placing her palm flat against the bark.

'If only this could talk, it could probably shed some light on what's going on here.'

'What happened back there?' James asked, not sure he wanted to know the answer.

Nova put her back to the tree, sliding down to sit on the ground, not seeming to care about the wet mud that oozed up out of the grass.

James crouched next to her. 'Are you OK?'

She frowned. 'Yes and no. I got something, I guess – the key locations of events in the house. Before we were interrupted, I think we were about to see how the entity was bound before.' She smiled suddenly. 'Oh…wait, that's good!'

'What? What's good about anything that just happened?' James asked, incredulous.

'The entity cared! It cared enough to stop us watching the previous binding, which means it's concerned that information could be dangerous to it. It sees enough power in me, in us, to go to the effort of disrupting things. Perhaps it doesn't fear us yet, but it sees us as worthy opponents.'

James nodded. 'Doesn't this mean we're in more danger from it, though, if it's feeling threatened?'

'I mean, technically, probably yes. But let's try and focus on the positives here. Just before the circle was destroyed, I was trying to get a read on the entities present so we'd know exactly what we're dealing with. I picked up on both and managed to distinguish between them. I saw them. Your Nathaniel, just as you described and…the other one.'

'And? Is he okay?'

'Nathaniel? Yes, as okay as a lost ghost can be.'

'And he's being held captive by the evil thing?' James confirmed, his previously hurt feelings soothed. Nathaniel hadn't been ignoring him; he'd been a prisoner.

Nova frowned. 'It's hard to tell if they're allies or if he's being held captive. I saw them both distinctly and separately, but there were energetic connections between them.'

James shuddered. 'What were they doing? And what does it look like, the energetic connection thing?'

'Nathaniel was just watching us; the other thing…it was moving, tendrils of crackling energy sparking from it. The shield I had cast over us was keeping it at bay, allowing me to observe it, but then it made a gesture, threw something physical over us, and you changed. Not to sound like I'm blaming you, but you sent out waves of energy that shattered the shield. What was it, the thing the entity threw?'

James looked away. 'It—it was parts of a photo of Will and me, one I ripped up in my room. I have no idea how that got into the garage.'

'The ward was down for hours; that thing could have done whatever it wanted in your room.' Nova sighed. 'It makes sense.'

'What does?'

'Your reaction was so powerful, it gave that thing enough power to—well, you saw.'

'Drag open the garage door and destroy our circle,' James said miserably. 'I'm so sorry.'

'Not your fault, but it's worrying. It must be very powerful to begin with, and if Nathaniel has joined it—'

'He wouldn't do that!' James retorted defensively, suddenly so sure of Nathaniel's allegiance.

Nova gave him a doubtful look and shrugged.

He had no idea how he'd explain his certainty if she pressed the matter; it was really just a feeling. Every time he recalled Nathaniel's eyes on his, their moments in the garden, his hand resting in his on the beach – James's heart kept insisting the ghost could be trusted. An evil being couldn't possibly have made him feel so safe.

'I hope you're right.' Nova got up, shaking her hands and rolling out her neck and shoulders like she was about to start a boxing match. James would have laughed if the situation didn't feel so dire.

'Time to go back in!' she announced.

'And do what?'

'We need to get to your bedroom, and then we start preparing to deal with them. It's going to be a long night, and we will definitely have to be strong. I'll talk you through how best you can help me, because I can't do this alone, James. I need your energy and I need your focus, and somehow, you must find a way of controlling your feelings about Will.'

James nodded. 'I—it just caught me off guard a moment ago; it won't happen again. I'm ready now. It won't hurt so much if it does it again.'

Nova nodded. 'If it does, try and channel your reaction into resistance, please. And it isn't likely to throw photos at you all night; you need to be prepared for other tactics.'

'Okay. Also, you said them? As in…'

'If Nathaniel is allied with the other entity, we get rid of him, too. There are no half measures here, James; there's no point removing one evil thing and leaving another, slightly less evil thing behind. Over time, he might be just as bad.'

'But he's not; he's a captive. He's not evil!'

'I'll try my best to be certain, and if that seems the case, then separate them. But James…you have to be prepared for the fact that it may not be possible. We might not be able to take that risk, and if things get too dangerous, then losing Nathaniel is the cost of getting rid of the evil.'

'As a last resort, though? An absolute, life-or-death last resort? Promise me?'

Nova nodded. 'I won't do it unless I have to, I promise. Hopefully it won't come to that, and once the evil is gone, we'll give him the choice on whether or not he wants to stay or go.' She picked up her bag and turned back towards the house. 'Once we go back in, I need you to do what I tell you, even if it's hard. Do *you* promise me?'

James knew she would keep her word, but he really wanted to give Nathaniel the benefit of the doubt and the best chance despite any risks, and he was concerned she might not be able to understand his emotional investment in that. He wasn't even sure he understood it himself. He nodded all the same. 'Promise.'

Nathaniel

'They're gone now; you've driven them away,' Nathaniel commented, staring in the direction James had left in.

'They'll be back,' the entity replied, 'and we'll let them pass. Humans are so predictable. They will hide in the bedroom, thinking I can't reach them.' It laughed. 'We wait, and at the right moment, we begin.'

'Begin what?'

'I've changed my mind. I don't want to take the father anymore; I'm going to take the witch.'

Nathaniel tried to hide his alarm. 'What? Why would you do that?'

The entity leant over his shoulder, filling him with revulsion as it invaded his space even more than the cords already did.

'She has power, power that will be mine once I overcome her defences. I can use her abilities to call in a friend to take the father, and then all three of us will be unstoppable.'

'You have a friend?'

The entity leered, revealing what looked like very sharp, jagged decaying teeth. 'I have many friends. So could you, if you hadn't hidden away here for so long…what, you thought you and I were the only ones who couldn't or didn't pass on? There are others floating around out there, listless and hungry. All desperate to find a living host to focus on – so you mind you always heed me, or I might decide to remove you back to this bodyless state and give the boy to someone more obedient and loyal to me.'

Nathaniel shivered, contemplating his best course of action once more. If it became impossible to stop the entity, should he possess James in order to protect him from something worse? Perhaps he could get him out of the house and then release him so he could go free.

Nathaniel had no idea what would happen to his own soul should he do that. His spirit seemed bound to this house, so he assumed the result would be oblivion, but his last act could save James from this nightmare.

'You say we'll be unstoppable, but won't we just be… humans?' Nathaniel asked.

'Think of James, of what he has, of what he is, and tell me you wouldn't feel unstoppable if you were him. That bright future ahead of you…'

Nathaniel made no protest, and the entity continued. 'You can't say it, not without lying. I can read you like a book. I can feel your feelings as though they were my own. Besides, we won't be limited to just *these* humans. When they grow old and weak, we'll find others and take them instead. We'll be immortal, ever-changing, becoming more powerful over time.'

Nathaniel remained silent, chilled as the full extent of the entity's vision sunk in. It was much more calculating than he had previously assumed. Less a manifestation of random malevolence and more a cold, insidious evil with deep, twisted desires.

'But why us?' he asked. 'Why do you think we can do all this? If there's all these lost souls like us out there, how come they aren't taking humans left, right and centre?'

'Because they lack my power and knowledge, Nathaniel. In life, I had some, but in death, I will be infinite.'

Nathaniel stared at the hazy features of the entity. Something about its grandiose vision of itself seemed somewhat familiar. 'Who are you, really? Why did you come here, of all places?'

A stone skittering across the driveway drew his attention to the pair approaching the house, and he wanted to cry out, to somehow reach James and warn him, but he knew if he played his hand too soon, all might be lost. So he did nothing but watch as they cautiously moved closer. He could sense their fear, and it tore at him, a wrenching reminder of his powerlessness.

He was startled when something he assumed to be the entity's hand, or the closest thing it had to it, clamped over his mouth. Confused, he wriggled as it dragged him across the garage into the darkest corner.

'Hush, let them pass,' it rasped into his ear as the cord around his throat began to crackle, a pressure that stole his voice away.

Perhaps he really should just accept he was a lost cause. There was no-one to fight alongside him, and even if there was, who was he kidding? He was under the control of the entity now. He had failed Arthur; he was always going to fail James too. He couldn't really be held accountable for falling under the sway of such a powerful force as the entity when there was no other path available to him, nothing to cling onto.

The sudden noise of running drew his attention. James had broken into a sprint directly into the garage, jumping up and grabbing the garage door, and as Nova ran under it, he slammed it down. She scrambled past, snatching at the door handle and disappearing into the main house.

Nathaniel blinked, feeling instantly more awake. Despite everything, James's closeness was still the only thing he could focus on. Everything else slipped away in his proximity; the ache in his heart since they'd lost contact was at the forefront of his awareness. He still felt the dread of the creature at his back, the silencing hand over his mouth, but they receded into the background. James's vitality was so striking, so bright, even amidst his emotional turmoil and terror, it was still like staring at the sun in human form.

Once the door was down, James hurdled his way through the room, somehow scooping up the candles from the floor with one hand as he went, turning through the doorway into the hall and up the stairs in a sequence of fluid movements.

Nathaniel gazed after them, struck by James's impressive speed and transfixed by the way his body moved.

The entity removed its grip on him, but its foul mouth remained near his ear as it whispered, 'Just think, all that will soon be yours.'

James

James charged through his bedroom door with such force that he had to throw a hand out to avoid a collision with his desk. Nova slammed the door shut behind him, and they both stood for a moment, recovering something resembling a sense of calm.

'We made it,' he said. 'Go, team.'

Nova glanced at the door. 'For now. I…that was too easy.'

'It was? You don't think we just caught it off guard?'

Nova shook her head. 'I sensed both of them still in the garage. The entity could have tripped us or something, but it didn't. It wants us back in the house.'

'Right, but we're protected in here.'

Nova nodded. 'We are, for now, but I don't think we should waste time.'

James passed her the recovered candles, and she returned to her salt circle from earlier. 'What next?' he asked.

Nova took a deep breath, centring herself. 'I'm going to call on the elements I work with for protection – my ancestors, guides and deities – and then I start the real work. Where's that pocket watch?'

James grabbed it from his desk and brought it to her.

She looked at it and quickly tossed it aside. 'It won't hold anything anymore; the crack in the glass makes it useless now. Never mind; I'll just try to banish it from this house.'

'Isn't that a bit crap, though? I mean, where will it go, wandering around the town haunting everyone?'

Nova ran a hand through her hair. 'I'm trying my best, James! I…have you got any better ideas?'

He shook his head. 'Nope, sorry.'

'Right, so, our priority is to get it out of this house and make sure you and your dad are safe. First, we need to try and separate it from Nathaniel.'

James couldn't hide his delight at her words. 'So, you believe he's good?'

Nova grinned back at him. 'I sensed fear that wasn't ours as we passed through the garage, and from what I saw, the entity was restraining him. I think he's being held captive by those energetic connections. If I'm wrong, if I can't separate them or if he turns out to be evil after all, we can fall back on our plan of banishing them both.'

James's heart skipped a beat, and he started praying to anything that was listening that they could be separated.

Nova closed her eyes and inhaled slowly. 'I can *see* the energetic cords in my mind's eye; I just need to cut them.'

She fell silent, and James waited as she began to draw symbols in the air with one hand, the other open in front of her.

'Pen knife, please,' she said quietly, and he placed it on her palm.

She continued to draw with one hand as she sliced through the air with the other, whispering under her breath. James waited for what felt like hours, and then she made a sudden downward movement. A small purple spark of colour flashed in the air for a fleeting moment, and Nova smiled.

'One down, just – oh wow – *six* more to go!'

James watched her intently as she repeated the process again, his eagerness for Nathaniel to be free making it really hard for him to contain his anxious, impatient energy.

Sweat was beginning to bead on her temples; her breathing was growing heavier, and he felt like a bad friend for taking so long to realise this process was intense and taking its toll on her. Hoping he could in some way help, he sat down, putting his back against hers and focusing on the intention to lend her any support and energy she needed, should she want to pull it from him. She pushed her back against his and whispered, 'Thank you,' before she carried on with her effort to free Nathaniel.

James was staring blankly at his bedroom door when he saw the next purple flash out of the corner of his eye and felt Nova sag slightly against him with relief.

'Just five more,' she whispered.

Nathaniel

Nathaniel watched the entity. Its attention was diverted, sensing what was happening up in James's room, and not on him. He inched away from it as it took up a position at the bottom of the stairs, enjoying a lessening of the oppressive feeling its proximity caused.

The sensation that hit him suddenly was entirely unexpected, and yet he immediately knew what it was: Nova had connected with his energetic field on a level deeper than he had experienced before. It felt like a warm blanket descending around him, covering his head and neck, soothing him, filling him with reassurance that he would be alright. A sudden haze of calm, and as he relaxed into it, he felt the sharpness of the first rip, a sudden stinging sensation as the first cord attaching him to the entity was cut with a little purple flash, freeing his right wrist. He flexed it, hope filling his heart at this lifeline. He hadn't been forgotten; they were trying to help him!

With that came a taste of freedom, a lifting of the heaviness that had clouded his mind since the moment the entity had breached James's room and dragged him down into its territory. Along with it, his motivation to fight was renewed; maybe all was not lost after all.

He willed Nova on, eager to be rid of the rest of the connections. He looked down at the bindings as she tugged at the second one, the sharp pain and then a further lessening of the skin-crawling discomfort followed by further release. He could feel them so clearly once they were gone, their precise location revealed by their absence. His impatience was overwhelming, his desperation to be completely freed before the entity noticed what was happening.

Nova latched onto the third and fourth cords, the ones around his ankles – when the entity turned sharply, its attention suddenly on Nathaniel. Its eyes were blazing, and his heart sank. This was too good to be true; of course it wouldn't let this happen right under its nose. It swept forward, and seized him by his collar.

'It's time!' it hissed with relish, dragging him along as it led the way to the stairs.

Nathaniel stole a sidelong glance at the entity as he felt Nova latch onto the red cord attached to his heart. He couldn't believe his luck – or Nova's skill at shielding her work perhaps – it hadn't realised he was being freed from its control yet.

'Time for what?'

It smiled. 'Chaos and claiming what will be ours. Sooner than I planned, but the witch is far more foolish than I could ever have anticipated!'

James

A low rumbling noise came from somewhere downstairs. Nova stiffened against him; she had heard it too, but she wasn't stopping.

James got up slowly. 'I'll distract it as long as I can,' he told her.

He moved forward cautiously and put his ear to the bedroom door, listening. The rumbling stopped, but then he heard the footsteps slowly coming up the stairs, loud, ominous and heavy.

'Dad?' he called out, knowing the tread was too heavy for his dad and besides, he was miles away, but still clutching at the hope that they had a human explanation.

That distinctive low laugh echoed in the hall outside, and his fear peaked, confirming without a doubt what he already knew: that definitely wasn't his dad.

He glanced back at Nova. She was deep in concentration still, eyes closed and hands moving.

James urged her on, hoping against hope to see the flashes of the remaining cords breaking, to know Nathaniel was free. He knew they were running out of time – the entity would be hellbent on preventing Nathaniel's escape and likely knew exactly what Nova was doing.

Two more purple flashes, one after another in quick succession. They were breaking faster now, and there were just two left. James considered opening the bedroom door, running out onto the landing as a diversion and trying to lead the entity elsewhere, but he never got the chance.

A moment later, many things happened at once: a flash of light, what sounded like a thunderclap but this time from just outside the bedroom, and the impact of what felt like a massive gust of wind hitting James directly, throwing him off his feet and back across the room.

He hit the floor hard, disorientated, and looked up to see a long crack snaking its way up the wall above the doorway. Before he could form a single word of warning, the wall crumbled as if hit by a mighty blow, and chunks of plaster and brickwork came crashing into the room. James stayed down, covering his head with both arms as debris rained down around him.

For a moment, all he knew was deafening noise, the pain of multiple objects hitting him, some heavier than others. Choking dust in his mouth and nose, coughing in the cloud surrounding him, barely able to open his eyes. He screwed them shut and tried to breathe as shallowly as he could until it passed.

In the aftermath, he looked up. The dark hallway was visible in the large gap, an entire section of wall was gone – and with it, the protection spell on the room.

James

James scrambled to his feet, blinking to clear his vision and brushing the worst of the filth from him as he frantically looked for Nova. That was when he realised he had a much bigger problem: she was unconscious. He was at her side in seconds, scooping her off the filthy rug and checking her vitals. She was breathing, but a trickle of blood at her temple and a rapidly forming swelling on her face indicated some of the rubble had hit her hard. Her spell bottle was shattered, the remaining neck of the bottle hanging in a jagged chunk from the cord.

'Nova? Nova!' he begged. 'Please wake up!'

Her eyelids began to flicker, and her hand twitched, giving him hope. But then she went rigid, her face turned to his and her eyes opened; they were gleaming red.

He froze, utterly terrified and completely at a loss as to what to do.

Nova's mouth twisted into an unfamiliar smile, and when she spoke, it wasn't her voice he heard.

'Good evening, James.'

James released her and scrambled backwards. 'Nova, NOVA! Fight it; please wake up—'

Her face twitched and spasmed as she straightened up to her full height and brushed herself off. 'Well, this is nice. I can feel a lot of power here.' The entity flexed Nova's arms. 'A lot of power, but not much common sense, luckily for me!'

'Get out of her!' James shouted, knowing he sounded desperate and panicked but also having no idea what he could do to fix this. 'This can't be happening!'

'Shut up, child!' the entity replied. 'It is happening, and the best part is you have the ignorant witch to thank for that.' It twisted Nova's face in a smug smile. 'Thinking she's so powerful, messing with my energy field, tampering with my cords – as if I would let anyone get away with that! So easy to turn that connection around, and now here I am, exactly what I wanted handed to me on a plate.'

James scrambled for the half-full mug of salt left on his bedside table and flung it directly into Nova's face.

The entity didn't even blink. 'Really?'

'Be gone, in the name of…I don't know…I cast you out; I—'

The entity tossed Nova's head back and laughed. 'Stupid boy! Just give up, will you? You won't have any worries soon; you won't have anything at all. Don't trouble yourself.'

James shook his head. 'No, Nova, I know you're stronger than this thing; fight it!'

Nova's body jerked, a horrible cracking sound coming from multiple joints. It looked as though there was an internal struggle taking place, and he felt a glimmer of hope – but when her body stilled, her eyes were still those of the entity looking back at him.

'Now, enough silliness, it's time to make things final—' Nova's body stepped forward, seizing James by his wrists. 'No point in wasting time, is there?'

He tried to pull away and found that he couldn't; the entity lent her hands a vice-like grip and inhuman strength.

It leered into his face. 'Nathaniel, do it now!'

Nathaniel

In the massive cloud of dust obscuring the threshold, Nathaniel couldn't see much, but he could feel James's undiluted terror pulsing through the atmosphere. And as the dust began to clear, his heart sank. Nova's body was still alive, but all her defences were down.

It didn't matter how prepared you were; it was awful to witness: The wrongness of an intrusive energy forced into a place it didn't belong. The battle of a trapped soul, the manipulation of a powerless body. The entity's inhuman voice coming from a human throat.

'Nathaniel, do it now!'

Familiar panic flared; this night was a horrific mirror of the one on which the entity killed Arthur, and Nathaniel couldn't go through that again. He had to get free; he had to flee from all of this while the entity was otherwise occupied within Nova, slip back into his secret space in the wall to hide. He could come out years from now, when it was all over. Guilt followed that thought. Was he going to allow himself to hide again and let someone he cared for die?

Besides, despite how much he might want to run, there was no longer anywhere truly safe for him to flee. It was pointless; the entity would be able to find him now if it really wanted to; the warding was destroyed.

He took inventory. His throat and midsection were still bound to the entity, but thanks to Nova's work, the tethers were much weaker; his mind was clearer now and his emotions discernible as his own. He almost had free will again, and here he stood at the moral crossroads he had dreamt of so often. This was his chance to redeem himself for failing Arthur, and even if he couldn't do anything to help, he would try. He needed to be strong.

James needed him now more than he ever would, and he didn't deserve a cowardly weakling; he deserved a fighter.

James was still releasing wave after wave of fear, enough to fuel the entity for hours, but Nathaniel could sense Nova's consciousness again, starting to spark up and fight back, distracting the entity.

Nathaniel began to pull at the cords, fraying them like old rope as they became weaker, tugging hard at the one at his throat, struggling to recover his voice.

Nova twitched. To Nathaniel's eyes, she glowed with a strange, sickly light, the mismatch between the energy animating her and her true essence shining clearly.

Nathaniel was pulled closer, the entity dragging on the cord at his throat, exerting what control it could over him, and as he reached Nova, he recalled the entity's instructions from earlier. He could do it; he could feel the possibility now.

It would be easy to do as he had been instructed: to tune into Nova's fear and drain it, feed on it, further weakening her resistance and driving her further under the entity's control. The longer she couldn't regain consciousness, the longer the entity had to carry out the remaining dark ritual to keep her under forever.

And as for James, Nathaniel could feed on his petrified reactions and fill himself with power – before the entity knocked him unconscious with his best friend's hands, allowing Nathaniel to take his form.

Nova's body shook violently with the entity's rage. James was still struggling to get free of its grip, but it was no use.

'*Nathaniel!* Hurry up and drain them!' it growled urgently.

Nathaniel's mind was spinning with how best he could do this. He could go along with it and save James at a later date, but he had to save Nova too somehow. She didn't deserve this fate…but he was running out of time. He paused, another sickening wave of guilt washing over him. If he went along with it, if he took James, would he ever be able to release him? Once he had a taste of his life, would he be able to give it up; could he trust himself?

'NATHANIEL!' The entity tugged hard on the cord at his throat, a crushing, choking sensation forcing compliance. He couldn't delay any longer; he had to do *something.*

Nathaniel placed a hand on Nova's back, starting to draw her energy into himself. He felt sick to know he was draining a human, something he had never done before. He knew how wrong it was, but he saw no other alternative.

He hated how good it felt, how much more powerful it was than draining devices and sucking the light from candles. The energy flowed into him, a surge of light and strength. He ignored the fear and emotions bubbling around and instead pulled in her life force, her pure essence. As he did it, he forced himself to concentrate, and a plan began to form.

He looked at James, struggling and confused at the hands of his best friend, and had to look away. He couldn't allow himself to be distracted; he needed to focus on what he could do.

It was a massive gamble – he knew that – but it was all of their best chances of survival. Using Nova's power, he turned his attention to the remaining two cords and, combining his own strength with hers, he severed them easily in a final flash of blue light.

The entity cursed, 'Stop being selfish, Nathaniel! Disobedience will be punished!'

When he judged he had enough power, he removed his hand from Nova and channelled everything into manifesting himself. James's eyes widened even more when he saw Nathaniel over her shoulder.

The entity let out a growl. 'Not yet, Nathaniel; the witch is still fighting me!' it spat as James wriggled free from its grip.

Nathaniel ignored it, moving forward and putting both of his hands on James's shoulders instead. James inhaled sharply, his eyes widening as he felt Nathaniel tapping into his energy source.

'Trust me, please,' was all Nathaniel said, hoping James would see the truth and intent in his face and know that he was trying to help.

As he collapsed to the floor, Nathaniel went with him, and as James's eyes locked onto Nathaniel's, he saw his shock, how bewildered he was.

'Nathaniel? Why?' he gasped out.

'Just trust me, please!' Nathaniel begged him again. For a long moment, they stared at one another, and then finally, James nodded, sagging back onto the dusty floorboards.

Without any time to waste, Nathaniel dug deeper, finding James's pure essence and stripping it from him, drawing as much of his energy as he could. Dragging it out from underneath the layers of heartbreak and fear, confusion and anxiety.

It was the most wonderful thing Nathaniel had ever connected with. The brilliance of James's essence was breathtaking, and he wished more than anything that the circumstances were different.

His yearning to bask and lose himself almost eclipsed everything else, but he managed to pull himself back. He mustn't get carried away, distracted from his purpose, no matter how intoxicating James was.

Just before James slipped into unconsciousness, Nathaniel pulled away from him and stood up. Nova's body was writhing, the entity letting out a foul stream of curses at her continued resistance.

Nathaniel moved quickly, releasing everything he had just gathered from James in a torrent and hoping it would be enough. He channelled it directly at Nova's authentic energetic signature, and the effect was almost immediate. Her body spasmed and locked into an upright position, suddenly very still. James's golden energy flooded her system; he could see it swirling around her heart, pushing back the grey tendrils of the entity, her own remaining essence flowing out to meet it. The light in her grew, visibly loosening the sickly grip of the entity.

Her eyes flashed from the entity's characteristic redness back into their usual hazel; a few flickers back and forth, and then they became clear and steady again.

She opened her mouth, howling as the smoky form of the entity burst forth, expelled from her body. She coughed, doubled over and looked as though she might vomit – then fell to her knees.

Nathaniel stood for a moment, overwhelmed with delight at what he had accomplished, and then realised he was in very real trouble.

James was coming around, clearly able to see the two entities in front of him now, but Nathaniel knew that was no use to him. There was nothing either of the humans could do to help him; he'd done his best for them, and now he would face the consequences.

The entity snarled, 'You little traitor; I'll DESTROY YOU!'

It lunged forward, and Nathaniel ran.

Nathaniel

Nathaniel fled down the stairs blindly, with no idea where he could go that would do anything but delay the inevitable. It wouldn't be long now before he ceased to exist, and he was frightened, but he consoled himself that it would probably be fast, and James would know Nathaniel had done everything he could to help. He would know how deeply he cared, even if he could never say those words to him out loud.

The entity's presence at Nathaniel's back drove him onwards, a desperate need to evade the terror for even a few more seconds. He felt its all-consuming rage as a dense pressure in the air just behind him, an icy-cold cloud of smoke about to envelop him forever. He tried one last attempt to leave the house, flinging himself at the back door into the garden, hoping that if he couldn't escape, at least he could pass amongst the trees one last time, choose the location of his last moments – but the invisible forcefield flung him back, as it always had.

The entity swept in, and he dodged to the side, making it as far as the corridor leading to the garage before it cornered him.

It advanced, its maw opening, its enraged state blurring its features into a monstrous visage. It was the thing he had always feared the most, and it was happening after all. This was how it would all end for him, after centuries of this strange existence.

At least there was meaning to it now. The events in James's bedroom finally made the years of torment worth it. He had held on to save them. He had resisted temptation, and he had done the right thing. He knew now the true measure of himself. When the chips were down, he had been brave and selfless; he had pushed away both the cowardly desire to hide and the darker inclination to take James's life for himself. Everything he'd ever wanted, and he had the strength to turn away because his morals were still stronger than his deepest longings. He could find peace in his last moments on the earthly plane and take that knowledge with him into whatever followed.

As he faced the looming energy, it started to feel almost like a relief, the idea of letting go and giving in. Sinking into the shadows and finally releasing his grasp on himself, his humanity. It was peace, of sorts.

The entity's smoky form surrounded him, the daylight fading away in the dark cloud blanketing his senses, the foulness making his skin crawl. When the entity spoke, its voice reverberated around him, coming from everywhere all at once. 'I offered you everything, and you threw it in my face, all for the sake of two worthless humans! I came back to help you, and *this* is how you thank me!'

'They aren't worthless, and you know it,' Nathaniel replied, finding his fear was oddly gone now he'd accepted his fate. 'And how was any of this for me? You're not making sense. You're the one who wants what the humans have more than anything; you're the worthless one, seething and wallowing down here instead of—'

Red eyes swam in the fog above him as the entity lashed out with what felt like a backhand to his face, the impact stunning Nathaniel. 'Shut up, you stupid little ghost!'

'You say *ghost* as though it isn't what you are too!' Nathaniel shot back defiantly. 'At least there was a reason for me to haunt this house. What's your purpose? You don't belong here; you're just—'

'BE SILENT!' it roared, the jarring pitch of its voice hurting Nathaniel's ears. 'Ungrateful creature, you should be so honoured I even noticed you exist!'

The entity closed in tighter, exhaling foul smoke into his face, drowning him. It felt like he was being dragged away, bound to it all over again, but this time forever, total absorption. There were no cords, no separation, just oneness and nothingness all at once. The boundaries of where he ended and it began were blurring; he could feel himself slipping. There was nothing anymore, just an endless dark void and then – the melding sensation stopped. He started to come back into himself, an awareness of his edges and selfhood. The darkness lightened to grey; the physical world became visible through the grey haze. Then the pressure lifted, and he could move again.

A howl of rage and pure frustration poured from the entity, an eardrum-shattering sound that made Nathaniel cringe.

The sound went on and on, but he realised suddenly that nothing was changing for him. He was not being bound to the entity, nor was it attempting to absorb him again as it had threatened so many times.

'Why can't I destroy you?' it roared, its distorted face terrifyingly close to his. 'I have eaten spirits before, but you—what *are* you?'

Nathaniel was lost for words. 'I…I don't know.'

The entity screamed again, recoiling from him and turning away, sweeping from the room and out of sight. Nathaniel remained where he was for a moment, blinking in the light from the hallway as he sensed its movement away from him and back to its preferred lurking area underneath the garage.

Tentatively, he stepped forward, running his hands down his arms, connecting with himself again as a distinct soul, separate from the thing that had tried to taint him with its closeness. If he were human, he would be in desperate need of a bath right now, something ritualistically cleansing.

But he wasn't a human. And yet, somehow, the entity was confused by what he was. It wasn't a question he had ever asked himself. He had been a human, then he died. Therefore, logically, he assumed he was a ghost. Had something changed recently, or had he always been somehow mistaken about what he was?

He shook himself. There was no time to waste in musings; the most important thing now was to make sure James and Nova were alright. He would have plenty of time in the future to ponder the nature of his existence.

He made for the stairs, a newfound confidence flooding in as it hit him: the entity had no power over him anymore. Unless it came up with some other way to hurt him, he was currently safe from it. For the first time since it had come creeping into the house all those years ago, he could step out from the shadow of that threat. He could exist without fear, at least for the moment.

He knew there were questions that needed to be answered, and he didn't have a full understanding of the situation yet, but for now, it had gone into retreat. It had given up trying to hurt him.

James

James drew in a slow, agonising breath. His throat was raw, his chest tight, and his whole body was heavy. He rolled onto his hands and knees and pushed himself into a seated position. Just moving felt like the hardest workout of his life. He blinked, trying to clear the fog in his mind, to find order in the blurred memories. There were gaps. He recalled the events of the last few minutes in snapshots only, still images with missing time in between. Staring at Nova's face and not seeing her looking back, bloodshot eyes, dilated pupils, a vicious stranger contorting her features. The grip she had on him with those unforgiving hands; he could feel bruises forming already, aching and swelling beneath the skin of his forearms.

And then Nathaniel, more solid than he'd ever looked before, his concerned expression, his conflicted, haunted gaze. His pleas for trust as he had somehow sucked the life from James, the blackness clawing at the edges of his consciousness, the sound of the blood whistling through his ears like reeds in a high wind. Then hitting the ground, Nathaniel stepping away.

Then what? He looked across at where Nova was crouching, her head down, breathing heavily.

'Nova…is it—are you…you?'

Her head snapped up, and there was clarity in her eyes; his friend was looking back at him. The relief was overwhelming.

'You're back! How…what happened?'

She moved to his side. 'We'll get to that, but are *you* okay?'

'Me? I think so, just really tired.'

'Okay, we're both alright, we think. That's something.'

'I'm having to fight to not lie down on the floor and sleep, though,' James admitted, 'which hardly makes sense considering how terrifying the last hour has been.'

'What happened to you while I was gone?' She shuddered, her words tumbling out in an anxious jumble. 'I remember the wall crumbling and then nothing – until I was suddenly aware my body was moving, had grabbed you, and I was here but not here. I could hear a voice coming out of my mouth, and it wasn't mine, but I couldn't say anything. I was aware; I could only see and hear these flashes, nothing coherent, and this other voice was talking *inside my head*, and something else was moving my muscles. It was…I was so scared I might never come back, never make it out or be me again!'

James reached out, and she came to him for a hug; she was still shaking.

'After you were knocked out and possessed, Nathaniel appeared. The entity was expecting him to do something, I don't know what it was, but he didn't do it. He told me to trust him and sucked out some of my energy. Then he touched you and vanished off somewhere.'

Nova pulled back and stared at James. 'Oh! I get it now! I think…I saw him too when he touched me, then I started to feel again…it was what gave me the strength to fight back and win.' Her eyes widened. 'And that was…your energy? It makes sense now; it felt so familiar. So familiar I thought it came from me.'

She looked around. 'Where is Nathaniel now? And the entity? Where did they go?'

James's heart began to race when he thought about the likely conclusion. 'I think he must have fled, and it pursued him.'

'We have to help him!'

'I want to, Nova, but I don't think I'd be much use to anyone right now; I'm so exhausted. And I don't think it's safe for you to intervene. I know you know a lot about all of this, so I don't mean to be rude, but I don't think this is going very well so far, is it?'

Nova sighed and stood up, going to the mirror and checking the swelling on her face, touching the dried blood on her head with a wince. She frowned, brushed the dust from her clothes and went to her bag, returning to James's side. 'I'm not giving up, James, and neither should you. There's no alternative.' She started pouring a circle of salt around the bed. 'We'll rest here a while and make a plan.'

James struggled to his feet and then collapsed onto the bed. 'Can the plan be waiting until I have the energy to run away forever?'

Caspian Faye

The appearance of Nathaniel at the foot of the bed made them both jump.

'That's not a bad plan, to be honest with you,' he said.

James struggled back into a seated position, Nathaniel's presence alone lending him a small amount of energy, his mood improving at the sight of him safe and well, if not alive, and if only for now. Then a thought struck him. 'Wait…are you—'

Nova rested a hand on James's shoulder. 'He's him, and he's clear of the entity's influence or control; I can tell. The cords are gone. Nathaniel, its, ah, nice to meet you properly,' Nova addressed him, and he bowed with a smile.

'And you, too. I wish it were in more favourable circumstances.'

James vaguely registered how cute Nathaniel's genuine smile was before he refocused on matters at hand. 'Nathaniel, can you help us out here? What exactly is going on?'

'Before we get to all that, I think I should put right the imbalance from earlier.'

Nova nodded and moved to Nathaniel's side. 'I agree; please do.'

He lightly placed an almost-transparent hand on her back for a few moments, closing his eyes. When he opened them, he beckoned to James, who got up with effort and came to stand where Nathaniel indicated. He placed his other hand on James's chest, a feather-light energetic touch that he could barely sense. He imagined it would be rude to step forward and watch Nathaniel's hand pass through him, so he remained still, and the illusion of two solid forms meeting one another remained.

Nathaniel closed his eyes again, and James waited. Suddenly, he felt a warm sensation where Nathaniel's hand was and the inexplicable sense of energy flowing into him, running down his limbs in threads, spreading out and expanding.

'I'm just putting back what I can,' Nathaniel explained softly, 'the excess of what I took from you earlier to help Nova. I took all I could safely take from you, just in case. But she only needed a little to fight her way back. The remainder I can return, and your body will recover the rest in time.'

A few moments later, he nodded. 'I'm finished.'

James stretched out his arms and yawned; he felt more or less normal again. 'That's so much better. Thank you so much, Nathaniel.'

Nathaniel smiled again. 'It's not much, but I'm glad it helped.'

'No, it's everything. What you did earlier, I can never thank you enough.'

Nathaniel looked down; his expression bashful but clearly delighted. 'Well, I couldn't have helped at all if Nova hadn't done whatever magic she did to free me.'

Nova turned back to them both. 'That was nothing compared to what you did, and we can never thank you enough, Nathaniel; James is right.' She took a deep breath. 'And obviously, we're about to ask for more help.'

Nathaniel nodded. 'Of course. The entity is…dormant for now, so we've got some breathing room. But that's all it is: a temporary setback in its plan. It'll be back.'

A wave of relief washed over James at Nathaniel's update, but it was soon followed by rising concern about what was coming.

'What's been going on, Nathaniel?' he asked. 'Where were you?'

'It took me captive for a while, after it broke the ward on this room the first time. I learnt as much as I could about its plans, but there's still a lot I don't understand about who it really is or was and why it couldn't absorb me just now. It caught me, and it tried but…I'm hoping maybe you'll be able to help me find some answers, Nova.'

She nodded. 'I'll try my best, but wow, this is a lot.'

'Shouldn't we do more to keep ourselves safe first?' James interrupted. 'This room is unwarded again, our protection bottles are smashed…apart from some salt, when it comes back, we're sitting ducks.'

Nathaniel

'I'll take care of that, don't worry,' Nova said, rooting in her bag and pulling out the ingredients for more protective spell casting.

Nathaniel watched as she deftly wove herbs and ribbons around one another, lit some incense and brought out more candles and pieces of wood. It all looked familiar, reminded him once again of Agatha and Arthur – but none of that had helped Arthur in the end.

'What's to stop it from just smashing up more of the house and destroying this all over again?' James asked.

Nathaniel gazed at him, impressed by how he managed to be so blunt and yet sound so kind about it at the same time.

'It's weak now,' Nathaniel offered by way of reassurance. 'It used a lot of energy over the last few hours, and it hasn't been able to replenish it yet. Maybe if we can do enough warding, it will hold long enough for us to work out how to banish it.'

'Why can't it just…do what you did earlier, Nathaniel?' James asked, his warm eyes curious.

Nathaniel fought to retain focus on the matter at hand; James looking directly at him after their time apart was an overwhelming experience. The closest thing he could compare it to was his vague memory of what it felt like to step out into the first days of summer heat.

'I…well, that's one of my questions for Nova,' he said, before adding, 'and you.'

James laughed. 'It's okay, you don't have to pretend I know much about this stuff; I won't be offended.'

Nathaniel smiled at him again. 'Good, that's the last thing I want.' He immediately felt silly, wishing he could have said something more intelligent or witty. He wanted James to like him so much it seemed to damage his ability to communicate. James was still smiling at him, though, their eye contact starting to feel like a conversation all of its own. Although he told himself sternly that it wouldn't do to get carried away again; it was just yet more wishful thinking on his part.

Nova cleared her throat. 'Right, best use this time to figure out what's going on. Nathaniel, fire away.'

'Fire what?' Nathaniel asked.

'It's just a phrase.' James reached out as if to brush Nathaniel's shoulder, and his fingertips grazed the edge of his energy, startling Nathaniel. He had *felt* it. Not just in the usual energetic way, but in an almost-physical sense, like in the garden, a little spark passing through him as a result of the contact. He looked at James, wondering if he had felt that too.

James pulled back. 'Sorry—habit. You just…'

Nova cleared her throat again. 'Let's get going. Come on, give me what you've got, Nathaniel.'

Nathaniel turned away from James with effort, fighting the magnetic pull constantly dragging his attention in that direction. 'I don't quite understand what happened earlier. The entity, it tried to absorb me, and it should have been able to. Many years ago, it absorbed other ghosts.' Nathaniel hated recalling those nights, but he made himself do it. It was important. 'It was during one of the séances the twins loved to have.'

'The twins being Arthur and Agatha Gadsby?' Nova interjected.

Nathaniel nodded, impressed at her research and how quick she was to piece things together. 'Yes, the first was a lost soul they often called in, a sailor who had died of old age near here and not quite realised he had passed. He was a gentle energy, harmless.'

'And what happened to him?'

Nathaniel paused, and Nova gave him an encouraging smile. 'I know it's horrible, but we need to know.'

'The entity absorbed him. He…the best way I can describe it would be to say it assimilated him, used the remnants of his soul to add to its power. I saw him screaming in agony as he tried to get away, and then this awful calm, this blankness came over his features, and he faded, dispersed into the entity's depths. Just…became a part of that shadowy mass.'

'And the others?' James asked.

'Arthur was the second, and…well, I didn't witness all of it; I couldn't bear…' Nathaniel paused, trying to keep his tone matter-of-fact and state the events of that night without being overpowered by the emotions attached to the memories. 'He was my friend; he was family. In a way that my blood kin weren't…' Nathaniel broke off for a moment to compose himself and then continued. 'Agatha saw everything; she helped him as much as anyone could have. He was possessed and then broke free but was possessed again. I think she told me a total of five times in all. Then his body gave out. He died fighting, but then before the light appeared for him, before anyone could do anything…it had already swallowed him up.'

'The light?' James asked.

'It's like a doorway that appears when someone passes, so their soul can leave this plane of existence.' Nathaniel explained. Nova nodded.

'Right, I get it. So, did you just decide to ignore the doorway and stay here when you died?' James blurted out without thinking, curiosity clearly getting the better of him.

Nathaniel didn't want to go into that now, so he just shrugged. 'After a fashion. Anyway, the entity, it threatened me: if I didn't help it to possess you, Nova, and if I didn't possess James myself and join it in its plans going forward, then it would swallow me up and use my soul for power.'

Both James and Nova exchanged worried looks.

'I wanted to warn you' Nathaniel pointed out, 'but I didn't have the chance, and besides, you wouldn't have heard me anyway, not with the spell bottle on.'

James clapped a hand over his mouth, 'Oh! I never thought—damn, I'm stupid sometimes.'

'No, it's alright; I understand!' Nathaniel reassured him hurriedly, trying to hide how happy he was at the revelation that James had not shut him out intentionally. 'It was good to protect yourself.'

'So…that was its plan, Nathaniel? That you would take my life?' James asked softly.

He nodded. 'Don't worry, I would never have done it under any circumstances!' he replied urgently. 'And if I'd had to possess you, then I had a back-up plan to get your body out of the house and set you free!'

James just stared at him; his face suddenly hard to read.

'Then what?' Nova asked. 'Talk me through what happened after you disobeyed it.'

Nathaniel tried to focus on her words, but his anxiety at James's inscrutable expression was distracting. 'It chased me. I thought it would follow through on its threat. Even weakened, it's so much stronger than I am. But when it came to do it, it just couldn't.'

'Couldn't? Why not? It grew a conscience suddenly?' James asked.

Reassured by his kind tone, Nathaniel relaxed. 'No, it physically couldn't. It had no power over me. I was thinking maybe the cord cutting Nova did earlier was the cause of that?'

Nova frowned. 'No, that might stop it attaching to you again, but it wouldn't have protected you from something like that.'

'It also, well, it asked what I am.'

Nova nodded slowly. 'Actually, I've been wondering that myself.'

'You have?' asked Nathaniel and James in unison.

'Well, yes. It's considered standard within the paranormal world that ghosts can feed off the emotions of humans and manipulate them to some extent, but that's just a matter of engaging with the energy they're giving off, draining energy that's already been released from the body.'

'Like the entity has been doing with my dad's heartbreak?' James clarified.

Nova nodded. 'Exactly. But what Nathaniel did earlier…actively engaging with your life force, transferring some of it to me so I could expel the entity and then transferring some back again, that's advanced energy work that should really only be possible in the realms of the living.' When they both said nothing, she continued. 'As in, living beings interacting with living energy.'

Nathaniel had never been so confused in his life, or death. 'Surely that just raises more questions than answers?'

Nova pursed her lips. 'In life, were you a magic worker? Advanced spell work and the like? Or some kind of energy healer?'

Nathaniel shook his head. 'No, I was, at best, a dabbler. A very mild dabbler. I was curious, and I'd heard whispers of people like me being able to work with the occult arts to be more…themselves. Making their outsides match their souls.'

Nova nodded. 'Go on.'

'So, I…well…people weren't that open, back then, about interests in such things. Do you know of the witch trials?'

'Of course, it's a painful but important time in history for someone like me.'

Nathaniel nodded. 'I'm sorry to bring it up.'

'It's alright; it's relevant.'

'It was something I kept to myself, my interest that is. Even before I ever really did anything, I was already being cautioned against being seen as different.'

Nathaniel thought back to the childhood friends who had started to distance themselves from him long before his family had turned on him. That had hurt worse. He had trusted them. They were supposed to love him for who he was; they were supposed to understand, to see him – but no one had, until Theodore and his coven.

'Nathaniel?' James's soft voice broke into his reverie.

'Yes, sorry. I—what was I saying? Oh yes, I was already considered…odd. But all I had learnt of was nature magic, sensing energy, tuning into it. Sitting in silence and finding peace in connection with the beautiful old tree out there, in the garden…' He sighed. 'Using my imagination…it was where I found relief, losing myself in a greater oneness, escaping into stories, leaving my body to explore other realms.'

Nathaniel glanced at James. 'But it wasn't enough. I wanted more, and when I met someone who thought they could give me what I needed, I couldn't resist. Theodore. He was a sorcerer, and I thought he would be my salvation. In more ways than one. I…well, I came to love him, and I trusted him completely and the coven he vouched for. So he brought them here one night under a full moon. We did a ritual. It had been planned for a while, but it all went horribly wrong.'

'Fascinating! And this ritual, how did it kill you exactly?'

James shot Nova a look, and Nathaniel smiled at him, touched by the concern for his feelings. 'It's alright, James. We don't have much time; directness is rather necessary. And it is quite fascinating, in a way.'

'These are painful memories, though. I'm sorry you have to drag it all up again and again.'

Nathaniel shrugged. 'It was so long ago, and the long stretches of sleep…they do help to numb the pain, make it more distant. Besides, my memory of the details and the ritual itself are still quite patchy.'

'Of course, I understand. I just wish there was a way to find out—' Nova stopped speaking suddenly, her face lighting up. 'I've got it!'

James smiled at Nathaniel. 'When she gets like this, something wild is about to happen. Best buckle in.'

Nova gave him a light shove. 'Wilder than this evening has already been? That'll take some doing…'

James nodded, 'I'd bet anything on it.'

Nathaniel was still enjoying the sense of connection from James's comment. Being included in their jokes felt like a warm arm around his shoulders.

Nova took a deep breath. 'Well, you're not wrong, James. I've got an idea, and I think if it works, it could be exactly what we need.'

Nathaniel and James both looked at her expectantly.

'It won't be easy, and I can't lie and say it isn't dangerous, but…we need to go back in time to see that ritual.'

James

'Not to seem like I don't have faith in you, because I really do, but also…what the hell?'

Nova shot James a determined look. 'I can do it, but I'll need both of you to help.'

James met Nathaniel's gaze. He saw fear but also strength and determination. The ghost nodded. 'I'll do what I can to assist. What do you need from me?'

'Thanks, Nathaniel. I'm going to cast a circle, and you and James will join me within it. I need you to focus on the night of the ritual as much as you can – the scents, the sights, details, the feeling of it. Your fragmented memories, patchy though they are, will provide an anchor point for me. Once I've located the right spot in time, we should be fine.'

'Hang on, *should*?' James interrupted. 'Nova, I know we need answers, but is this a risk that's actually worth taking? Can't we just try and see a residual echo like earlier?'

'No, a residual echo won't hack it! I need detail; I need to see and hear. We need our own timeslip in technicolour surround sound.'

'But the risk, Nova, it—'

'James! After the last few hours, I'm done playing small. We're in too deep for that now, and we're dealing with big, powerful forces. If we don't rise to the occasion, we'll drown, and I'm not choosing that for us.'

The hairs on the back of James's neck rose. 'Isn't there a third option? We don't rise to the occasion and risk getting in further than we can handle, and we also don't stay here to drown. We get out now.'

Nova stared at him. 'Run away?'

In the silence that followed, Nathaniel spoke quietly. 'I can't run away. I can't leave this house.'

James looked at him, saw the sadness in Nathaniel's expression before he covered it with a forced smile and hastily added, 'But you should run away if that's what you want. It's a good idea!'

James shook his head. 'I didn't mean run away, more retreat and get reinforcements.'

'Would you be safe here if we were to do that?' Nova asked Nathaniel.

He gave a little shrug in response. 'No way to say for sure, but I think so. I think it can't hurt me anymore – or at least, not for now. You two are the only ones in any actual danger from it.'

James thought about Nathaniel left here alone, his future safety uncertain, and he shook his head. 'No, if we can't all go, I don't want to go. Let's get on with this.'

Nathaniel's face brightened. 'I…that means a lot, thank you.'

'Well, we're a team now, aren't we?' James replied, eager to reassure him he wouldn't be left behind.

Nathaniel moved into the circle in response, his expression now set to one of resolve. The decisive movement was all Nova needed, and she started lighting her candles and incense again, pulling out a battered old book from her bag and leafing through it until she found whatever she was looking for.

James sat down opposite Nova and waited until she looked up, giving him a nod. 'Focus your energy on me. Listen to my voice and copy my chant as closely as you can, got it?'

He nodded, allowing her to take his hands in hers. He was caught between anticipating what was to come with a thrill of excitement and his fear of the same. The whole situation felt so far out of his comfort zone, but Nova's soothing voice and the flickering of the candlelight was hypnotic. He could feel his consciousness changing as the moments slipped by. He began to lose track of time, his eyelids heavy and drooping almost all the way closed as he focused on Nova's voice, copying her intonations as much as he could. At some point, she stopped chanting, and his awareness shrank right down to the dance of the candle flames and the steady hum of energy around them. Then he became aware of chanting again, but it wasn't Nova's voice; it was other, unfamiliar voices. With effort, he forced his eyes further open. They were still in his room, but it didn't look like his room as he knew it. It was full of antique furniture, lit with an old lamp and candles, and inhabited by strange people.

Nova was also looking around, her eyes wide. She shot him a look of awe and tightened her grip on his hands – in an effort to contain her reaction and not freak out, he assumed. The shock that it had worked was also flooding through him, waking him up more effectively than a double espresso.

He glanced at where Nathaniel stood, and his breath caught. Nathaniel was transfixed, silent tears running down his face as he stared at the other people in the room.

James followed his gaze to where the strangers were gathered in a circle near the bay window. A handsome, theatrical young man dressed in a velvet cloak who appeared to be the leader immediately drew his attention. Undoubtedly, this was Theodore.

James saw a slight resemblance to himself in the stranger's features and wondered what kind of person he would have been if he'd lived back in those days. Then the coven members began to spread out and lower themselves to the ground, forming a circle, and his attention was drawn to the frightened-looking youngster who crouched on the floor amongst them. It was unmistakably a much younger Nathaniel.

It looked like him, and yet not like him at all. James could see hints of the Nathaniel he knew. He wore the same clothing, and as he looked on, he recognised familiar mannerisms. The way Nathaniel stared at the people around him, seeking reassurance. The familiar tilt of the head, the way he pursed his lips and stuck out his chin, choosing to put on a brave face in this uncertain moment. James recognised that well.

But despite the echoes of the boy he knew, there was more that was unfamiliar to him. James was struck by his frailty, the way in which he seemed somehow caved in on himself, not wanting to take up space. His body looked half-starved and his face sunken. The distress in his eyes, alternating with faint flickers of hope and badly concealed fear. He seemed less real somehow, despite appearing in solid human form. Oddly, the Nathaniel who was living in that past moment looked more like a ghost than ever.

James stood up, transfixed by the potential he could see, the truth that was yet to be revealed. He took a step forward without realising and felt Nova's hand on his trouser leg.

'Don't leave the circle!' she hissed. 'You could get stuck in the wrong time.'

He stopped, feeling sick at how easily he might have done it.

Nathaniel, however, was drifting closer, almost standing on the edge of the circle.

James leant forward. 'Is that—'

Nova nodded. 'I think he's fine. He's timeless; he was there then and is still here now.'

James hoped she was right and they weren't causing some catastrophic time rupture by allowing Nathaniel to wander around.

'So, now what?' he asked.

'Uh, maybe you could stay still so I don't have to worry about you getting stuck in the wrong time and place?'

'Sorry.' James sat back down and watched in silence.

The magic workers had joined hands around Nathaniel's past self, who was lying on the ground, arms outstretched. One of the cloaked figures leant forwards holding a ceremonial knife and drew a symbol in the air with the blade before lowering it and making a series of light cuts across Nathaniel's palms. He was biting hard on his lip, his hands clenching into fists when the knife was withdrawn, his blood trickling out onto the floor in crimson threads. His fear was now obvious, but so was his desperate need to go through with this, whatever it was. James recognised his spirit in that alone.

The magic workers began to chant, their eyes closed as they raised their arms over the shaking boy on the floor. He lay wide-eyed, staring at the ceiling above.

Nathaniel still stood watching his own history play out before him, but as the chanting continued, he stepped closer, kneeling down beside his past self and reaching out a hand.

James gasped, but Nova shook her head. 'It's fine. I think.'

Nathaniel gently rested his outstretched hand on his younger self's forearm, and James watched as his bloody fist slowly unclenched.

For a long moment, they seemed frozen together like that: the two Nathaniels, past and present, both crying silent tears in unison.

Then something changed in the room, a shift in energy. The candles began to flicker aggressively, the spell workers' chanting intensified, and Nathaniel's younger self let out a gasp, his eyes widening and his body spasming as his back arched, lifting his torso off the ground.

The spell workers' heads turned; glances were exchanged from beneath the hoods of their cloaks, but they carried on. The leader gestured to them not to stop. Living Nathaniel spasmed again, letting out a scream, and Nova clutched at James's hand again.

Nathaniel leant down and started whispering to the past version of himself, who was thrashing around, his limbs snapping out and twitching unnaturally. With one final scream, the broken boy shuddered and fell back to the floor, his eyes still wide open but his body motionless. Nathaniel stood up and backed away, as if giving the past events space to unfold; whatever he had said, he was done now.

For a while longer, there was only the increasingly desperate chanting of the spell workers; their leader wasn't permitting them to stop.

Nathaniel reached the salt circle and stood beside James. The tears had stopped flowing, but his eyes still held residual sadness. James wished more than anything that he could get up and hold him, wrap his arms around a solid version of him and give comfort. He couldn't imagine what he had gone through then, what he was still going through as he relived it all.

Nova swore, drawing James's gaze back to the ritual. Immediately, he saw what had prompted the reaction: past Nathaniel was dispersing into the air. A golden light from within him was emerging, but his body was drifting apart in a mist of tiny particles, spreading out and fading away. As they stared, his physical form slowly vanished, leaving only the golden light, hovering and humming, its edges blurring as it moved. It began to shrink, growing smaller and smaller until it vanished.

One by one, the spell workers broke the circle as they panicked. One of them stood, looking all around, gesturing wildly as another frantically rifled through their leather satchel. The others followed, their panic infectious.

'What have we done? What have we done?' one of them repeated.

The leader stood, his eyes filled with rage. 'You broke the circle, idiots! The spell has failed! All that preparation for nothing, damn you!'

Another one, shaking their head, began to gather all the magic accoutrements from the floor, fumbling in haste. 'We should never have done this! We've gone and *killed* him!'

At this, two of the witches fled out the bedroom door, the others quickly following on their heels. The leader pulled the hood of his cloak up and gestured to the remaining coven member, a very nervous-looking young man. 'Make yourself useful for once. Clean up this mess and then get out of here!'

As the man scrambled to follow the orders given, the leader took one last look around the room, tossed his cloak over one shoulder, lifted the sash window and slipped through into the night. The last remaining member of his coven snuffed the candles out and climbed after him, leaving the room in darkness. A few moments later, a golden pinprick was visible, hovering and growing in size again.

The golden light gradually began to take shape; slowly it re-formed into Nathaniel as James had always known him.

He looked around and then down at himself, his expression excited by his new form. He moved to the mirror, and his overwhelming joy became apparent. He ran his hands down his torso, checked his face, spun around, and only then seemed to notice he was in darkness, alone.

James looked to present-day Nathaniel, curious to see his reaction, but he had stepped away and averted his eyes, turning his back on his past self. James looked back at the moment from the past and finally understood what he did not want to relive: the realisation that was coming.

James watched as Nathaniel's past self ran to the lamp to light the room and better see his new reflection, but his hand passed right through it.

He staggered, his face full of confusion as he tried again and again to touch it before reality hit him.

For a moment, he froze, staring into nothingness as he tried to grasp his situation. Then something seemed to break within him, and he dropped to his knees, letting out a whimper of despair, curling into himself, his head in his hands.

Nova turned away. 'We've seen enough.'

She blew out the candles within their circle, and the old room faded, taking Nathaniel's past with it, until they were back in James's room in the present moment.

James looked around at the return of the brick dust, debris and mess, and still preferred it to what he had just witnessed. He looked at Nathaniel, but he was still turned away, hugging himself with both arms.

'Nathaniel, are you…' James trailed off. Asking if he was alright just seemed so ridiculous. He took a deep breath and tried again. 'Nathaniel, I'm here.'

He didn't turn around or acknowledge James's words.

James turned to Nova, expecting to see her face reflecting his own sadness, but her eyes were shining. 'I know what happened! And it's okay – we can *fix* it!'

Nathaniel

Nathaniel didn't want James to see him cry like this, but he also did. It was very confusing. Part of him wanted the privacy of retreat, to go back into the familiar, comforting, darkness of the wall. To sink back into sleep and the safety of not feeling. To accept that his future lay in not having, in not being. The other part of him wanted to turn around, wanted James to look at him with those eyes full of empathy, to open his arms and tell him he didn't deserve what happened to him. That he didn't deserve the horrible accident and, in the aftermath, to be abandoned by Theodore, the one person he thought really cared, when he needed him the most.

He felt it all again, his frustration rising that all the years since had not lessened the impact of the abandonment. He didn't want Theodore anymore, had not wanted him for years – but the longing for someone to stay was agonisingly powerful. It was all he wanted, back then and still now, if he was honest. Someone to stand up and be counted, someone to remain at his side and mean it when they said they were there for him, someone to make him feel less alone, someone to prove to him he mattered.

In the early, disorientating days following the ritual, he had thought of nothing else, his existence reduced to a hopeful vigil for Theodore's return. Sitting in the window every night watching for a sign; a note, a letter, a signal – anything to show him he wasn't forgotten. When nothing came, he told himself his beloved was merely delayed by planning a new spell, researching and gathering supplies.

But time wore on, and one day, his mother entered his room in her mourning black, with a pinched, tight face. She stood with her rigid back and dry eyes, indicating to her maid to clear away Nathaniel's things. Most of it he didn't care for, but he still screamed at them both to stop. Neither of them could hear him, completely oblivious to his objections. When his mother had pulled out his journals, his cherished, battered journals full of his stories, he'd howled at her. The tendrils of loose hair framing her face had fluttered, and yet she still hadn't reacted. Instead, she'd walked to the window and closed it, tossing his journals into a sack for disposal. Looking at them discarded, never to be opened again, was the moment he realised his mortal life was truly over.

The crushing certainty hit him then: no-one was coming for him, and Theodore was gone forever. Accepting the horrible truth, that the one person he had counted on, who knew him intimately, had decided he was worthless – what did that say about him, really?

Time had passed, more time than he had perhaps realised. When his mother left that afternoon, she turned the key in the lock again, perhaps out of habit, perhaps intentionally, and although the locked door was no barrier to Nathaniel anymore, he still turned away and stepped into the wall for the very first time.

Nathaniel sighed, his heart heavy as his non-corporeal body recalled the energy of that day. He wasn't sure why he'd felt compelled to speak to his past self when he knew his words would fall on deaf ears, but somehow, it had still felt important to do. To send himself some loving energy, to whisper the words he longed to hear, both then and now. *'You are not alone. I'm here; you've got me. You've always got me.'*

He drew his arms tighter around himself and looked at the wall. Perhaps it would be for the best if he went away again now. He ran it through in his head. His existence was overcomplicating this whole situation for James and Nova. If he vanished, they could leave, not held back out of a sense of loyalty to him. Ultimately, their safety was much more important. It meant the world to him how much they had done already; he shouldn't allow them to do more.

Without him as a consideration, James could get on with his life. Nathaniel could be strong, exercise self-control and stay away, hiding in the wall until James left. One day, long after he'd gone, Nathaniel could come out again and look back on these days as the best of his existence.

He resolved to do it, but he couldn't resist one more glance at James. He wanted to remember his beautiful face for eternity.

James was staring at him, his eyes alight. 'Did you hear that, Nathaniel?'

'What?'

Nova stood up. 'We can fix it! I finally understand what happened to you, and we can bring you back!'

'Bring me back? From the dead?' Nathaniel shook his head. 'I can't allow you to even try that. I know enough to be certain that's incredibly dangerous dark magic and unlikely to work in the way you might hope.'

James stood up too, his gaze moving to Nova. 'Are you really suggesting necromancy?'

She shook her head. 'No! Not at all! The thing is, Nathaniel *isn't dead*!'

James stared at her. 'Have you lost it?'

Nathaniel moved back to her, reaching out a hand that passed through her arm. 'What is a ghost if not the essence of the deceased?' he asked.

'Look, Nathaniel, the coven you knew, they were good, just not good enough.'

She walked to the bay window, gesturing at the spot where moments before they had watched a ritual from several hundred years ago. 'They had the right idea, and they managed the first stage of the spell. They separated your essence from your physical form, but they never completed the spell. They didn't reform your body around your essence; they just…left you, floating.' She gestured around the space. 'You never actually died; you just got disassembled.'

James moved to join her, looking around as though he could somehow find the answers in thin air. 'What does this actually mean for Nathaniel? What can we do?'

Nova grinned. 'I won't bore you with a lecture on the intersection of physics and magic, but essentially, we can give Nathaniel physical form again, and we'll be working *with* the forces of nature, not against them.'

James frowned. 'If nature wanted him to be in physical form again, why isn't he already?'

Nova shrugged. 'I'm not sure. Perhaps the entity in the house is somehow preventing that harmony, disturbing the laws of what should be. Or maybe…wait—' She started pacing, her eyes flicking from side to side and one hand turning in the air as though she was trying to physically grab her next thought.

James stepped closer to Nathaniel, so close he could feel his breath when he whispered. 'She always does this when she's thinking. Give her a moment.'

Nathaniel's non-corporeal heart was beating faster than ever before, his limbs shaking, his muscles clenching wildly. Desperate hope filled him; this level of wanting was beyond anything he'd ever experienced.

Suddenly, Nova stopped dead in her tracks. Her head snapped up, and a wide grin spread across her face. 'Yes! That's it!'

Nathaniel managed to form words, but it was an effort, his voice cracking, 'Yes, what? Is there really a chance, Nova?'

Nova reached him in a few bounds, her eyes flicking between James and Nathaniel. 'I think I've got it. It's so simple! And it's been happening all along, right in front of me.'

James nodded. 'What? Nova, speak non-witch to us, please!'

She gestured at them. 'Both of you, face each other.'

James turned to Nathaniel, and he felt a flutter at their proximity.

'Look at him, James; concentrate!'

'What do I do, Nova?' Nathaniel asked, fighting hard against familiar feelings of overwhelm.

'Just be seen; just look back at him.'

James gave him a reassuring smile, a little raise of his eyebrows as if to say things would be alright. Nathaniel stared into those warm eyes and thought once again he could do this for a thousand years and never get bored. James put out a hand, and Nathaniel rested his on James's palm, feeling the energetic crackle of connection.

He was struck again by how curious it was that someone could cause such overwhelmingly powerful feelings within him and yet feel so safe and grounding all at once.

The world receded; everything melted away as he continued to look back at James. He couldn't help noticing every tiny detail: every little freckle dappling his skin, the flecks of colour in his irises, and most of all, the beautiful soul that was so clear in his eyes. His heart fluttered again with just how much he wanted to make James happy. How he wished to devote his energy to making him laugh, to lightening his load in life and healing old hurts, if he only had the opportunity. The feeling of love growing within him felt uncontainable, as though it was expanding through his energetic field and radiating out into the world. He projected it towards James, wanting to share it more than anything.

He noticed then that the flutter in his heart had become a steady pounding; it felt more solid now. He put his free hand to his chest and felt a tangible firmness he hadn't felt since childhood.

James noticed the movement, his gaze flicking down for a moment. Without pause, he reached his free hand up and placed it against Nathaniel's chest. His eyes widened when his hand didn't immediately pass through but instead found some slight resistance.

Intuitively, he didn't push; he gently rested his hand there, on the boundary of Nathaniel's tentative form.

In that moment, something burst into life within Nathaniel. His heart was truly alive again, and it was racing. James gasped as his hand finally rested against something solid.

He closed the fist of his other hand, but Nathaniel's fingers were still not quite there, and they lost contact as his hand slipped away.

'Slow down; it's going to be a long process,' Nova murmured. 'Don't panic; just keep going.'

Nathaniel focused on the gentle pressure of James's hand and used it to pull himself back from the disappointment of not being complete yet. He looked back up into those earnest eyes, allowing their depths to draw him in again and soothe him. To have the undivided attention of such a wonderful being felt like oxygen, like he was just learning to breathe.

'Thank you,' he said softly, knowing there were no words that could do this justice.

James gave a tiny shake of his head. 'I'm barely doing anything.'

Nathaniel felt his throat tighten with emotion. 'It's…you're doing everything. You're bringing me to life.'

He could feel his torso more now and his shoulders growing heavier, more solid. He smiled, felt muscles move in his face for the first time in hundreds of years.

James smiled too. 'You know, you really light up when you smile.'

Nathaniel's smile broadened at that, and James's did too.

'And I can see the colours in your eyes so much clearer now, it's like you're moving from low resolution sepia into full colour high res!'

'What?'

James laughed. 'Sorry, it just means I can see you clearer now. You're brighter, richer, more defined.'

Nathaniel realised he had relaxed into the process without realising it; the gnawing terror that it wasn't going to work had subsided. He was smiling, the joy of every moment with James eclipsing all else.

He was almost there; a dream he hadn't even allowed himself to dream was coming true.

Only then did he realise how fully he had previously relinquished the spark within and resigned himself to his half-life, to the isolation and invisibility. Drifting onwards in his seemingly endless, meaningless existence until he one day faded away completely or the world ended, whichever came sooner.

As his heart sparked fully back into life, an intensity of feeling came flooding in. Alongside the love he felt came pain with a razor-sharp edge, the shadow side of the light. As he truly connected with himself, a terrifying but exhilarating new emotional range presented itself. He leant into it, embraced it, allowed more tears to well up and run down his face. James's eyes turned sad, the laughter fading from his face. He raised his other hand, reaching for Nathaniel's, and this time, their fingers met. James closed his slightly, and Nathaniel felt the pressure. It prompted more tears, but he let them come.

This was human. He was becoming real, finally grounding into the moment, being truly present. He wondered for a moment if this was what being human felt like, and he had merely forgotten – or if his human existence as he recalled it hadn't also been a kind of half-life. A rehearsal, a prologue for what was coming next, for the exciting new life he was now eagerly anticipating, despite the challenges it would likely present him with.

James's eyes were tearing up too, and Nathaniel's heart gave another pang at his compassionate nature and the deep, immeasurable gratitude he felt at the knowledge this wonderful soul existed and cared about him, of all people. He took a deep breath in and tried once more to put his feelings into words.

'To be known by you, to be seen by you, to exist at the same time as you, I am so lucky,' Nathaniel whispered.

James drew in a breath and opened his mouth to respond, but he never got the words out.

The bay window shattered inwards, an explosion of glass shards peppering the air. Nova threw herself forwards and down, taking James to the ground with her. Nathaniel stayed where he was; centuries of being unaffected by the physical had left him without his old reflexes and the habit of reacting to such things.

It was a new kind of fear when the glass spray hit his left side and he *felt* it. He looked down. Most of the glass had fallen through him – but some of it had struck him. He raised his left arm; there were actual cuts on his hand. He stared at them, strange red ribboned lines in his skin. He raised a hand to his face, and his fingers came away with what looked like traces of blood, but he had no time to fully examine himself.

Nova scrambled quickly to her feet, looking shaken. Nathaniel looked between her and James. 'Are you both alright?'

Nova nodded. 'I...I think so. I had my back to it.' She rubbed the back of her neck and pulled her hand away with blood on it. 'I might need some plasters later, but it all feels minor.'

James stood up. The right side of his face and body had been hit, but they all looked like light wounds. 'I'm okay too. What the hell caused that? Is it—'

The chaos that erupted answered his unspoken question; the entity was back and somehow stronger than ever. The desk turned over with a crash as pictures were torn from the wall and flung in every direction. James's mirror toppled onto the ground with an ear shattering crash. Nova moved first, catching James by the arm and dragging him towards the door. Nathaniel followed, feeling a new kind of fear now that he was semi-vulnerable to physical attacks.

He looked back, realising that seeing the entity was a little harder for him now, as was sensing it. He hadn't felt it coming up the stairs. Whether that was because he was so absorbed in James or because he was losing touch with those abilities now that he was becoming a physical being again, he wasn't sure.

The three of them fled down the stairs as an awful, guttural roar came from the bedroom behind them. Nathaniel stumbled on the stairs, suddenly aware that gravity needed to be considered once more, especially as the hand he threw out to steady himself was only half effective. Luckily, the banister provided enough resistance to slow his forward momentum before his fingers slipped through it. He steadied himself and continued down after the others.

As they reached the hall, Nova pointed toward the backdoor. 'The garden, quick!'

James slowed. 'But can Nathaniel—?'

'Worth a shot; move!' Nova urged.

James led the way, heading towards the kitchen, but as he rounded the first corner, a cupboard door flew open, smashing into his face and sending him backwards into Nova. Nathaniel managed to dodge a triple collision as both of them hit the floor hard but in doing so went halfway into the breakfast bar. He stepped out of it with an uncomfortable wrench and paused for a moment to gather himself. The physical laws governing how he could move through the world in his in-between state were maddeningly inconsistent and possibly dangerous.

James

James blinked, trying to clear his vision as he disentangled himself from Nova.

'This is getting old fast. Are you okay?' she asked.

James put a hand to his face, the swelling already beginning around his left eye socket and down onto his cheekbone. 'I'll live. You?'

She stood up slowly. 'I think you absorbed most of my fall, thanks.'

'Don't mention it.'

James straightened up and watched Nathaniel stepping partly out of the breakfast bar. It was like looking at a double exposure photograph: unsettling but mesmerizing.

'Let's get out of here.' He made a move towards the door into the garden but felt the air turn icy and knew instantly they weren't going to make it without something else going wrong.

Nathaniel moved faster than the star goalie on James's old football team, skirting the breakfast bar and skidding to a halt in front of James and Nova moments before the kitchen windows imploded in another shower of glass.

James had time to duck down far enough behind him to protect his face and watched as the splinters of glass mostly glanced harmlessly off Nathaniel. The brunt of the impact caused a ripple in his energetic field, but very few pieces penetrated it.

Those that did left a mark, but even as James stared, those marks seemed to be fading, and there was no visible loss of blood.

'You're a marvel; this defies logic!'

Nathaniel turned to him, his head cocked to the side. 'After everything that's happened, this is what you've chosen to be amazed by?'

James grinned. 'I guess so. You just saved me from yet another glass shower, so yeah, I'm pretty impressed.'

Nova moved past them both, crunching through the glass and reaching for the door handle. 'Mutual admiration later, guys, please! We need to—OUCH!'

She withdrew her hand from the handle immediately, holding it up. Her palm was bright red and rapidly blistering. She ran to the sink, fumbling at the tap and holding her hand under the cold water.

James seized a damp tea towel and wrapped it around his hand, trying the door handle. It wouldn't budge. He put all his body weight behind it and still nothing. 'Shit!'

He ran to the sink and handed Nova the tea towel. She ran it under the cold water and wrapped her burnt hand with it as he returned to the door. He kicked it hard, and it felt like concrete.

'There's no give in it at all...'

Nathaniel moved to join him and laid a hand on the door, closing his eyes for a moment. When he opened them, he shook his head. 'It's no use; it won't open. The entity is—'

All the cupboard doors in the kitchen swung violently open in unison, Nova moved first, getting clear just in time as their contents were flung out in all directions. She ran to the hall, and James followed, sensing Nathaniel on his tail. As they cleared the threshold, James glanced back to see the kitchen drawers slamming open, cutlery and knives rising from them of their own accord.

Nathaniel saw it too, his eyes full of fear as he pointed towards the sitting room. 'Go!'

Nova was already halfway there, and James followed, skidding to a halt and slamming the door behind them.

'The entity, it wasn't retreating to lick its wounds like we hoped it was; it's seeped into the fibres of the house and, I think, drawn strength from the...from the feelings I couldn't avoid earlier. I'm so sorry. My remembered pain, the intensity of what I felt just now, it's fed it, and it's so much stronger than it was!' Nathaniel apologised.

Nova swallowed hard. 'Oh, I didn't even think about that. I was so focused on getting answers and helping you. *I'm* sorry!'

Nathaniel shook his head. 'Don't apologize for what you've done for me.'

The sitting room door suddenly shuddered under impact, with the sound of something thudding against it. A peal of laughter echoed around the hall, and Nathaniel turned to James with fear in his eyes. 'I don't think we have much time. We're trapped, and that thing is out to end this.'

Nova glanced around, 'We have a little time. I can feel this room has some basic warding left over on it, I presume from Agatha's work right after Arthur was lost, but it won't hold for long.'

The door handle rattled.

Nathaniel startled. 'We need help, and we need it now. Nova, Agatha.'

Nova nodded. 'Yes, what about her?'

'You need to call on Agatha. She'll help us, if she can.'

'Okay, I can try. Summoning a soul back…that's fairly advanced work, but I can't think of anything else. Do you have anything of hers?' Nova asked.

Nathaniel paused for a moment. 'The spell in James's room was made by her, but that's been destroyed…I don't know where the ward is hidden in here.'

Another thud on the door, this one harder than the last, making the hinges creak.

'Arthur's watch!' James shouted as the thought hit him. 'Would that work? It wasn't hers originally, but they were twins, right? So, they were close, and it would have been hers after he passed?'

Nova looked at Nathaniel. 'I think that could work. What do you think?'

The sound of splintering wood came from somewhere in the hall. Nathaniel nodded decisively. 'I think it has to.'

He moved towards the door, and James felt his heart lurch; he didn't want Nathaniel going out there alone.

'Nathaniel, wait!'

Nathaniel turned back. 'It has to be me. You can't go out there, and neither can Nova. Whatever it throws at me will do much less damage.'

'Less damage, maybe, but you're not indestructible! And it might be able to hurt you in other ways we don't know about. I can't let you go. I'll go! I'm fast; I'll be fine!'

Nathaniel shook his head. 'No, I couldn't stand it if—'

The sitting room door swung open, and Nova vanished out into the hall, leaving them both staring after her. As soon as James recovered himself, he realised several things, the first being there were several knives lodged in the door. The second being that several more were now flying across the hall at him and Nathaniel. Nathaniel turned to face them, deflecting the first few as James moved out of the line of fire, slamming the door shut.

Nathaniel turned back to him, an odd smile on his face. He held up one hand, and James saw a few drops of blood beading on his palm. 'Look, *look*! It's actually bleeding. I'm more here than I was even a few moments ago!'

James tried to share in his joy, but all he felt was fear for his safety. 'But the more here you are, the more you might get hurt!'

Nathaniel nodded slowly. 'I suppose that's the price of it.'

He reached out with his injured hand, his fingers grazing James's shoulder but still passing through without a solid connection. He sighed. 'I'm sorry; I just wanted to try. To see if I could.'

James registered the noise of hurried footsteps above and immediately felt guilty for allowing Nathaniel's presence to distract him so thoroughly from the danger Nova was currently in.

'We need to distract the entity, keep it busy somehow!'

Nathaniel nodded. 'Let me. You stay here and be ready to help Nova.'

James felt his protective impulse again. 'But I want to keep you safe!'

Nathaniel turned to face the door. 'I know, but I'm not some fragile little ghost; I can handle it.'

He stepped across to the wall and stopped. James watched as he raised a hand, running it along the wall and realised what he was doing: testing it. But he couldn't do it anymore; he couldn't pass through.

Nathaniel reached out for the door handle instead and closed a hand around it, trying hard, but the handle didn't move. James wondered what he was feeling, stuck in between two realities, physically limited like a human but not fully able to interact like one yet either.

He wondered if Nova and himself had done something dreadful, if they had trapped Nathaniel at a midpoint that was even worse than where he'd been. Then he pushed the fear away; that was a problem for later, after they all survived the homicidal entity.

James joined him at the door. 'Here, I'll get it. Are you ready?'

Nathaniel nodded, and James pulled it open, watching him sprint out into the hall and into the kitchen, dodging flying objects as he went.

Nathaniel

Nathaniel moved like he had never moved before. He looped around the kitchen, making sure he had the entity's attention, and then fled back out into the hall, leading it towards the garage. He only needed to keep it moving until Nova could return to the sitting room and summon help; if Agatha heard their pleas and answered the call, he was sure they would be fine.

If she didn't – or couldn't – then he wasn't sure if they'd be fine at all. He frantically wracked his brains as he ran, desperately trying to come up with a decent backup plan.

He couldn't see the entity in the same way as before, but he knew it was on his tail – he could feel an icy breeze just behind him and a sense of wrongness in the air. As he reached the garage, he turned and looked back. When he really concentrated, he could make out the shape of it, the glow of its eyes, but it was fainter now. He could hear Nova's footsteps on the stairs, and he put on an extra burst of speed, vaulting over James's weight bench and twisting away, staying just out of range of that chilling touch.

A dumbbell sailed through the air and smashed into the wall, but he was well clear of it and out the door, feigning a route back to the kitchen and turning suddenly towards the sitting room at the last moment. He made it seconds after Nova, and she slammed the door behind him the moment he made it back in. It immediately shuddered under the impact of the entity renewing its efforts to gain entry, further infuriated at being teased and thwarted.

'We need to hurry this along!' James shouted.

Nova finished laying out what she needed and pulled out Arthur's watch from her pocket. 'I'm going as fast as I can. Both of you, sit down either side of me.'

Nathaniel sat down; he could almost feel the texture of the rug underneath him. It was hard not to be distracted by all these new things he was noticing despite what was unfolding.

James sat too, his knee coming to rest against Nathaniel's, a gentle pressure that immediately absorbed his attention. He tried not to look down at the point where their energies met, not to show how much it meant to him that James had sat so close and seemed so comfortable.

It made his leg tingle – reminding him of their time together in the garden – and made Nathaniel want to smile, an impulse he stamped down on immediately on account of how inappropriate it would be at such a time.

James

Nova arranged the pocket watch carefully on the floor, placing it between them, open with the initials showing. She straightened up and looked at Nathaniel. 'Can you focus really hard on your memories of Agatha? The more emotional the better – that should be enough to anchor this so we don't accidentally reach out to the wrong spirit.'

James couldn't help the anxiety he felt. 'Nova, what if we summon something really bad? We aren't going to make things worse, are we?'

The almighty crash that followed in the hall prompted her to snort. 'Do you really think we could make things much worse?'

Nathaniel leant forward. 'Well, actually—'

Nova held up a hand. 'That wasn't a real question. Okay let's get on with it before this house is reduced to rubble.'

James winced, the splintering sounds from the hall suggesting the complete destruction of the coat stand. 'Yeah, I know the extensive repairs aren't the most pressing issue right now, but also there's not much point banishing the entity if there's no house left for us to live in!' he said, trying to lighten the moment.

'There is: you won't be dead or possessed.' Nathaniel pointed out. 'That would be a significantly worse outcome for you.'

James glanced at him, wondering if he'd ever secretly hoped for someone he liked to die in the house and keep him company.

Nova gestured for them to settle down. 'Don't break the circle, please. Close your eyes and focus.'

For a few moments, James heard only his own loud breathing, the rush of blood in his ears and the pandemonium in the hallway. Then something shifted; the temperature dropped, and he began to feel as though someone was watching them.

Nova must have felt it too – she immediately called out, 'Agatha, are you here?'

James opened his eyes and followed Nova's gaze. She was looking into the corner of the room, where a faint grey figure was beginning to form.

He heard Nathaniel gasp; he had seen her too.

As they stared, she appeared more solid, drifting towards them. He could pick out details of her dress; it looked like Victorian mourning wear from what he remembered of history class. Her hair was scraped back into a tight bun, but despite the severe nature of her appearance, her eyes were kind and focused on Nathaniel.

She smiled gently. 'Hello, my boy. It's so good to see you again.'

Nathaniel was smiling, despite the tears forming in his eyes. 'You too, Agatha. I've missed you so much!'

She nodded. 'And I you. Leaving you behind was one of the hardest things I've ever had to do, but I *had* to do it. You'll understand soon, if you don't already.'

Nathaniel nodded. 'I think I do. it wasn't my time.'

Her smile broadened. 'Indeed, it wasn't.'

Nova took a deep breath. 'I hope it isn't now, either – but it might be, without your help.'

Agatha turned her head, fixing Nova with her calm gaze. 'You are powerful, aren't you?' Then she looked at James; an involuntary shudder ran down his spine when those translucent eyes were trained on his. 'And you – thank you for what you've done.' She looked between him and Nathaniel. 'It's good to see that some things turn out for the best with the passage of time.'

James found her to be both an unnerving and comforting presence all at once. Her knowing looks made him feel as though he was utterly out of his depth, but her sage manner was reassuring in their current circumstances.

She moved right up to where they stood, and the temperature plummeted. She reached out and ran one of her hands along Nathaniel's cheek. 'I'm so glad I could come back and help – and that it was I that you thought of in your time of need.'

Nathaniel nodded. 'I would always think of you.'

Caspian Faye

A thunderous noise from the hallway drew their attention away for a moment, and Agatha sighed. 'I wish this was a pleasant social visit, but alas, our time is short. To pressing matters…'

Nathaniel bit his lip. 'I…I have an idea. It might not work, but Agatha, Nova, would you be able to hold the entity in place for me? Give me a little time to try something before you rid us of it?'

Agatha nodded. 'Of course; that shouldn't prove too difficult between us. What do you want to try?'

'Something I think might weaken it considerably, among other things. I don't want to make any promises, though – as I say, it might not work.'

'Intriguing. Well, we'll see soon enough'

She moved to the door, pulling herself up to her full height with resolve and casting shapes with her hands. 'Right, I think it's time to let the entity in and end this once and for all, don't you?'

Nova's eyes widened as she realised what was happening. 'I…are you sure? Are we ready?'

Agatha continued to draw symbols in the air. 'It'll happen sooner rather than later, and I doubt any of us will ever feel ready for such an encounter.'

'Ah, yes, spot on, actually,' James agreed, privately thinking years of paranormal study wouldn't be enough to make him feel prepared to face what was out there.

All of them turned to watch the door as Agatha finished her sequence of movements.

James stepped forward and pulled the door open, bracing himself for whatever was going to come next. The next thing he knew, he was flying backwards, hitting the floor so hard he was completely stunned. He stared at the ceiling, unable to reorient himself before something hit his midsection, the air driven out of his lungs by a crushing force. He gasped and choked, feeling sick and winded. It reminded him of the worst tackle he'd ever endured on the football pitch, one that had left him doubled over on the grass, feeling like a fish pulled from the sea. He sucked in a half breath and tried to roll onto his side but was slammed back onto the floor. Pressure was building on his shoulders; something was pinning him down. He tried to push back, but he wasn't strong enough. The vague outline of something grey and dense above him was swimming in and out of focus: red eyes and a snarling mouth.

Something was constricting his throat now; a strange whistling sang in his ears, and he realised he was about to pass out. The horror at what that would likely lead to flooded through his body, and he struggled harder against the force above him, but it did him no good.

Just as reality was fading, he heard a voice say, 'Not again!' and suddenly, the weight was lifted. He was panting, and his arms felt bruised, but he was alive, and he was still him.

He sat up and saw Agatha and Nova flanking the entity. The grey shadow reminded him of an angry wasp trapped in a glass as it lashed out erratically against the invisible binding the two witches had cast together. It was clearly testing them; James could see the tension in Nova's rigid posture, but her face was set in a determined expression he knew well.

Nathaniel was at James's side, eyes wide and full of concern. 'Are you hurt? It moved so fast…I…there was nothing I could do in time!'

'It's not your fault,' James replied.

Nathaniel bit his lip. 'Well, I—'

'Now!' Agatha shouted. 'Nathaniel!'

Nathaniel gave James a nod. 'Later.'

He turned and stepped between Agatha and Nova, drawing himself up to his full height and facing the entity.

James suddenly found the energy to get to his feet; his fear for Nathaniel's half-life was very motivating. He wanted to do something but had no idea what and, being someone who hated it when people pointlessly said, 'Be careful' in films, he kept his mouth shut.

The entity's approximation of a mouth opened wide in a hideous mockery of a smile as it loomed over Nathaniel, that jarring laughter echoing around the room again.

Nathaniel stayed exactly where he was, grounded in stillness. 'Come on, then,' he said, his voice devoid of emotion.

Caspian Faye

James flinched as the grey mass flung itself at Nathaniel with all the force it had just thrown itself at James with, but it had no effect. Nathaniel's lack of solid mass rendered its physical assault pointless, and it couldn't absorb him, either.

As it howled in impotent rage again, Nathaniel extended a hand into the heart of it and closed his eyes. It began to flicker, becoming a more solid grey, then the surface began to swim with shifting colours, like oil on water.

Agatha gasped, and James knew whatever Nathaniel was doing, it was turning out the way he had hoped. A purple hue began to gather around Nathaniel's hand, slowly gaining size.

James's mouth dropped open as the purple began to take on the shape of a human, facial features beginning to appear. Nathaniel's eyes were open now; he was staring at the person slowly taking shape with shock and joy.

Agatha and Nova were shaking with the effort of holding the entity in place, but neither looked as though they were anywhere near giving up.

As the human's features became clearer, James finally understood. The colour faded; lines became more definite and, with a jolt, Arthur Gadsby stepped clear of the evil that had kept him prisoner for so long. James stared at the man he'd seen in the old photograph Nova had sent him what felt like a lifetime ago.

He looked exactly like the photograph, his spirit form slightly faded in the same way the image was. He stumbled forward, blinking in confusion at his surroundings. His gaze landed on Nathaniel, and he stared, his expression incredulous, then his gaze travelled to his sister and his mouth dropped open. 'Agatha…*Agatha*!'

The entity let out a screech, and Arthur turned to look back at the thing that had taken his life all those years ago. It was still a myriad of colours, but it seemed to be glitching, expanding and contracting and folding in on itself, its energy crackling and spitting.

'It's so much weaker now!' Nova panted. 'We've contained it; now we can banish it forever!'

Arthur stepped alongside his sister, extending his hands in a similar way. 'I'll help you; damn this thing to hell!' he shouted emphatically.

'Wait!' Nathaniel stepped forward again. 'Just a moment.'

He extended his hand again, his fingertips grazing the edge of the entity's energetic field. Another purple hue began to form; slowly taking a human shape and developing facial features. At Nathaniel's hand, a kindly faced old man gradually appeared, stepping free and blinking, looking around in a similarly dazed manner.

'You're free now,' Nathaniel said. 'You can go wherever you need to.'

The ghost James guessed was the sailor Nathaniel had spoken of looked around the room and then stepped behind the twins, drawing himself up tall as if to offer moral support in the absence of magical skill.

The entity was still struggling, spluttering and fuming, a stream of incoherent nonsense coming from it that more resembled growling than actual speech.

'It's over,' Nathaniel said. 'It's time for you to let go now. Surrender and choose peace or be banished!'

Nathaniel

Nova's eyes flashed gold as she drew on more power reserves to keep hold of the wriggling entity.

'I can bind it easily now; I can feel it!' she called out. 'Someone get me a container of some kind and we'll be done with it! But this time, hide it somewhere deep where it'll never be released.'

In response to her words, the entity screamed. In that scream, Nathaniel could hear frustration, anger, hatred, but underneath all of that…pain.

For a split second, he considered containing the entity once more, but then he realised if they did that, there would never be an end to it. No matter where they hid it, it would one day be found by some unsuspecting person and released again, even more pent up and deranged than it was now.

Nathaniel realised then that unexpectedly, he pitied it for the emptiness it must be feeling to be so hell-bent on causing destruction and misery to everyone it encountered.

'I want it gone more than anything, but I don't want it to suffer,' he said with certainty, feeling his words right down to his core. 'I've spent years fearing and hating that awful creature, but it must be so miserable to have become what it is.'

He looked at the thing that had tormented his waking hours and nightmares for years and extended the energy of compassion towards it.

Agatha shrugged. 'Very well, then; we'll encourage it to move on. I guess if it will go, that'll be for the best – for all of us, the entity included.'

Nathaniel paused, recalling all the times he'd dreamt of taking revenge on it for the pain it had caused him. It was a relief to let that go. 'I never want to be near it again; I don't want to feel that energy, ever, but I do wish it the best.'

The entity's writhing slowed; it seemed to be processing his words. Slowly, its boundaries shrank; it grew smaller until it began to take on the shape of a person.

'I'm not scared of you,' Nathaniel said quietly, 'not anymore.'

The entity faded to grey, slowly taking on the shape of a young man in a cloak, and Nathaniel's jaw dropped open. For a long moment, there was only silence as he and the entity stared at one another. Then the entity spoke. 'Now you know.'

Nathaniel finally found his voice in his shock. '*Theodore*! How could you?'

James

James stared wordlessly at the source of their terror, the mysterious sorcerer from Nathaniel's days, and wondered at how ordinary he looked now.

James hated to admit it to himself, but when they'd been watching the past unfold, there were moments when he'd understood why Nathaniel had been so taken with Theodore. Seeing him command a circle of magic followers all firmly under his thrall, there was something seductive about that level of power and influence. Not to mention he'd worn it all very well: on Theodore, a cloak had looked dashing; his dark, all-knowing eyes and thoughtful pout seemed both wise and very sexy. It was carefully constructed and thoroughly fake, he thought, but annoyingly, it had worked for him, nonetheless.

But now Theodore was unmasked and not looking at all sexy *or* terrifying. The years as a malicious entity had done him no favours. His dark eyes were vindictive and hollow and his hair bedraggled; he looked remarkably human, not powerfully monstrous. It was odd to think they had suffered so much because of the malice that dwelt within this pitiful being.

The entity looked down at himself, realising he had been revealed as he once was, and then his head snapped back up, staring defiantly at them all.

'Why, Theodore?' Nathaniel demanded. 'Explain yourself! All these years, all this time – why?'

Theodore looked at Nathaniel, a mix of emotions flitting across his face. 'You think this was my choice, you stupid boy?'

'Manners!' Agatha snapped, and Theodore's gaze flicked in her direction momentarily before he returned his attention back to Nathaniel.

'I'm here because of you!' Theodore said. 'Surely that much is obvious.'

Nathaniel shook his head. 'Obvious? What's obvious about it?'

'The ritual I performed on you was the defining achievement of my mortal existence!'

James's stomach turned at the glow in Theodore's eyes as he elaborated.

'You remember, up until that night, all we'd been able to accomplish were relatively minor spells. But I knew I was destined to be powerful; I just had to prove it, to my coven and myself.'

'By destroying me. *That* was your greatest moment? Your grand plan?' Nathaniel asked in a flat tone.

Theodore waved a hand impatiently. 'No, no, not exactly! Rituals such as the one we enacted upon you carry risks, but it wasn't my intention to harm you. I never lied to you, Nathaniel. I always meant to separate your soul, transform your physical body as we discussed and simply reunite the two afterwards. I knew I had the potential, and I did succeed in separating your soul, which at least proved I could perform magic of that level and complexity. After that night, I knew I had great abilities; I just needed to refine them.'

'So…I was just a pawn in your sick, selfish game?' Nathaniel asked. 'You're so much worse than I ever suspected.'

'Stop taking everything so personally! You have such a narrow view of it all. A man like me cannot be held back by the interests of a single soul!'

'But I thought…you said you loved me, Theodore! How could you have done that to someone you loved?'

'If you would just let me finish?'

Nathaniel looked like he was about to laugh but indicated to Theodore to continue.

'As I was saying, after that night, I knew I needed to refine my powers. Fine, that ritual hadn't quite been a *full* success, I'll admit, but I was halfway there.'

'Can you even hear yourself? You count what you did to me as a partial success?'

'Nathaniel, do stop getting caught up on the outcome. Think of the work itself! I'd succeeded in separating you from your body; it was just the part where we re-formed your body that failed. Although, it did show me the time had come to cut my pathetic coven loose…'

Nathaniel rolled his eyes. 'Oh, of course! It was a ritual you led, but it wasn't your fault it failed? How silly of me not to realise that.'

Theodore raised an eyebrow. 'Giving me cheek now, are you? I see you've changed for the worse.'

'And of course you've changed for the better,' Nathaniel shot back. James couldn't help the snort that escaped him.

'You're right; I have.' Theodore replied without a hint of shame. 'It was nothing short of genius how I refined what I'd learnt that night. I designed a ritual to regenerate and reform my body in whatever way I chose. Eternal youth and endless improvements.' He paused with a smile, looking expectantly at Nathaniel. James wondered what reaction he was seeking with his bragging, but whatever it was, he didn't get it. 'I could have done it alone, too; I didn't need the coven's help! Of course, their subsequent betrayal derailed my plans, but I suppose that's what I get for trusting those who lacked my vision. Left without a body of my own to transform, the only course of action was learning to possess other beings – well, if I wanted to live, at any rate, and to be anything other than another lost spirit.'

Nathaniel shook his head. 'You never cared about helping me. I was an experiment to further your own quest for power.'

'Will you stop making all this about you?' Theodore snapped, 'It's tiresome! And do let me finish a bloody sentence! I'll have you know, I was going to come back here once I had it all perfected and bring you back. It would have been such a triumph for me …' His gaze turned distant as he smiled vacantly, captivated by his own fantasy.

'So, what happened?' Nathaniel asked. 'How did the coven betray you?'

'Pathetic worms waited until I was mid-ritual and separate from my body, then they made sure I could never return to it. Terrified of my potential, I believe… The decapitation I might have been able to fix with enough effort, but they burnt my limbs to ash too…scattered pieces of me widely…there was no reforming then.'

248

Nathaniel's mouth fell open, 'Theo, that must have been painful.'

'Don't get soft on me, Nathaniel. I don't need your pity. Besides, they got what they deserved.'

Theodore smiled again, and a shiver ran down James's spine. He was fast reconsidering his earlier thoughts about the human form being less frightening. 'I knew who destroyed my body; I watched them do it. I knew exactly who to seek revenge upon, and the perfect means.'

'What on earth has any of that got to do with Nathaniel, though?' James burst out, unable to contain himself. 'Why come back here and torment him, as if he didn't suffer enough because of you?'

Theodore turned slowly, his lip curling as his eyes raked over James. 'Spare me the dramatics. You don't have to play the gallant hero; he's already smitten.'

James felt a strange lurch in his chest. 'I'm not playing at being anything. Just answer my question!'

He glanced at Nathaniel, who seemed frozen in place, his eyes averted. Theodore was still smiling, and James loathed the sight of him.

'All good things take time, boy; you'll learn that one day. First, I had to make sure the traitors suffered and died in agony, which was fun.'

James stared into Theodore's soulless eyes, searching for a shred of remorse, but he could see none.

Theodore turned back to Nathaniel. 'The very last one was sneaking around your garden, you know, trying to find a way to communicate with you. He died under the tree with our initials carved into it – how wonderfully poetic is that?'

Nathaniel swallowed. 'You're vile, Theodore.'

Theodore laughed. 'Sticks and stones, dearest one… When he died, he fled into the light, and I suppose I could have followed then, but after all the lives I'd taken, I didn't really fancy facing those consequences. Perhaps the powers that be would make an exception for a sorcerer of my calibre and understand I had no choice – but I'd rather not take the chance. Besides, I wasn't finished with my work.'

'So, you just hung around in Nathaniel's house?' James asked.

Theodore shook his head. 'For many years, I couldn't enter the house. I waited until I was given a way in, by them.' He gestured at Agatha and Arthur. 'Their warding kept passing spirits out, but their meddling created a portal in, a doorway.' He sighed. 'You can understand, after all that time, well, it's only natural I was…angry.'

Agatha gasped, a hand going to her mouth, and Arthur looked pale even for a ghost.

'But why?' Nathaniel demanded. 'I don't understand. Angry? That's what you call it, that inhuman rage? That spiteful, vicious behaviour?'

James knew before Theodore spoke that he was going to hate the answer.

'Nathaniel, dearest, you need to understand the cumulative effect here.'

'I do understand it, Theo! You're talking to someone who was trapped in this house for centuries, same as you!'

'Perhaps, but we are very different, you and I. You may have chosen to spend your centuries crying over past hurts or wilting over dashing young men, but me? I had things I wanted to accomplish with a strength of motivation you cannot imagine. I was betrayed, tortured, thwarted over and over, and after all that, I see a fine prize right in front of me' – he pointed at Arthur – 'and he denies me. I came so close to having a form again I tasted it, a handsome, vital form, and then what? I'm pushed out, the prize crumbles into death and I am locked away, confined, trapped, choking…' He broke off. For a moment, James glimpsed what looked like genuine pain. Then Theodore blinked, straightened up and forced a laugh.

'No, you must see, Nathaniel, things have been unjustly hard for me. There is nothing more intolerable to me than failure…and that ritual with you was both my greatest triumph and my abject failure rolled into one. How could I rest after that? I really did want to fix it all for you, make things good between us. And I would have done right by you, made us both immortal, unstoppable…allowing you to share in my glory – if you were a good boy, of course – and even tonight, after everything I have suffered, didn't I try to give you a handsome form and a new life out of the goodness of my heart? The opportunity for us to be together again, after all this time. To have the life we never got to have before.'

James had to clench his jaw to hold back the tirade he wanted to release at Theodore. He was boiling over with anger, but he knew it wasn't his place to intervene. Besides, Nathaniel didn't look like he needed or wanted any help.

'Theodore, after everything you have done, the last thing I would ever want is to be with you, in life or in death.' Nathaniel remained calm as he continued. 'You were allowed back in here by means that were out of my control. But I don't want you here, nor does the current owner of this home. You will achieve nothing by lingering. It is time for you to move on.'

Theodore drew himself up to his full height. 'How dare you speak to me like that? You think you can judge me, Nathaniel? As if you're some paragon of virtue, not the little coward who hid for years, quaking in terror at the very idea of me.'

James looked at Nathaniel's placid expression and felt a strangely intense relief at the complete lack of impact Theodore now had on him.

'Theodore, you're wasting your energy trying to hurt me. I don't care much at all for your opinion of me, not anymore,' Nathaniel stated.

Theodore glared at him. 'I don't care! I don't care if you care or not, this place is mine now, MINE!'

'Enough!' Agatha cut in, her tone firm. 'Enough of this grandstanding and petulant nonsense. You know that's not true. Unfortunately for us, we unwittingly allowed you to infest this home. It is long past time you ceased your evil and departed this plane of existence.'

Arthur put a spectral arm around her shoulders, his eyes full of tears. 'Well said, sister.'

She glanced at him, both of them smiling an identical smile at their reunion.

Arthur looked at Theodore. 'You robbed me of my life, parted me from my family and kept me here, forcing my sister to move on without me.'

Theodore stared back at Arthur, unmoved by his words. 'You think I should regret that? You asked for it.'

'I did no such thing! I fought you until my very last breath. You have caused decades of misery, and it must end. Now.'

'Says who? Perhaps I'll break free and absorb you again, and maybe your sister too while I'm at it!'

Nathaniel erupted into laughter. James studied his expression; there was a lightness there he hadn't seen before. He was feeling something similar himself. He couldn't even imagine how much deeper that went for Nathaniel.

Theodore glared at Nathaniel, but when he spoke, his tone lacked conviction; he didn't even seem to believe his own threats anymore. 'Shut up! I'll wipe that smile off your face!'

'Stop that talk; you know you lack the power to do any such thing! You are no match for us,' Agatha said.

'You're not even a match for me alone anymore. I could banish or bind you by myself. Your power is gone!' Nova put in. 'I can feel it – it was mostly borrowed – and your heart isn't in this fight anymore. Surrender!'

'Give up and *go away*,' Nathaniel added resolutely.

James

A brief silence fell, and James watched as the sorcerer slowly accepted his situation, the bravado seeping out of him as reality crept in. His head dropped for the first time, the arrogance on his features faltering. Finally, he looked up, his gaze landing on the twins.

Agatha fixed Theodore with a level stare. 'Despite your past, despite everything you have done, we offer you compassion. We will help you move on.'

'I don't want to move on!' Theodore retorted, but with less certainty than before. 'I told you.'

Nathaniel stepped forward then, placing his fingertips on his old lover's shoulder. 'We will help you. The others will be going on to find their peace; they can show you the way.'

Theodore looked down at Nathaniels' hand, the remaining defiance being replaced by defeat. 'Why would *you*…help me?'

'I forgive you, Theodore. What's done is done. Let's resolve this for everyone's good, shall we?'

'You forgive me? I didn't even apologize!' Theodore responded, his tone incredulous.

'You didn't need to. My compassion is not dependent on your apologies. Your words mean nothing to me now, but I would see you find peace,' Nathaniel replied softly.

'But…I can't. I can't find peace!'

'Why not?' Nathaniel asked.

'You know! I don't know what's next, what awaits me. A being such as me is not made for damnation! It's too late for me to pass on in search of some fluffy notion of peace!'

'But is it better to linger on the physical plane?'

'If I remain here, I know what to expect. If I go on, what awaits a soul like me on the other side? Can you tell me that? I don't think so.'

Nathaniel frowned. 'I admit I don't know, but you don't have a choice. For once in your existence, Theo, you aren't going to get your way. If you do not pass on, we will banish you from here, and who knows where that will send you – I certainly have no idea. You may run into other very powerful energy workers who won't show you a shred of mercy. You could end up bound again, for much longer than before, perhaps for centuries. Maybe an eternity.'

Theodore said nothing, just stared at Nathaniel, his expression unreadable.

'I think it's time to be brave, go on to whatever's next with no idea what awaits you – that seems much more fitting for a great sorcerer than lingering on the mortal plane, hoping for the best.'

Theodore looked down, apparently considering his words for a moment, and then looked back at Nathaniel, a resigned look on his face. 'Very well, then,' he answered simply. 'I will move on…better that than be bound again…somewhere I cannot speak, move nor rest.'

Nathaniel looked to the twins, and Agatha gave him a nod. 'I'll see to it. But first…'

She beckoned to Nathaniel, and he walked into her open arms. 'So wonderful to see you one last time. It feels like only yesterday we were parted.'

'And you, too. I've missed you. I've held you in my heart all these years, even as I've forgotten many others who've dwelt here. You and Arthur gave me the love I never had and always wished for. My family.'

Nathaniel turned to Arthur. 'I'm so sorry I couldn't save you before.'

Arthur looked at him in surprise. 'What on earth are you apologising for? I meddled with forces I couldn't control. Alas, the consequences were not favourable for me – or you. I should be apologising to you. My foolishness was my fault and mine alone.'

'Well, maybe I could have done *something*; maybe—'

'"Maybe" is a waste of time; what's done is done. And besides, what you did today, Nathaniel, was spectacular. Thank you.'

They held each other for a moment in a tight embrace, and as they broke apart, Nathaniel gave him a shy smile. 'I always wished I could do that.'

James stepped alongside Nova, who was quietly observing their exchanges. She gave him a sidelong look and mouthed, 'Jealous? You aren't his favourite housemate!'

He was about to pull a face at her but was struck suddenly by the accuracy of what he'd initially assumed was just a joke. He paused as it all sank in, and he acknowledged the spike of emotion he felt at Nathaniel's affection for the Victorian ghost for what it truly was.

It was a lot to process on top of everything else, and James noted he would have to express gratitude to Nova for her perceptiveness, her ability to see how he felt before he had fully admitted it to himself. James smiled at her, his best friend since primary school, and felt like he was seeing her in a new light, as a powerful force to be reckoned with. He was in awe of how fearlessly and selflessly she had thrown herself into this battle, risking everything to help him out when he really needed it. He resolved when everything had calmed down to take a moment to tell her again how much he loved and appreciated her.

Arthur stepped back, smiling sadly at Nathaniel. 'Well, we'd best get on, I suppose. Until we meet again.'

Agatha nodded. She waved a hand at the sitting room door, and the doorway began to glow.

'Before we go, a moment with you.' She crooked a long, elegant finger at James, and he walked towards her, feeling like he'd been called to the headteacher's office. She laid a hand on his elbow and leant down to whisper in his ear. It felt like taking a hat off in a snowstorm.

'Be gentle with his scars.'

A shiver ran down his spine that had nothing to do with her icy breath. 'I will,' he murmured, unable to trust his voice to say more.

'Look after him, won't you? Not that he needs it, but he deserves it.'

James nodded, his head still spinning at the oddness of being given relationship advice by a Victorian ghost. 'Of course. I promise.'

'Because he'll look after you; I know that.'

James nodded again. 'I know that too.'

'The odd lover's tiff I shall permit, but so help me, if you ever hurt him unduly, I will be coming back. And it won't be a friendly visit, so be warned.'

He pulled away to look at her, and she was smiling, but there was an unsettling steely light in her eyes.

'You can trust me, Agatha.'

She laid a hand on his shoulder, the cold radiating through his clothing.

'I hope so. I hope to see you both again one day, a long time from now, with many stories to tell me.'

'I'll do my best; I can promise you that.'

She seemed satisfied, stepping away from him and taking her brother's hand.

With the other she waved again at the sitting room doorway, and the hall began to take on a luminescence. She looked back at James, Nathaniel and Nova. 'None of you are to go out there until the glow fades, understand?'

With her other hand she seized Theodore by one of his wrists, pulling him in line beside her like a disobedient child. He bristled at her touch but tolerated it. Arthur stood by Agatha's other side, the sailor with him.

'You can release the containment spell now, dear,' she said to Nova, who sighed with relief and dropped her arms immediately, starting to massage out one of her wrists.

The luminescence grew, reminding James of videos he'd seen of the aurora borealis. When it reached a vivid green, Agatha stepped forward over the threshold, and all hell broke loose. Theodore twisted violently away from her, tugging himself free and back into the room. Arthur and the sailor had already stepped ahead and began to fade into the light, but Agatha managed to step back, reaching for the escaped sorcerer.

The speed with which Theodore moved gave James only enough time to register his trajectory and brace himself. When the impact hit him, it wasn't quite as bad as before, but it still drove the wind from his lungs and sent him to the ground. He tried to fight back, but his hands passed through Theodore like an icy mist. James struggled against the crushing pressure on his chest, his heart hammering as his throat began to constrict. He gasped for air, his fingers clawing at his neck in a desperate attempt to buy himself more time. As his vision started to grow dark, he wondered fleetingly if this really was it this time – then a blinding flash and sudden relief.

James screwed his eyes shut against the brilliant white light, only blinking them back open when it had faded. The air above him was still shiny somehow, and he sat up slowly, dazed and ready to thank Agatha and Nova – but it was Nathaniel standing over him, breathing heavily, an arm outstretched and his grey eyes blazing with rage.

'What…what did you?' James gasped.

Nathaniel blinked as if coming back into himself and looked around, seemingly as confused as James. He glanced over at Agatha and Nova where they both stood staring, arms still raised from the binding incantation they'd begun.

'I don't actually know.' Nathaniel panted, 'I just…I saw him about to harm you, and I didn't know what I was doing; I just—'

'You obliterated him.' Nova broke in quietly, 'Shattered him into pure light with one hand gesture. I've never heard of anything like that before.'

Agatha drifted over, her head cocked to one side. 'Neither have I, my dear. I'm starting to see why Theodore was so obsessed with you, Nathaniel.'

Nathaniel turned to her. 'What do you mean? I didn't even know what I was doing.'

Agatha nodded sagely. 'Even more impressive. Your abilities are innate – hence the desperation to win you to his side.'

'I wonder how much of the ritual was really him and how much of it was you…' Nova mused.

'Well, I didn't deliberately disassemble myself!' Nathaniel retorted.

'No, but you did reassemble yourself, in a way.'

'But I couldn't have done it without James,' Nathaniel said loyally. 'And you too, of course Nova.'

Agatha smiled, patting down the front of her dress and clearing her throat. 'Anyway, I'd be best be getting on. That doorway is a lot of effort to keep open.'

James stood up, one of his hands rubbing his throat, which was still quite sore. 'Wait. Can you explain a bit more about what just happened before you leave us?'

Agatha looked between him and Nathaniel. 'I have no answers for you; I think that's something you'll have to work out for yourselves. Good luck.'

With that, she turned, giving them all one last wave before she stepped forward and into the afterlife. The remaining trio stood in silence, watching as the glow faded from the hallway, leaving behind a stillness that the house had not known for centuries.

Nathaniel

Nathaniel stared into the hallway as the lights faded, stunned. He remained in stillness, staring after the departing soul of Agatha, with his turbulent emotional state matched only by the relentless flurry of thoughts flying through his mind. Theodore was no more. Nathaniel had tried his best to help him – he had, hadn't he? – but Theodore had chosen not to accept it. He had tried to hurt James; Nathaniel had had no choice but to do what he did, whatever that was.

What had he done? He couldn't begin to understand. Maybe it would take time before he did, but he knew for certain he had found true closure now. He had looked into the face of his first love again, the man who had hurt him in a way that felt endless, the heartbreak he had felt anew every time he awoke, carried for centuries like a faithful dog; he could finally let it go.

Now he could see Theodore for what he really was. Having looked upon his real face, heard his honest words, he finally knew it really had been about Theodore all along. The way he had behaved said nothing about Nathaniel and everything about the manipulative sorcerer. All those years of feeling like he wasn't worthy of love, wasn't likable, wasn't worth anything to anyone, all because someone who wasn't capable of love had deceived him – it was absurd. He smiled; he felt the weight of this burden as it began to lift. It was time to forgive his younger self for being taken in by a charismatic showman who had known just what to say.

He took a moment to pity Theodore, a soul so lost he had thrown away a genuine love and a life full of potential in the pursuit of power, a pursuit so obsessive it had corrupted him into the monstrous entity for so long, a jealous vindictiveness that wouldn't let him accept peace when he was offered it.

There were no words for the sense of relief Nathaniel felt at the freedom from the terror – a final, absolute relief, not a temporary binding this time but a proper resolution. That darkness was gone, and it was never coming back.

Not to mention the lightness he felt at releasing the guilt he had carried for Arthur's fate. What happened to him hadn't been Nathaniel's fault, and no one blamed him. Arthur was safe now; he was at peace. So was Agatha, lovely Agatha.

And tonight, Nathaniel had been brave. He had really helped, and now James was safe too. He had saved him.

James. He could feel his presence as always, so powerfully. That ability had not lessened since becoming a more physical being. He knew exactly where he was and how he was standing without having to look. He could even imagine the expression on his face as he too processed the events of the evening. He wanted to look at him, but somehow, Nathaniel couldn't bring himself to turn and face him. Not now. Because what if…what if now everything was done, James wanted to go back to his normal life? Go back to settling into his new routine, making new, normal friends from this century. Get along with finding another boyfriend, someone like Will.

Or even worse. The way James had looked up at him, the uncertainty in his voice when he asked Agatha for an explanation… Was James frightened of him now? Of his newly discovered ability… Nathaniel couldn't bear it if, after everything, things ended like that. To look into James's eyes and see fear would be excruciatingly painful; he couldn't risk it. He turned his back, grasping frantically for a plan.

Where could Nathaniel go?

He started to panic. The wall wasn't an option anymore. He couldn't go back to sleep there; he couldn't even get in it anymore. That particular safe space – or perhaps, on reflection, a trap that he'd never clearly seen for what it was – was a thing of the past. Over and done with. He couldn't go back to sleep; now he knew he wasn't a ghost.

He wasn't a human, either, though. Maybe with effort he could be, but he'd never be normal in the way he was certain James wanted.

He needed to test something.

He looked into the hallway. The lights were definitely gone now, and it was safe to go out there. He walked forward, over the threshold and into the gloom, without looking back.

The first cold light of dawn was filtering into the kitchen through the broken windows as he continued in. He didn't bother trying the doorhandle. He put his hands on the windowsill and pulled himself up, hesitating for a moment before swinging his legs over the edge and letting go.

For a split second, he feared the familiar resistance, the containment within the house, but it never came. He dropped smoothly to the ground; he was outside. He paused and took a breath, tasting crisp, fresh air again. He could leave the house now. He might not be fully physically present like a normal human, but he existed enough in the physical reality to not be constrained by his old limitations. He was finally free.

At least he could leave now. Go somewhere, go anywhere…the possibilities were endless and overwhelming. There was a whole world out there, a world he knew was vastly different from the one he had once known.

He could feel the ground; the wet grass was cold underfoot. He crouched and ran a finger along a blade, gathering the icy dew. He could feel it in a way he hadn't since his human days. He surveyed the garden he remembered so well, raw emotion rising up his throat at how beautiful it all looked. He was out here again; his wish had come true. He could walk here again, and how wonderful that it was all still here, even if it was no longer his.

'A long time since you last walked through here, isn't it?'

Nathaniel turned. James was standing in the open doorway, leaning against the wall. He seemed casual, not fearful at all, and Nathaniel felt a little relief. Either James was hiding it well or his opinion of Nathaniel hadn't changed.

He nodded in response, and James jumped down the steps, coming to join him. His purposeful walk and the intense look in his beautiful eyes took Nathaniel's breath away. He panicked. He wanted more than anything to stand still, to be close to James – but suddenly, he felt so unsure of what to say to him. He turned and walked away, trying to gather himself. Now that the entity was gone and they no longer shared battle lines, everything felt different.

His mind was blank. After all the personal conversations they'd had, after every intimate detail Nathaniel had shared, he now struggled to know what to say. There was so much unsaid, so much he thought he perhaps could never – or should never – say. After everything they'd been through, now that it was all done, somehow Nathaniel was overwhelmed by uncertainty.

He began walking towards his favourite tree, the site of so many of his most private, sacred daydreams. He wondered what James would think if he could see inside Nathaniel's mind, if he knew the fantasies he had, the constant longing he couldn't seem to shake. He was glad James was behind him and couldn't read the emotions on his face.

He couldn't bear it if James knew he was unable to stop hoping that working together to clear the house of the entity meant something deeper, that what had passed between them was more than camaraderie. He wished more than anything that the ritual in the 1700s hadn't gone wrong, that James had lived back then. That they had met in different circumstances, in another life. He would happily have traded all the centuries of his existence for one mortal life span with James. But wishing changed nothing; he knew that. He had to look at the facts.

And in the cold light of day, it seemed likely that someone as kind as James was just being nice, helping Nathaniel because that was the kind of person he was. Someone who helped people, who cared, a kind nature that extended to humans, nonhumans and partial humans alike.

But there was a world of difference between kindness and wanting what Nathaniel dreamt of. And the idea of expressing any such hopes made him feel more vulnerable than he thought he could stand. The worst part was he knew James would never mock him; he would be kind about that, too, which would make it so much harder because the truth would remain the same. James wanted something different to anything Nathaniel could ever give him. It could never be the way his heart yearned for.

Wouldn't James want a normal, fully physical human from his own era, someone who would understand him and be bound by the same laws of physics as he was? Someone who he could have a normal life with. Someone who didn't have the potential to blast souls to pieces. Someone like Will, but better. Nathaniel picked up his pace as he reminded himself James deserved what he wanted: a happiness unspoilt by complicated histories, strange paranormal phenomena and miserable memories.

Yet he knew James was still walking behind him and was now drawing level. Perhaps James suspected what lay in Nathaniel's heart and was about to make things clear, to say a final goodbye. This was it. Nathaniel would say farewell to the garden he loved so much and the boy of his dreams, and then he would take his leave, go out into the world and make his way somehow. He'd been brave before; he could do it again. He was no stranger to painful goodbyes.

He reached his favourite tree and stopped, extending a hand towards it. He knew he wouldn't feel the comforting rough bark under his palm as he used to, but he would be able to feel its energy and connect to that familiar life force. He glanced up at the faint carving; it was still there, but slightly faded by time. James followed the direction of his gaze, and Nathaniel knew it would be obvious to him what it signified, the heart with an N and a T carved into it. Nathaniel stared, thinking of all the years that had passed and all that time the tree had borne a piece of his history.

James gasped suddenly. 'Nathaniel, your hand…'

Nathaniel jolted and looked down at his hand as James reached out, catching it in his.

'You're hurt; you're bleeding.'

Nathaniel froze. James was holding his hand, properly *holding* it. He flexed his fingers; they were solid. He stared; there was actual blood pooling on his palm from a wound that wasn't healing immediately.

'I must have cut it climbing through the window…' he murmured in awe.

He looked up, straight into James's shining eyes, and felt a smile spreading across his face. Regardless of his soon-to-be-broken heart, this was still beyond any magic he'd ever known.

'I'm here. I'm actually, really *here*.'

James nodded, still holding Nathaniel's hand. 'You are. You did it.'

Nathaniel shook his head. 'No, *we* did it! Thank you for seeing me…for making me feel seen.'

'I…it was the least I could do, the very least.'

'But it was everything, and it means the world. It *gave* me the world…it means more than I can ever say. I don't have the words…'

James's expression turned serious. 'Well, maybe you don't need words.'

For a long moment, they stared at one another, the fully formed heart in Nathaniel's chest beating furiously. James's eyes were so full, so bright, so vibrant. As he stared into their depths, something clicked suddenly into place, that regardless of what happened next, what James meant to him was no delusion – no one could ever take that away. His feelings were real, and he would always have them. And he would treasure them forever.

James was running his thumb back and forth across Nathaniel's hand, a gentle movement that soothed him and gave him just enough encouragement. He decided that despite his fear, he would try because he had to. If he'd learnt anything from recent events, it was that he should always try. If he didn't, he would never know. He hadn't gone through centuries of loneliness to let a chance at something different pass him by without even trying. What was the point of it all then? So he opened his mouth, took a steadying breath and finally voiced the question.

'James…I'm not sure if—I mean, I would love to stay, but I can go, if you'd rather…get on with your life in peace? I assume that's the case, and I understand, of course.'

James's eyes widened, and he shook his head. 'What…no, that's not what I would rather at all.' He paused and looked away, a slight flush tinging his cheeks. 'I don't have the words either. I…' His free hand reached up to Nathaniel's face, gently tracing along his jawline, tipping his chin up. 'Can I just…?'

Nathaniel stared at him, frozen by this turn of events and stunned by the uncertainty in James's tone. For a long moment, he couldn't even find his voice, so he reached out instead, his uninjured hand connecting with the firmness of James's waist and pulling him closer.

'Of…of *course*…' he murmured in response.

A moment later, their lips met, and Nathaniel's mind emptied of all thoughts as his being flooded with pure joy. Time stopped as their kiss deepened; every part of him was singing, melting, on fire. Nathaniel began to feel light-headed and realised he'd forgotten to breathe. As they broke apart, he gasped for air, grateful for the solidity of James's arms keeping him upright. James smiled, drawing in a deep breath himself, and Nathaniel realised he was helping keep him upright too.

'Oh! I need to fix something!' James said suddenly, his eyes alight as he pulled his pen knife from his jeans pocket. Nathaniel released him, and he leapt up the tree, his hands and feet finding Nathaniel's old footholds with ease. When he clambered back down, Nathaniel looked up at his handiwork and laughed. The T in the old carving had become a fresh J.

As they walked back up to the house, Nathaniel felt as though he was in danger of losing his physical form again, carried away to another reality by pure elation. This was an outcome he hadn't allowed himself to anticipate, and he couldn't quite get his head around the surreal nature of it all.

'That was…*I've* never been kissed before,' he said trying to articulate a realisation that was just forming.

James looked at him with amazement, giving his uninjured hand a gentle squeeze. 'That is just crazy to me.'

Nathaniel tried again. 'No, I mean…Theodore did, back when I was human, before…but it was never me being kissed; I was never really there. I've never kissed or been kissed as *myself*. Kissed for me, because someone wanted *me*.'

James stopped in his tracks and turned to him. 'Oh! I get it.'

'You do?'

'Yes, and I'd go for your second, third, hundredth kiss right now, but it's seriously cold out here, and Nova is making us coffee.' He paused and grinned. 'I can't wait to see you drink a coffee! There're so many things I can't wait to watch you taste.'

Nathaniel stared at him, wondering how it was even possible that all his wildest dreams were coming true, that this was really happening.

James raised a questioning eyebrow. 'And…there's plenty of time for that, I hope?'

Nathaniel thought it unlikely he would ever answer a question more emphatically, even if he lived for a hundred more years. 'I'll give you all the time I have, gladly.'

The smile James gave him in response made Nathaniel's heart expand with uncontainable bliss.

As they continued on up to the house in a comfortable silence, Nathaniel stepped ahead, taking great delight in holding the door open for James. Everything was so vivid now: the sharpness of the cold metal handle against his now-warm hand, the colours of the morning sky, the smell of the coffee coming from the kitchen. He felt at home, finally, in every way possible.

As James brushed past him, he felt every nerve sing and knew it had *all* been worth it, for this.

James

As James settled onto one of the battered barstools at the breakfast bar, Nova put the cafetiere down and turned back to the toaster, filling it with bread. 'Don't know about you two, but I'm starving!'

James nodded. 'Yeah, count me in!' He started filling mugs with coffee and looked at Nathaniel, waiting for his response.

Nathaniel looked down. 'Um, I'm not sure yet.'

James grinned. 'Are you trying to remember what hungry feels like?'

Nathaniel nudged James gently with his knee. 'Is it that obvious?'

James placed a mug of coffee into his hands and gazed at him, lost in the miracle that he was. All he wanted to do was touch him, but he knew he needed to pace things. Nathaniel was only just human again, which must be an adjustment. Never mind that it might be a bit rude with Nova still here.

He was fighting the urge to pinch himself constantly. On paper, his life lately had been an absurd rollercoaster of utterly improbable events, and yet, in this moment, everything felt so right. He pushed his knee up against Nathaniel's, his mind wandering back to that moment in the garden when they'd first shared a bench.

He couldn't remember the last time he'd felt so grounded, so present and so comfortable. Nathaniel's energy was so calming, and he felt at home with him in a way he'd never felt with anyone else, including Will. He realised he could just relax and be himself, be nothing but his raw self without any filter, without any pretence, and it would be okay. Nathaniel made him feel like he was enough, like he would always be enough. That they were a team, that he could share anything and it would be held carefully. His heart would be safe.

He, too, felt he was seen.

The back door creaked open with a soft meow, and James looked down. 'Oh, wow, Posey, have you learnt to open doors now too?'

She trotted into the kitchen, her tail high, and went straight to Nathaniel, rubbing up against his shins. James laughed. 'Thanks for the seal of approval, baby. I really like him too.'

Nathaniel bent down and ruffled her fur. 'Hello again! I'd forgotten how soft cat's fur is.'

The door swung further open as James's dad followed Posey in, awkwardly navigating the debris whilst juggling an overnight bag, laptop and coat with his uninjured hand.

'James! I've been so worried about you; I just broke the speed limit to get back. You didn't answer any of my calls. Are you alright? Nova, you're both okay? What happened? How was your night…' James's dad trailed off as he looked around, taking in the destruction and the bedraggled, battered state of the kitchen's inhabitants. His eyebrows shot up when he saw Nathaniel, the morning light illuminating his frock coat.

'Ah, hello there. Who on earth are you?'

'It's a pleasure to meet you, good sir,' Nathaniel replied getting to his feet and delivering a bow. 'I'm Nathaniel, and I'm not a ghost – well, not now, at any rate.'

Frank dropped his keys onto the counter and his belongings to the floor, looking at his son with utter confusion. 'You know what James, I think you'd better pour me a very strong coffee.'

'You got it, Dad!'

Frank nodded. 'Cheers, much appreciated. I—' He stopped, staring out at the destruction in the hall. 'Oh, God. Are you sure you're definitely, okay?'

'Definitely,' James reassured him. 'Never better.'

'Actually, you know what? Hold the coffee for now, I think I need to go and have a lie down. Is it…safe…for me to sleep?'

'Absolutely, sir,' Nathaniel replied. 'The entity is gone now; you won't be possessed.'

'Well, that's a relief, thank you. Very helpful,' Frank answered with a faint smile. He had turned rather pale and grasped the countertop. 'I just need a moment. I didn't sleep last night with worry, and I…if you're really okay, then I'll see you all later. And deal with this mess.'

He left, and Nova frowned. 'Is he going to be okay?'

James nodded. 'Yeah, I think so. He's just stressed and stuff; he'll be more himself after a nap. And some extensive repairs on the house.'

Nova winced. 'Yeah, I can't even imagine the bills he's anticipating.'

'Can't you just magic it all back the way it was?' James joked.

Nova shook her head. 'Nope, sorry, you might just have to get a job!'

James's phone buzzed, and he drew it out of his pocket; it was Will.

'Whoops, my screen got cracked at some point last night. And oh, wow, sixty-three missed calls from my dad,' he commented before he opened Will's message.

Sorry baby, I might have been a bit harsh with you in my last message. Maybe we could chat soon about being friends? X

James stared at the screen and realised how little he felt in response. A part of him was tempted to ask Will if Stevie had dumped him already, but he put that impulse aside. Instead, he sent back, *I think it's a bit too soon for that conversation. Wish you all the best though,* and put his phone back in his pocket.

Nathaniel sipped his coffee and smiled. 'Thank you, Nova, that's, wow…for my first drink back, this is perfect.'

The toaster pinged, and Nova threw the slices of toast onto a plate and put it down between them. 'I hope my toasting skills are also worthy of your first breakfast back!'

'I know very little about toasters and toasting, but I bet they will be, thank you.'

'It's all in how you press the button, you see; takes a skilled chef to make toast,' Nova quipped as she rooted around in the cupboard. 'Urgh, that bloody entity smashed all the jars!'

'There's marmalade in the fridge, I think,' James suggested.

Nova grabbed it and turned to the cutlery drawer, which was hanging open on damaged hinges. 'Ugh, crap! All the knives are on the floor. Fancy some washing up?'

'Washing up? You know, ghost stories massively gloss over the minor inconveniences that come along with homicidal entities haunting your house.'

Nathaniel and Nova both laughed in time with one another, and James looked contentedly at them both sharing a moment. Then his gaze moved to take in the warm rays of sunlight filtering through the kitchen, illuminating everything as the dust settled on his new home, and despite the mess and the work ahead, he knew everything was exactly as it should be.

Acknowledgements

Thank you first and foremost to the incredible Joshua Dean Perry of Tiny Ghost Press, without whom Nathaniel & James's story would just be an abandoned world gathering dust. I am endlessly grateful to have found such a wonderful, caring home for something so close to my heart, and to have the opportunity for such a joyful creative process. Thank you for believing in this tale. It means the world.

To everyone else at Tiny Ghost Press another huge and very heartfelt thank you. To Reuben Davies-Hoare, Thomas Shah, Lewis Hughes for the incredible social media marketing, Melody Jaikes for all her hard and detailed work on the copy edit, and to Fiona O'Shea for the beautiful cover design and bringing the boys to life.

Nova, my chosen sister – thank you firstly for the honour of using your name - and secondly for your inspiring strength, kindness and presence in my life.

Izzy – my anam cara, thank you for being my witch/astrologer on speed dial or voice note - (and for all the times you've saved me.)

Loren, a set friendship that actually became a real life one - thank you for all your support over the years, with my early tentative writing – and everything else.

My Mum Jo and my Dad Stephen – thanks for the books I was given, the stories I was told and the creativity that was always encouraged.

Anna, thank you for being my friend – and my writing friend - and all the chats on the creative process we've had. It's been terrific motivation along this long road.

Guy, thank you for reading my previous books, letting me know what they meant to you and encouraging me to keep writing.

To Doug, Chrissy, Sage & the team at Delaney Grey Management – thank you for being a consistent light in my life & for all the years of support along my journey.

Jo - thank you for the years of friendship (and ghost hunting! We may not be on the trail anymore, but I have endless fond memories of that time.)

The four (Dan)iels (not a boy-band, but would make a great one.) Thank you for the therapy, for always making me feel seen & safe, rebuilding my faith in humanity and giving me creative outlets when I needed them; films, photos, scripts- or listening to me recite a summary of my first draft on a Menorcan beach at midnight and not telling me to shut up.

The three Amys and two Hannahs (not sure what it is with awesome people in my life and recurring names, but it's clearly a thing) thank you for the sanctuary in which I felt safe enough to take my first steps out of the wall, the support and the community right when I needed it the most.

To Sebby– thanks for the flexible work schedule when I needed to vanish off for a bit and scribble away.

And to Laura for your "coffee and fresh air" wisdom.

You have all helped more than you will ever know.

To Maia & Mosi for inspiring Posey the cat – amongst so many other gifts you brought to my life. I will miss you both forever, my weird little goblins.

And finally, to the LGBTQ+ community – thank you. Our defiance, strength and resilience in the face of this world makes me proud of us every day. I hold onto hope that one day it will be easier – but in the meantime, we move forward. Love to you all.

The Author

Photo by Olivia Spencer

Caspian is a writer and performer based in London. He attended drama school and has a background in acting, with experience across film, TV, stage and live events. Alongside this, Caspian has also trained as an energy healer and has a keen interest in healing modalities, mental health, paranormal investigation, fitness and cooking. When not writing or performing, Caspian is most likely to be found at the gym, listening to a spooky podcast, on a beach or drinking large amounts of green tea while reading.

A ROMANCE TO HOWL HOME ABOUT

TAKE HOME THE BEST SELLINH

THE ALPHA'S SON

SERIES...OUT NOW!

AVAILABLE IN PRINT, EBOOK, & AUDIOBOOK

WWW.TINYGHOSTPRESS.COM
@TINYGHOSTPRESS